FAKE
MAKE OUT

FAKE OUT MAKE OUT

KATE WILLIAMS

First published in the UK in 2026 by
INK ROAD
an imprint of Bonnier Books UK
5th Floor, HYLO, 105 Bunhill Row, London EC1Y 8LZ

A CIP catalogue record for this book is available from the British Library.

ISBN: 978-1-78530-916-8

Also available as an ebook and in audio

1

Typeset by DataConnection
Printed and bound by CPI Group (UK) Ltd, Croydon CR0 4YY

FSC www.fsc.org MIX Paper | Supporting responsible forestry FSC® C013604

The authorised representative in the EEA is
Bonnier Books UK (Ireland) Limited.
Registered office address: Block B, The Crescent Building
Northwood, Santry, Dublin 9, D09 C6X8, Ireland
compliance@bonnierbooks.ie
bonnierbooks.co.uk/InkRoad

For the readers, the runners, and those in the waiting room at the rheumatologist.

1

CHARLIE

OK, we all know Mondays can feel like a marathon, but today feels more like a full-out sprint. Limping through the unrelenting Florida heat with my arms full of sandwiches is not how I imagined my first day as the executive assistant to Oliver Hawkins, CEO of FIRE – the world's biggest organizer of extreme endurance sporting events.

My first challenge as Oliver's assistant: lunch.

A meeting got rescheduled that would prevent the entire C-Suite from having lunch and it's my job to make sure the plates keep spinning. I should excel at this. I've been an elite athlete my whole life. Blood, sweat, and tears are part of the equation. Required. But that's not who I am anymore.

My days of actual races are gone. Getting back to the office in time is the closest I'll get to race pace nowadays.

Trying to jog back toward FIRE's headquarters in these low heels and a pencil skirt, I promise myself I'm focusing on my new dream. FIRE groupies from around the world would jump at the chance to have this job, this access to Oliver. I've seen the FIRE logo on bumper stickers, next to 26.2 and 140.6 ovals. I've seen it on calf tattoos and finisher shirts at run meets. And now I'll get to help make these epic events happen. It's enough. More than enough. It has to be.

The blazing sun reflects off the shiny glass skyscraper on the edge of Tampa Bay. *Don't sweat on the sandwiches, Charlie!* I scold myself. The box in my arms is in the direct splatter zone; at least the bag on my elbow is safe. Although it keeps smacking against my thighs as I bobble, which is annoying.

The first day at a new job feels like the first day of school. New outfit. New supplies. Where do the cool kids sit for lunch?

I hustle as best as I can from the parking garage, juggling kale Caeser salad wraps and quinoa burritos. Rushing toward the door, I grab the long metal handle and pull. *Ouch, hot!* I yank it again. Nothing.

Oh crap. My badge! In all the chaos of collecting orders, I must have forgotten my ID badge on my desk. Sweat pools under my arms, drips down my lower back. Every place I do not want it. It's bad enough these sandwiches are wilting as I melt into a puddle. I could reach into my purse for my phone to call Shauna from HR, but I need both hands to manage this load. I would have to put the box of sandwiches on the ground and, while they are wrapped, I don't think that's for the best.

Being locked out on my first day, with famished executives waiting for me to feed them, is a nightmare. Hungry CEOs are not happy ones.

I reach for the handle with my index finger one more time. The door doesn't budge.

Come on, universe. Let someone – *anyone* – walk toward the front door right now. I let out a grunt of frustration and throw my head back, looking to the cloudless sky for some kind of assistance. Imploring the universe for help is surely the first sign of heatstroke.

And then, like a mirage, I spot someone walking toward me.

I adjust the glasses that slide down my nose by brushing them against my shoulder.

Help! I will him to come closer.

The man is tall and lean. He strides toward me like a hero in the midday sun. The broad shoulders, the dark hair, those forearms. Is he about to save the day and then sweep me off my feet?

The embroidered ballcap reading NAVY and his Annapolis T-shirt suggest he's an officer, so not a real-life knight but close enough. My shoulders relax, the tightness in my throat eases.

I flash him my most earnest smile, hoping I don't appear too sweaty or gross. Then again, I'd take this very attractive stranger's pity if it got me inside.

"Would you mind giving me a little help?"

He stops a few feet away and his eyes scan my face. I fidget under the scrutiny of his gaze.

A strange expression crosses his face before he responds. His thick eyebrows pinch together, a thought he is keeping to himself.

He does not return my friendly tone or smile. His face is stone: his chiseled jaw, his unwavering scowl. The only movement he makes is to purse his lips slightly as his gaze narrows on me.

"I forgot my badge," I explain with a nervous laugh. His expression remains inscrutable.

His gaze turns into a sneer, his words clipped and direct: "I don't think so."

The debonair but disagreeable stranger, now directly in front of me, takes a deep inhale. Is he smelling me? No, wait. It's the sandwiches! *Why is he smelling the friggin' sandwiches?*

He shakes his head. "We have a strict no-guest policy." Again, the man assesses me with his deep brown eyes. I'd think he was checking me out if he wasn't so confrontational. He's sizing me up as if I'm here to attack the office with turkey on rye.

"I work here, I just need help opening the door," I tell him as politely as I can, but my patience is thinning. "If you could *pl—*"

He cuts me off. "No, you don't. *I* work here and I know everyone in this office." The man reaches into his bag and grabs his key card. Key card! The ticket to air-conditioning!

"Look, it's my first day and I'm really in a jam." I roll back my shoulders, channeling all the confidence that I have left and hoping he'll remember some time in his life when he needed a helping hand. "I'd really appreciate it if—"

No such luck. He interrupts me again. "Nice try," he says with a wink. A wink! As if this is some game to him.

He swipes his badge and opens the door slightly, blocking me easily. Crisp cool air wafts out of the building. I want to swoon into it.

I think he is about to pull the door closed behind him when he stops. *Oh, maybe he is going to help me after all!?* Instead, he asks, "Who is this food delivery for?"

"Oliver Hawkins," I reply.

The man in front of me laughs. A sharp bark of delight at my answer. I clam up before I can clarify – again – that this isn't a delivery, and I have a lunch to set up because my job is on the line. My new start. The first day of the rest of my life, in fact.

"I'm running late," he says with a scoff. "Tell the Order to try harder next time."

He pulls the door closed behind him, hard, leaving me in the broiling sun.

The order? I triple-checked the order. I just forgot my badge!

My mouth drops open as I see him saunter through the lobby. Panic swells, rising from my toes, my back, and up to my throat. I wouldn't be this freaked out if I hadn't thought help had arrived.

Don't cry, I remind myself again. *I am a grown woman, goddammit,* I am not going to cry on my first day. But when I'm angry, I cry. And I am fuming. The nerve of that guy!

What do you call a knight-in-shining armor who turns out to be a villain?

My new coworker, apparently.

One tiny tear manages to escape, and I tell myself it's just sweat.

2

DECLAN

The Order has really outdone themselves this time.

"What. The. Hell?!" I hear the annoyingly attractive – and now more than a little exasperated – young woman shout from the other side of the glass doors. I cast one discreet backward glance. She is glaring at me like I have ten different heads.

It would be just like the Order to send an operative right here to the head office to weasel their way in and get intel. It's already clear they have one mole within our organization; with a second set of eyes and ears, who knows what they could accomplish.

An attack on Oliver or any of our other operatives. Hack our network. Plant a listening device. More of the sabotage that we've been dealing with for the past six months.

Fresh off a red-eye flight from Helsinki, I nearly let exhaustion cloud my judgment at the sight of her damsel-in-distress act, arms full of sandwiches and a large bag hanging off one elbow. With her chocolate brown hair pulled up, some ends sticking out, and frazzled by the humidity, she looked eminently kissable. Not to mention those toned legs . . .

Enough, Declan.

I shouldn't think the worst of people. But an attractive young woman who looks exactly my type, standing outside the FIRE headquarters?

Six months ago, I would have trusted a pretty face and a plausible story.

Now I know better.

The gym attendant, an amiable guy named Brian, waves at me when I enter. "Hey, man, it's a little late for you to be in here." He's right. I'm usually finishing up a punishing training ride when he arrives for the day. My gaze flits to the stationary bike.

"Red-eye got in late. Just gonna hop in the shower." If my flight had arrived on time, I would have gone home, knocked out at least thirty to forty miles, showered, eaten a real breakfast, and then come into the office. Instead, I have barely enough time to clean up before the meeting, and I do not have time for chit-chat.

Starting to clean down the equipment, Brian says, "Bummer. Where did you go?"

Great. First a turbulent all-night flight, now this.

"Helsinki." My reply is terse, hoping he'll get the message. I'll take turbulence over small talk any day of the week.

Brian cocks his eyebrow. "Business or pleasure?" he asks, not getting the message at all.

Definitely not pleasure. My mood sours further. I haven't had a vacation in two years, and dating requires too much of a time commitment. Even if there was someone I wanted to make time for, the risk isn't worth it.

I tell him the truth: "Business." But not the whole truth. "We're hosting our first ultra-marathon in Finland. Athletes will finish under the midnight sun on the longest day of the year."

Brian already knows I work for FIRE. Has asked me a few times about upcoming events that he swears he is going to sign up for. He seems like an alright guy, and I have a dossier on him that proves he isn't connected to the Order. Still, I generally don't trust people who ask so many questions, not in my current line of work.

Brian moves on to cleaning the next treadmill. "Well, I bet it was a lot cooler there than it is here," he says.

I nod, signaling the conversation is over, and head toward the men's locker room.

The shower stall at the end of the row is open and I set down my duffel bag. I'll re-wear the wrinkled clothes I wore at meetings this weekend.

As I take off my faded Annapolis T-shirt, my phone pings.

I glance at the notification.

Oliver Hawkins

Crisis in Kandy. Mostly under control now.

My shoulders deflate. *We can't go a full twenty-four hours without an international incident to resolve.* I shake my head.

Then my phone rings. It's Oliver, impatient for a response to his message. "Great work with the peace talks this weekend," he says without so much as a hello.

What I told Brian was true. I was traveling for business, but the ultra-marathon planning meeting and permit application was a cover for a top-secret meeting between warring world leaders and military officials to hammer out the final details of a peace treaty. When you have the right contacts in every major city in the world, you can get a lot done.

"I'm glad it's finished," I respond, careful to manage how much information I reveal while in a public place. I didn't see anyone from the other offices in the gym on my way in, but I can't be too careful. "Oh, and we are all clear to use Senate Square for the race village." I slip between topics seamlessly. Secret missions to race operations in a second.

I was surprised when I first learned about FIRE's clandestine arm. It makes sense, though. Sport brings people together. It tears down borders in an instant. When you stand on the start line, when you're gassed mid-course, when you're giving it everything you have to get to the finish, it isn't about the flag on your arm. What your government is or isn't doing to help. These venues are the best way we can get meaningful peace on paper, to stop evil masquerading as capitalism.

This past weekend was all conference rooms, handshakes, and civilized discussions. Much calmer than my other recent missions.

"Excellent," Oliver replies. "Let's get the team up to speed at the Monday meeting. We had to bump it. You're on your way in?"

A meeting first thing after a delayed red-eye across the Atlantic? I'd rather chew glass.

"Yep, just got to the office," I tell him, stifling a groan. "I'm about to shower. Then I'll hop upstairs."

I expect him to hang up, but he adds, "Charlie, my new assistant, started this morning. I'll do intros at the meeting."

Right, another new assistant is starting today. Oliver didn't have the team interview this one. I can't say I blame him entirely. After what happened six months ago, we're all on edge. Oliver wants to bring in his own guy to manage his schedule, I get it. He needs someone he can trust. That he doesn't entirely trust me to vet this new assistant still stings.

"Great," is all I manage in response.

Oliver disconnects the line.

I shake off the feeling that things will never be the way they were before. Back when Oliver still trusted the team, when he had no reason not to. When *I* had no reason not to.

I finish undressing and step into the freezing water, opting for a cold shower to shock my system. I will the ice-cold water to wash away the sinking feeling that I'm always one step behind.

Wake up, Declan. I need to stay sharp, stay alert.

I'll never let my guard down again.

3

CHARLIE

"You have no idea how much you are my hero," I tell my favorite new coworker, Ana, as she helps me carry the sandwiches from the elevator into FIRE's lobby. "I can't believe I forgot my badge."

Ana shrugs, scanning us into the office. "Happens to the best of us." She's about my age, wearing fitted black jeans with a floral-print silk button-down, her long dark brown beachy waves effortless and glam at the same time. "Shauna said you needed some staff gear, but let's get the suits their lunches first."

That's right. During my tour of the office, Shauna told me to link up with Ana Alonso in merchandise.

"That would be fantastic." A smile instantly spreads across my face as we cross the threshold. My skin prickles. I could blame the goosebumps dotting my skin on the air-conditioning, but I know that isn't it. "I don't think I'll ever get over the cool factor here," I breathe.

Ana laughs and flashes me a smile. "That's why we all stay. The hours are long, other sports pay better, but you'll never have a cooler business on your résumé than this one." Ana explains what I already know. What I'm already feeling. The array of Emmys, ESPYs, and other awards filling the built-in glass bookshelves to the left of the entrance is only part of it.

We head toward the executive conference room past a TV screen in the lobby playing the same promotional video on repeat. Finish-line smiles flash to the sound of drums beating a resounding conclusion. Athletes of all ages, races, and abilities celebrating. A voiceover accompanies the music, reciting the company motto, the words spoken at the start line of every race:

The race is not given to the swift, says the familiar voice as images of pro triathletes and ultra-marathoners pop up on screen. *Nor valor to the brave.* Runners jump for joy, falling to their knees at the finish line, exhausted and euphoric.

But to those who, the voice continues, a drumbeat punctuating each word, *Endure. To. The. End!*

The final four words remain on screen before the company logo appears beneath them. The letters of 'FIRE' morph into two friends lifting their arms in between two mountains, symbolizing one challenge accomplished and another on the horizon.

"So, did you move here for the job?" Ana asks, drawing my attention back from the video.

"Yes!" I say, a little too eager to please. "From Oregon."

"Oh my gosh, we did an open-water swim on the Oregon coast last year and it was so beautiful!" Ana gushes, and I can't help but think about what my first event as FIRE staff will be.

The entire office is adorned with inspirational quotes on the walls, along with high-quality finish-line photos. A mosaic of vintage race bibs and finisher medals screams endurance-athlete culture.

In the conference room, Ana helps me set up the beverages and sandwiches on the back table, which is much easier than anticipated with an extra set of hands.

"OK," she says, "time to do a little spin." She eyes me up and down. "Shauna didn't know what sizes to grab for your staff gear." The downside of being hired directly by the CEO without going through the standard process: Oliver never thought to ask my size. What will my new colleagues think when they learn it's my family connection that secured me this job?

Turning in a circle, I admit, "I feel like one of those hot dogs left to roast all day at the gas station."

She laughs at my joke. "Ha! But you look like a cute hot dog."

I wiggle my eyebrows and roll my eyes, accepting her compliment. "Any chance you can get me a polo shirt in the next fifteen minutes, so I don't have to wear this sweaty button-down at the meeting?" I ask and gesture at my shirt: rumpled, wrinkled, and beginning to stink.

"Fifteen? I can do better than that. You're about my size and we've got one full set of staff gear left in the merch closet that should fit." Ana winks. "Wait here. I'll be back in five." After that horrible interaction at the front door with Mr. Meanie, I think maybe I've made my first friend.

It hits me for the umpteenth time today. *I work for FIRE!* The butterflies have redoubled their efforts. *Damn, this is so cool!*

While I wait for Ana to return with a clean shirt, I fish my phone from my purse and check my email. Shauna already got my phone synced with the FIRE cloud. Sure enough, there's a cascade of calendar revisions for Oliver that I've been copied on. Meeting requests for Oliver with local sports officials in different cities around the world. There's an invitation from the head of the World Games Organizing Committee – I'll wait to respond on that one. I need to have my head right.

The final request is from the prime minister of Luxembourg. *Wow, I guess our ultra-cycling race there is a big deal if the head of the entire country is asking for a meeting with Oliver.*

My rapidly expanding to-do list is coming together in my mind as Ana rushes back in. She hands me a forest-green polo embroidered with the FIRE logo. "Here you go."

"You have saved me again!" I tell Ana. "I seriously owe you."

"First round is on you for happy hour," she says as we part ways at the conference-room door.

"You bet. Thank you, thank you!" I say and walk-run to the bathroom to change into the new top.

A quick glance in the mirror and it's not a completely mismatched outfit. I can make this work. I feel the seconds counting down to my first meeting with the executive team as I undo my ponytail and finger-comb my hair.

I pop by my desk to lock my sweaty blouse in the bottom drawer so any odor doesn't escape. My smile falters as I spot the second large feature at my desk. The quote in bold forest-green block letters on the wall behind my chair. *It's not personal*, I tell myself. *There are quotes all over the office.*

Quitters never earn a line in the history books.

I can't help but bristle. As if I were destined to end up here, to sit as Exhibit A proving this quote to be true.

I shake the thought from my mind because I have no time for self-pity. It's like I'm staring down a race clock again. I decide that the rest of today will be better. No more run-ins with judgmental douchebags, I hope.

Checking the time, I make a beeline for the break room to mix Oliver's requisite shake before the meeting.

"Charlotte, is everything OK?" Shauna from HR sidles up next to me and continues walking with me toward the break room. It's weird to be called by my legal name, but, of course, it's on all the paperwork she had me sign: NDA, Healthcare, retirement savings, and other benefit registrations.

"Exec meeting starts in three minutes," I tell her. "And I'll need every second to whip up Oliver's shake."

Shauna is about ten years older than me, with an impeccable tan, blond highlights, a bright tropical-print pantsuit, and an even brighter smile. "*Run, walk, or crawl*," she says and points at the quote on the wall leading to the company kitchen with a knowing smile.

This is the official rule for crossing the finish line at any FIRE event. While elite athletes like my dad can win his age group, many sign up just to do the thing, to finish before the race cut-off. Finishing at all is a huge accomplishment.

We both laugh, and I'm relieved by her generosity.

"Do you need a coffee?" Shauna offers. "You must be exhausted with the time change from the West Coast."

"You're so kind. I'll be good," I demur, not wanting to explain I don't drink coffee unless it is a half-caf iced latte, so really one-eighth caf in the entire mug. I worry it sounds too high-maintenance. Although my radical shift in diet *is* high-maintenance, the head of HR doesn't need to know that on Day One.

"Let me show you what you need for Oliver's shake," she says. It's strange how everyone here calls him Oliver – so formal – when to me he's always been Uncle Ollie. I watch Shauna pull out the items needed for his protein and collagen shake, committing their location to memory.

When the blender finishes groaning, I pour the concoction into a glass with the FIRE logo etched on it – the liquid matches both the consistency and color of a murky mud pie.

I'm about to walk-run out of the break room when a woman in three-inch heels, their soles crimson, click-clacks imperiously toward the water cooler. Her flowing raven tresses fall perfectly across her shoulders. Her outfit is impeccable, her cheekbones high and sharp. She makes quite an entrance.

The woman doesn't so much as glance at me or Shauna until the head of HR clears her throat.

Shauna starts the introductions. "Celine, this is Charlotte Ross. She's our new executive assistant."

I smile and timidly extend a hand. Celine assesses me, considering if she should accept. "Everyone calls me Charlie," I add nervously, my fingers itching to grab the hair tie on my wrist and put my hair up. As a lifelong runner and then a coach, a ponytail was practically a uniform. For my first corporate job, I took time to blow-dry my hair this morning. The Florida humidity had other plans.

"Celine Charboneau," she says, a French lilt to her words. With tight lips, she offers me a limp hand and a quick shake. "I run our public relations." *PR? More like* Project Runway. I thought I would be comically overdressed today in a navy pinstripe pencil skirt and blue button-up. Given the attire of the women with me in the break room, I now know I'm woefully underdressed.

"It's so nice to meet you," I reply, but Celine is already breezing through the exit with her full bottle of water. There's no time to contemplate her cold greeting.

I thank Shauna again for her help and hustle into the conference room, placing Oliver's shake at the head of the table before I take a seat in the back corner, pen in hand, ready to learn and take notes.

A man in his mid-forties wearing an eccentric plaid button-down, a smartwatch on his wrist, and a micro laptop tucked under one arm, is the first to enter. He walks right toward me, beaming. "You must be Charlie." He extends a hand. I stand to greet him. "I'm Ian Turner, chief technology officer and the head of network security."

Isn't CTO and head of network security the same thing? I want to ask. But I don't. His title is a mouthful and sounds redundant to me, but some people like having long titles.

"Welcome aboard. I know Oliver can be busy, and I am too, but if you need anything, never hesitate to reach out," he offers with a nod. Ian glances at his watch. "Oliver should be here momentarily. He's still on with the Sri Lankan minister of defense."

What in the world does the minister of defense have to talk about with the CEO of an endurance-sports company?

"Right," I say. "Of course." I must have misheard. Ian must have said minister for sport. I'm overwhelmed by how much there is to learn, so I don't question it. I took so much for granted in my last job. I knew everyone; they knew me. Now I'm starting from scratch.

Ian glances at the platters of sandwiches that Ana and I laid on the back table. "I hope you won't think me rude if I abandon you for a chicken wrap, Charlie."

I laugh and take my seat. "Not at all. Although I'd recommend the mojo pork sandwiches – I saw them making it fresh."

"Don't mind if I do. Always good to have insider intel." He strolls toward the buffet table.

Uncle Ollie strides purposefully into the room, talking to the CFO – Finn. He cuts an imposing figure. Oliver Hawkins is an endurance-sports icon. He looks like he just stepped off a cover shoot for a glossy sports mag: gray polo and green chinos, his salt-and-pepper hair buzzed.

"Charlie, you're in the room. You're sitting at the table," Oliver commands without looking at me. My cheeks heat and I move from my inconspicuous corner to a chair at the middle of the table. When I sit down, I hazard a glance over at Oliver and he gives me a wink. "You've got this," he mouths, and I feel a surge of confidence. He takes a sip of the shake and doesn't immediately spit it out. *Phew.*

I'm taking in the view of the bay from the windows as the execs grab their sandwiches. The midday sun is dazzling on the calm water, shooting rays in different directions. I'm struck once again by the epic nature of this job, this office, this company. *It's an epic job because I can still do epic shit!* I tell myself.

"Where's Davidson?" Finn asks.

Tearing into his sandwich, Oliver replies, "On his way – caught the red-eye back last night."

The sound of footsteps hurrying toward the conference room distracts me from my thoughts. I turn my head in time to see Mr. Douchebag-at-the-Door waltz in.

He appears freshly showered and cleaned up, he's lost the baseball cap, and his hair is slicked back and tidy. He is wearing a FIRE polo, the same one I have on, and khakis. He looks every bit the polished professional. Not the troll-like guard who leaves people sweating in the sun with their arms full that he is.

"Sorry I'm late," he announces, not seeming especially contrite, and takes the seat opposite me.

It isn't until he sits down that our eyes lock. I catch a brief expression of shock before he composes himself. His dark brown eyes turn stormy, as if he still doesn't quite believe that I belong here. As if *I'm* an intruder. He shoots Oliver a look.

"Declan," my uncle begins, "this is my new executive assistant, Charlie Ross."

I smile and nod at the various executives now seated round the table. My title may be executive assistant, but my primary role is to help Oliver do his job. Today that was to finish my onboarding and make sure the executives had lunch. Tomorrow it could be tracking down delayed event incident reports or getting a shipment of finisher medals through customs. *Keep the plates spinning* is what Oliver told me. After helping my dad as his assistant coach for years, I knew I could tackle this too.

"Everyone, Charlie is my new right hand. Anything you need from me goes through her first."

I can still feel Declan's gaze boring into me. When I lift my eyes to his, I want to shout, *I told you so!* at him, but that wouldn't exactly be professional. Instead, I say, "I think we met downstairs earlier."

He swallows, and for a moment I feel the same exhilaration I used to get when I passed someone on the track. But that feeling is quickly replaced with disappointment. The person who didn't let me in the building is a senior-level member of the team. *Declan Davidson*. I recognize the name from the empty office opposite my desk. He'll be sitting across from me every day. Silently judging my ability to do basic tasks, I'm sure. Seated beneath the most befitting quote: *Quitters never earn a line in the history books.*

"Welcome aboard," Declan mutters, his words insincere.

The meeting commences and beneath my pasted-on smile, I feel myself deflate. All that confidence and excitement for starting a job at FIRE seeping away. I contemplate throwing in the towel, telling Uncle Ollie this was a terrible idea, but then the quote above my desk becomes an epitaph. And Declan, who clearly thinks I don't belong here, would be proven correct. How long until they find out anyways?

That I'm the girl who forfeited her spot to race at the World Games in Auckland four years ago. I'm the girl who took an assistant coaching job and had to see the looks of pity on everyone's faces. The girl who quit said coaching job because she couldn't stomach watching her dad coach another team to victory at this summer's World Games when it wasn't something she'd ever be able to achieve herself.

Charlie Ross: *the girl who quit.*

And if I leave now, if I let even one person here see me back down, then it becomes true. I need to prove to this team – including Declan Davidson – and more importantly *myself*, that I can do this.

I will not be the girl who quit. Not anymore.

4

DECLAN

Well, this doesn't happen often. But I was wrong. I don't plan on admitting it aloud any time soon.

I grimace at the memory of leaving Oliver's new assistant locked outside in the midday heat, then try to cover it by cracking my knuckles.

She should have clarified who she was. And Oliver should have let me and Ian interview her as well. There were a lot of mistakes along the way that led to this situation.

Ian gives his update: "Our new servers have been installed and the team is making sure we have more than enough capability for all our events this season." The need for new servers *does* support the race-day app that will allow loved ones to track their athletes on course. They also support the new massive firewall we had to install after a series of hacks into our secret database compromised our encryption. At least Ian's update doesn't require him to lie or carefully place his words. Nothing the new assistant can't hear without revealing our clandestine operations.

Charlie is across from me, taking notes. She is focused. *That's a positive.* I assess her once more. Instead of seeing her as a potential threat, how could she be as a coworker? A possible asset for our covert operations? But first, can we even trust her?

She has changed her attire. The forest green looks good on her. Not that I care what she looks like.

Finn is boasting about the bottom line: "The latest merchandise campaign has boosted quarterly revenue." *Good. We need all the extra revenue we can get if we are going to combat the Order.*

Each of the executives provides their update. I'm debating how to handle mine. We have sensitive items to address and with a new person on the team who has not been read in on our covert operations this will get tricky.

"Declan, can you update us on your trip to Helsinki?" Oliver prompts.

I relay the same information I told him over the phone to the rest of the team. The permits for our midnight finish have been secured.

"Are all the documents signed?" Ian asks.

Out of the corner of my eye, I see Charlie's head pop up. She must have caught this question. Because to the uninitiated it sounds like Ian wasn't listening to my update and is asking a redundant question. But I know what he is really asking. He is confirming the peace treaty.

"Yes," I reply, my tone clipped. "Can you catch me up on Kandy?" I could wait until Ian, Oliver, and myself can connect. But Oliver decided to have his new assistant in here. He can find a way to talk around it.

"Minister Atapattu will meet with us when the team arrives for the race. We'll work closely with his team and see to it no details *slip*. Ensure a *seamless* event," Oliver relays.

It sounds like our usual jargon. But the words Oliver has used clue me in.

Slip – as in someone is letting information slip. Based on our past conversations with the minister of defense, I can guess there is someone in Atapattu's department who is slipping information to a local cartel that is terrorizing segments of the capital city, and they need to be stopped.

Seamless – no loose ends. As in, we will engage with each member of his team to determine who the leak is and identify them. From there, we can assume the minister of defense will dismiss them from their post. Or will follow the leak to identify members of the cartel. Either way, we'll have enough people on site, enough eyes on the course and his team, to make sure we find the answer.

Charlie cuts in. "Should I add any specific meetings to the agenda for when the team arrives for the triathlon?"

First day. Only female in a room full of men. At least four years younger than me, which means she's two or three decades younger than everyone else. She's speaking up right away. That takes confidence. I have to admit I'm impressed.

She isn't hiding behind any "it's my first day" excuses. But she hasn't been fully vetted. Oliver hired her without talking to anyone else. Did he check that she wasn't sent by the Order? Has she already been briefed on us by her handler?

"Yes," I say at the same time as Oliver says, "Exactly. We'll confirm details with his team over the coming weeks."

The thought of these missions used to give me a thrill. My time in the navy gave me the skills to do this job. I loved serving my country, but I couldn't shake the feeling I was expendable. An interchangeable cog. At FIRE, I thought I could really make a difference.

My mood sours thinking of how I started here. Xander Caruso recruiting me. X.C., my mentor. My friend. My final memory of him flashes in my mind. His confusion just seconds before we were both blown into Osaka Bay. Fighting the waves only to realize X.C. wasn't next to me. We'd been betrayed on that mission and X.C. paid with his life. If I had been faster, my thoughts sharper, I could have saved him. Saved us both. The guilt is as suffocating as the frigid water he never surfaced from.

It was Oliver's faith in my ability to help stop the Order and hold their members accountable that kept me going. My trust is still in tatters.

It makes me a better agent, I tell myself. *Trust was a weakness.*

That's why I'm still here at FIRE. To stop the Order.

Everything else? It's just another contract signed. Another city to host an ultra-marathon, an endurance triathlon, some new spin on a death-defying open-water swim. Meet with the head of local police to help weed out an informant selling secrets to organized crime. Make sure the weak link in a local crime family is intercepted by the authorities. And on and on and on.

I used to think we were making a difference, a dent in the evil in the world. Now it's like an arcade game of whack-a-mole with no prizes to be had. Only more work to be done, more ruin to unravel.

I eye Charlie and catch her assessing me. She looks away quickly, suddenly engrossed in her notes. And now I have a new challenge. To root out if she is, in fact, just a new executive assistant or if she is here to sabotage our mission.

I add one more to-do onto the pile.

5

CHARLIE

By Wednesday, I've found a great route to get to the office with minimal traffic. I've located the forms I'll need for an inventory restock. And, thanks to Ana, I've sampled the best Cuban food I've had in my life at a café not far from the office.

But I have not met with my boss yet to discuss his expectations or any goals for my position. That is about to change.

"Ready?" I lean into Oliver's office. We have our one-on-one on the calendar, but that doesn't mean he hasn't been pulled into a new emergency or a report of some kind.

"Yes! Charlie, come on in." He gestures with a wave and pushes the papers in front of him aside. They go into a haphazard pile that has me itching to straighten it. His cluttered shelves around the office are full of trophies, medals, and photographs of Oliver and various coaches, athletes, celebrities, and heads of state.

I'm settling into one of the cushioned chairs in front of his desk when he dives right in. "How is your first week going so far?"

The thing with Oliver Hawkins is that when you have his attention, you have all of it. For better or worse. He can be kind of intense that way. I think I once heard someone say "cluttered desk, organized mind." It must be true because Oliver has the sharpest mind of anyone I've ever met.

"I like the office, and having a desk is a nice change," is the first thing that pops out of my mouth. I wince. It sounds silly, but it's true; I do love it. The buzz of phones and chatter of coworkers is a pleasant white noise, an ambient soundtrack to a peaceful work environment. That's what I wanted in a new job. There is also the undeniable cool factor.

"Well, half the team is either heading to a race or heading back from one. Great for concentrating when we are in season, not great for tracking people down," Oliver explains. "But this is an office job. Sitting is the new smoking. If you need a standing desk to get on your feet, let me know," he says, before giving a slight grimace. He realizes the double meaning of his words. That I'm off my feet, literally sitting at a desk all day. Which is a legitimate health concern. But his phrasing also reminds me that I'm *off* my feet, as prescribed. No running. Nothing to stress the body too much. "You let me know at the first signs of any—" Oliver begins, but I cut him off.

"I don't need bubble wrap." I spill out the same words I said to my mother two weeks ago when I told her I'd accepted this job. Yes, it will have a certain level of stress. But I've been healthy for four years now. And while I loved being my dad's assistant running coach, I do not miss the blistering sun on a long training day. Or the smell of the locker room that would permeate the coaching office. I don't miss the looks either. Pity or judgment. I hung up my running shoes years ago and then, a couple weeks ago, I hung up my whistle too.

Oliver pushes his lips together, holding back whatever he wants to say. I understand his worry. But I'm not a child. I can make my own decisions, take an exciting job opportunity, and monitor my own health.

"Maybe I'll put in a request for a standing desk," I offer. Not that I think I would actually enjoy one of them, but to show him that I took his words at face value.

Oliver nods. "What have you got for me?"

I go through the list I've collected. Requests for his time, mostly from people outside of the company. In house most people run things to their manager, then director, then their C-level if needed. The executive team brings the big-picture items to Oliver, the rest he trusts the team to handle.

"Um, the president of Croatia wants to meet when you are in Dubrovnik for the marathon relay?" I say, but the words come out as a question. I'm not entirely sure it isn't a prank.

But Oliver doesn't skip a beat. "Ah yes. He's a good friend. I'll get back to him today and confirm a time to meet. I'll make sure you have the details for my schedule." Oliver says this quickly, rushing to get to the next topic.

I nod and make a note. I knew FIRE was a big deal in the endurance-racing world. To have the attention of world leaders, though. I'm astonished at what Oliver has built. But I guess he never does anything halfway.

We go over his full itinerary for the next four weeks. Not only is he attending two of our events in North America, but he is racing one of our events in Brazil at the end of the month, which means I need to make sure all his gear is with him too.

"One final item," I begin, a little nervous to even mention it. Because, depending on his response, I will either have my faith in Uncle Ollie confirmed or shattered. "Titus Kilbride is registered for our ultra-triathlon in Miami." The man is notorious. An ex-senator accused of sexual harassment and assault by multiple female staffers. The trial was all over the news, but the case was dropped on a technicality. The consensus is he did it; the prosecution just can't prove it. "Do we really want him on one of our courses?"

Uncle Ollie nods his head, thinking of his response. "Hmm, I do believe in the justice system. Even when it doesn't work as well as it should. I'm happy to relieve him of his money if he wants to spend it."

My childlike admiration for my dad's best friend, my uncle, one of my sports heroes, buckles. "But won't it tarnish our brand?" Most everyone agrees he is guilty and getting away with it. Not to mention that he poses a potential security risk for our female athletes, and the damage his association could do to our brand is significant.

"Should we be in the business of judging people?" Uncle Ollie's face is unreadable. He leans back in his chair, as if the burden of this topic is heavy enough to push him back. "Do we decide that his punishment for his crimes is that he can't subject himself to seventeen hours of voluntary torture? I don't like the guy. But cancelling his registration doesn't feel like justice."

The potential headlines flash in my mind. If FIRE refunds him and bars him from competing, the logical next question is, on what grounds? We could have a PR nightmare because "he is a jerk" is unfortunately still not a crime. I let out a frustrated sigh. "Could I throw a stick in the spokes of his bike tires?"

Uncle Ollie leans in and gives me a wink. The same one he would give me when he would sneak extra cookies onto my plate at one of my parents' BBQs. "I like that plan. Has some wrinkles in it, though. Primarily, you getting charged with assault. Then he sues the company and we may have to go under, due to a mountain of legal fees." He is silent for a moment, as if he is actually considering this. His playing along pacifies my concerns. He locks his eyes with mine before raising one eyebrow. "Or what if we could get him to admit to his crimes on course? Get incriminating evidence?"

I laugh, because that has to be a joke. A daydream. That this notorious predator could be put away. "Like he'd confess so easily."

Oliver resets in his chair and shrugs. "You'd be surprised what smug criminals think they can get away with. He thinks no one can touch him. He'll forget the part of the athlete waiver that says we record all of our events. The assumption is that it is for marketing and promotion. But he doesn't know that we could pick up the audio."

That's the stereotype of criminals; they slip up eventually. Get too bold. But what does Uncle Ollie know about criminals? It would be nice to see the guy behind bars, but we're not trained to coax out confessions. Best we can do is hope he has the worst day of his life on course.

"I hear your concern, Charlie. Let me think on this," Oliver says as he checks his smartwatch, which is actually a top-of-the-line fitness and biometrics tracking device. "I have another meeting in ten and I still have one topic for us to go over."

"Sure thing, what is it?" I ask, trusting he will circle back to this problem.

"You're brand new – what are your impressions of the team so far?" he asks, his hands behind his head, reclining in his chair once more.

"Oh." My shoulders relax at this question. I was expecting a new laundry list of items to complete. I think about his query, realizing there are office politics in play. I don't know enough about them to answer carefully. I choose the brutally honest route. "Everyone is on their A game, that's for sure." You have to be an elite athlete to win a FIRE race and you need to be elite in your profession to work here.

Oliver nods, but I sense this isn't the answer he was hoping for. "Charlie, I know you are a hard worker; you're a team player."

I nod along, eager for this praise.

"But you are also very trusting." As he says this, something in my gut reacts. Because I tend to believe the best in people. I trust people until they give me a reason not to. And the only person to betray that trust thus far in my life has been, well, me. My body. "I need you to be on the lookout for me. Someone on the team . . ." He pauses, searching for the exact right way to phrase his next words. "I think someone is sharing company secrets."

I sit back. As if this knowledge is a hot stove that I've skirted too close to. What Oliver is concerned about makes sense. With success comes competition. Each year, more race operators try to put their own spin on FIRE events. Mimicking distances, course venues, and sometimes even the branding.

"Can you keep an eye out for anyone acting suspiciously?" Oliver tasks me with this secret responsibility.

Immediately, I think of Celine and her cool attitude. About Declan and his refusal to let me in the building. What am I looking for? Watching out for? Will I know corporate espionage when I see it?

6

DECLAN

One more meeting and then it is the weekend.

An hour and then I'm out of here.

Home, changed, and ready to ride.

Just me and the bike. The sound of the chain and wheels rolling and the freedom of the road. If I hit all the traffic lights right, I might be able to get back from my twenty-mile ride before the sun sets. With three months to go until my 300 km cycling race in Athens, I can't slack on my training if I want to place in my age group. All that stands between me and my evening is one final meeting.

With my water bottle in one hand and my notepad in the other, I head out of my office to the conference room. My timing is horrible, because Charlie Ross hops up from her desk at the same time. Her perky ponytail bobs along, all she needs is a yellow pencil in her hair and she'll have the quirky librarian look down. The glasses, the hair. The pencil skirts that are professional yet still highlight her sculpted calves. She has her security badge on a lanyard round her neck, as if she is trying to rub it in my face that I left her stranded outside on Monday.

"Hey, Declan." She makes eye contact, which means we'll end up walking to this meeting together.

I give her a nod in response.

"So, you were just in Finland?" Charlie asks. Her tone is so peppy and upbeat, I wince as if I've been hit in the eyes with direct sunlight.

"Yes. And?" I answer, not sure where her line of questioning is going.

"Oh, I saw a headline that the peace treaty was negotiated there. I've gone years of my life not thinking about the country and then two times in one week: Finland!" She talks with her hands and it only accentuates her prattling.

"Hmm," is all I can muster in response. *She knows something. I don't know what, but she does.*

Charlie presses her lips together. I hope my short responses are enough to end her questions. I'm all for helping the new team member out, but her direct questioning, the timing of her arrival, are too uncanny for me.

We pass by accounting in silence, for which the number crunchers are likely grateful. This corner of the office is the quietest, even with half the race operations team out on site all year.

"So you're the VP of strategic operations?" Charlie pries once more.

"Yep," I respond, happy to see the conference-room door just ahead. I won't have to deal with her inane babbling for much longer.

"What does that even mean?" she asks. "I mean, sorry, that came out rude. But we have race operations, so how is strategic operations distinct from that?"

I stop short a few paces before we reach the conference room. Charlie stops a half-step later and turns round. Her blue eyes gaze up at me behind those librarian glasses. She is searching for something. She could be trying to make small talk, get the lay of the land in the office, but my instincts are telling me that there is more to her sudden appearance and expedited hiring process. I answer her query: "Business development. Making contacts with decision-makers in each market."

"That sounds fun," she replies with a nod.

I brush past her and enter the conference room. There are two open seats left, thankfully on opposite sides of the room. My options are the chair next to the A/C vent or Celine from PR Celine is good at her job, but she can't take a hint. I'm not interested in anything other than the necessary professional interactions with her. I elect to sit near the A/C.

The meeting is productive and efficient. Each department head gives a brief update, a few even cede their time so others can go over more pressing topics. Trey, who leads our corporate travel logistics, asks for an update on the visas for the executive team. Charlie provides her update succinctly. I have to hand it to her, she's on top of things. That's a good sign. But then, of course, Little Miss Questions pipes up.

"I have one name from the previous executive list that I can't get a hold of. Is Xander Caruso still traveling with the same itinerary as Oliver?"

The room shifts. Everyone was quiet before, but now it sounds like they are all holding their breath. They are all frozen. And instead of looking to Charlie, who was just speaking, or Trey, who could easily have deleted X.C. from the list, I can sense that the whole room is focused on me. I look over and Ian Turner has shifted his gaze back to Charlie; his expression mirrors my own.

I flex my hands as if I have some imaginary stress ball in my palms. The motion helps, fractionally. "He's no longer with us."

We never recovered his body from the bottom of Osaka Bay. But Shauna still sent the obituary in a company-wide email. They brought in grief counselors for employees to talk to. I worked from home for a few weeks to avoid questions. I needn't have bothered. The rumor mill turned out enough theories.

X.C. might have looked fit, but he had a heart condition. Went for a run before one of their meetings and dropped dead.

Well, I heard X.C. was wasted and drove his rental car into the water. It's a miracle Declan made it out alive.

None of the rumors got close to the truth and that was just fine. Let people create their own story.

Charlie glances over to me and I can read the look on her face. The "oh, I've stepped in it" expression.

Next to her, Celine catches my attention. She rolls her eyes at Charlie's expense. I may not like Charlie very much, and I certainly don't trust her, but no one likes a bully either. I ignore Celine's non-verbal commentary and resume my notes.

The meeting ends a few moments later. I stay back as everyone else filters out – everyone except Ian. "We need to talk to Oliver about his new assistant." His terse words confirm that he shares my suspicions.

"Couldn't agree more," I say before we both march over to Oliver's office. Charlie is sitting at her desk, already dutifully typing her meeting notes.

Ian walks right past without giving her a second glance. He starts right in before the door is closed. "Oliver, Charlie is asking a *lot* of questions."

I'm only a few steps behind him, hurrying to join him in Oliver's office. I close the door behind me. My frustration is now directed at Ian as well. His premature comments were sloppy. There is no way Charlie didn't hear Ian's opening complaint.

Oliver is standing at his desk, packing his laptop, notepad, and USB drives into a FIRE-branded messenger bag. "It's her first week; of course she's asking questions. She's learning the ropes around here."

"I think you misunderstand. She's prying. Asking about my trip to Finland. Asking about what I do here," I emphasize to Oliver.

Oliver rebuffs my statement. "Those are perfectly reasonable questions for a coworker to ask another."

Ian lets out a sigh and crosses his arms. The man is 6' 4" and not one to speak up much, if at all. He is a tech guy through and through; he would prefer to communicate with robots in binary code than with humans in words. The fact that he is bringing this issue to Oliver speaks volumes, or it should. "I don't know where you found her. We know nothing about her past. Her allegiances."

Oliver stops his preparations to leave. "I'm sure you could ask Charlie about all of that. Her last job. Where she went to college. How fast she can run a mile."

I put my hands on my hips. I hate to have to spell it out for Oliver. "She could be a plant from the Order! Have you stopped to consider that?" In the six months since X.C. and I were burned on a mission in Osaka, we have had multiple covert operations go sideways. Bad intel, informants tailed and bullied into hiding, and then a direct threat to one of our events. An explosive package left in the transition area of one of our triathlons, the metallurgic signature matches a known associate of the Order. It could be multiple individuals or organizations colluding against us, but it fits that it would be the Order. They clearly have a mole within our organization to keep that flow of intelligence running. We've swapped out security clearances, repositioned team members, and found nothing. That my mission in Helsinki was successful means that we've thwarted the Order's attempts to infiltrate us. Or the mole got wise and realized we were on to them, prompting the Order to send a new informant.

Ian backs me up. "The World Games are later this summer and we are less than five months out from our Exponential Endurance Championships. We've got too much on the line to chance a new potential threat to our security."

Oliver takes off his glasses and cleans them with the hem of his polo. It's a stalling technique I've seen him use before, a way to gather his thoughts. "You're right, we can't be too careful about who we trust. Which is why I wasn't excited about the idea of hiring someone with the espionage experience that you suggested." He levels his gaze at me. "The last two you sent me," he says, addressing Ian, "were keen to do all the clandestine work but couldn't manage the calendar. Horrible executive admins *and* I couldn't trust them. Charlie has my absolute trust, can do the job, and most importantly isn't previously trained in deception." There is a note of finality in his voice, but my doubts linger.

"But *how* do you know you can trust her? How can we?" I protest.

He points to the far wall of his office with the start-line quote on it. "You know the origin of that quote? *The race is not given to the swift, nor valor to the brave, but to those who endure to the end*?"

"Ecclesiastes," I retort.

"Matthew?" Ian guesses, both of us referring to a biblical origin of the quote.

"Partially correct." Oliver nods. "But the first time I ever heard it was from my college roommate. It was his personal mantra. He uses it all the time in his run coaching now."

Ian and I are silently waiting for Oliver to elaborate further. When he does, he only gives us a name: "Tom Ross." In my periphery, Ian's shoulders sink, his guard dropped.

Tom Ross, Mr. Run Barefoot, coached the US track and field delegation to multiple gold and silver medals in the World Games four years ago. Best-selling author, Tom Ross. In terms of famous runners and running coaches, he's a big name. No one outside our little niche knows who he is, but everyone inside of it does.

"And, let me guess, Charlie *Ross* is his daughter?" I ask, finally putting the pieces together.

Oliver gives me a nod. "And my niece. I know I can count on you to show her the ropes. She'll be on site with me next weekend in Kalispell, but when I'm out of the office, can you look out for her?"

I manage to squeeze out "yes, sir" through my tight jaw. Oliver leaves and pats Ian on the shoulder on his way out.

"Have a safe trip," Charlie chirps behind me.

Our operation has never been more vulnerable, we are still reeling from the chaos the Order has caused, and now we are stuck with an inexperienced nepo hire of an executive assistant.

This is worse than a plant. At least that person can be dismissed with cause. Oliver's "niece" is not going to be up to this task and we are all going to pay for *her* ineptitude. And *his* weakness in hiring her. Best to keep my guard up. Ian turns to me and gives me a "what are you gonna do?" look before walking away.

I close Oliver's door on my way out and avoid eye contact with Charlie as I walk to my office. I'll be using this frustration on my ride tonight, knocking out twenty miles in an hour, easy. Maybe forty minutes.

From behind me, Charlie calls out, "You know, Ollie isn't really my uncle."

I turn to her, letting my pent-up frustration out. "They never are!"

It may not be Charlie's fault that my mentor was murdered in front of my eyes. That the operations FIRE runs to keep the world safe from nefarious scum are compromised. That my instincts are all screaming to trust no one. But she is getting the brunt of it.

Her assertion that she and Oliver aren't blood related does nothing to reassure me or make this any less a clear case of nepotism. If anything, it is the worst-case scenario. Not qualified for the job and a potential liability. The Order aren't above bribery. If she has any student loans or debts in the family, they can use that as leverage.

Charlie cocks her head to the side and gives a laughing smile. "Did you just angry-quote *Pretty Woman* to me?"

The most irrational response! How am I supposed to work with this?

She grabs her purse and locks her computer. "Have a good weekend, Declan." She waves and bounces out of the office as if her presence hasn't caused a massive disruption. I want to slam my office door. I want to tell her to her face that I think she shouldn't be working here. I want to shout.

Instead, I pack my things, head home, and plan to pound out these training miles. To focus on the road, and the bike, and to forget for a while.

7

CHARLIE

"This place has the best frozen margaritas!" Ana declares as soon as we enter the bar for the after-work drinks I promised on Monday. It may be open-air, but the music is loud and the growing crowd of Friday-night revelers are fighting for dominance.

The bar sits on a tiny shell-laden beach on the bay. Ana assures me that the best thing about Florida is that you can go to an outdoor bar year-round. My poor frizzed hair begs to differ. The theme here is very beachy, with thatched roofing over the bar and mixed drinks available in plastic coconuts.

"You've got to try one!"

I nod my head as she leads us forwards. Because I hadn't thought through the whole ordering drinks part of the evening. Training always came first in college and that meant no drinking for me. And then my immune system decided to attack my muscles and that settled it – no alcohol ever. I promised her I'd get the first round and I'm happy to have a friend to go out with. Finishing out my first full week in a new city, at a new job, is cause for celebration. *Maybe one little drink can't hurt.*

Ana pushes into the throng of people pressed up to the bar for their orders. I pull my oversized purse closer to my body. Not that I'm afraid anyone will try to run off with it; it is far too packed in for anyone to make an escape. I'm more nervous about it knocking into someone and inadvertently starting a bar fight.

We get to the front and Ana waves down the bartender. The tall, tan, skinny woman behind the bar with wild fuchsia curls and a sleeve of tattoos on her right arm gives us a nod.

"Good, my ex is serving tonight," Ana mentions as we wait our turn to order.

"Is she going to give you a healthy pour or a weak one?" I ask, trying to gauge if this is a friendly ex or not.

"Oh, she's going to be jealous that I'm here with you." Ana pauses mid-thought. "You're awesome, honey, but not my type," she says before continuing her original explanation. "She's going to pour well and even offer one on the house. You may not have to pay for any of my drinks tonight."

"Win!" I say, raising my hand for a high five.

Ana claps my hand. "Double win. I talked Trey into switching the room assignments, so you'll be bunking with me on site in Kalispell." This is welcome news. We'll be flying out for the marathon weekend in northern Montana on Thursday.

"Thank God. I was terrified I might have had to share with Celine," I say. I could only imagine the judgment she would pass on my night guard and flannel pajamas. I stop myself from complaining further. If Ana and Celine are buddies, then I might have just stepped in it.

"Ha! I would not subject you to that in your first month on the job," Ana retorts before scanning the bar for her ex again. She is working her way toward us, mixing drinks as fast as she can.

"What is Celine's deal anyways?" I ask, trying to get a better understanding of why she was so unwelcoming.

"You mean she wasn't on her *model* behavior?" Ana asks sarcastically.

"She was a supermodel?" I gasp.

"Super, maybe or maybe not. But yeah, she used to model professionally," Ana responds. "The reason I don't like her has nothing to do with her good looks. It's not her fault she's gorgeous or that she had a job that played to her strengths."

I nod in agreement. I wouldn't want my appearance used against me, not that anyone is lining up to do that any time soon. "So why don't you like her then?" I catch on Ana's phrasing.

"We're women in a male-dominated industry in a male-dominated office. She should be lifting up other women, others around her. But no," Ana begins.

It's a dynamic I didn't even realize I was used to. Growing up in sports meant mostly being around guys. Teammates, coaches, trainers, athletic directors. There have been shifts and better representation, but it isn't even close to parity.

"Everyone at FIRE is competitive, and if you had yet to notice, running, cycling, triathlon, and swimming are all individual sports, if you catch me."

I mull over her analogy. "So Celine buys into the macho alpha-male bullshit?" My mind flashes on Declan and his less than warm reception and continued antagonism. Like going to Oliver to complain about me for . . . asking questions?

"Hook, line, and sinker," Ana says, leaning against the bar. "She benefits from it, so why change it?"

I think back on Oliver's request to keep an ear out for anyone passing company info to our competitors. If Celine is really cut-throat and competitive in business, she may be tempted to sell company secrets. I file this information away.

"Can we please talk about the superwoman transformation from workplace Charlie to Friday-night Charlie?" Ana changes the subject, eyeing my outfit. The dress code at FIRE allows for casual Fridays. I paired my best jeans with a blouse today but chucked it into the back seat of my car after work and changed from heels into sandals. The camisole I wore under my blouse is light and low-cut, ideal for a hot open-air bar.

"What? It's a beach bar. I'm dressed for the beach," I explain. "And I usually wear contacts, but the pollen count in this state is off the charts. Figured wearing my frames at work would give my eyes a break, but I wanted to look cute tonight, so I popped in my backup contacts before we left." I pat my oversized purse as I say this. I've learned the hard way to always be prepared with backup contacts, solution, a case, and glasses. *You never know.* Ana accepts this explanation without commenting on how I live my life around my allergies, around what my body demands. *Maybe it isn't that uncommon after all.*

Ana peers down the bar again and waves to the woman she identified as her ex. The woman gives a reluctant smile and Ana turns round to me. "I know that smirk. Lucy will be over in a moment. I apologize in advance for her being a smidge territorial." Ana adjusts her outfit, checking the buttons on her blouse and smoothing out her hair. We are indeed the same height and size, but Ana is still rocking her work heels and a few inches taller because of it.

I'm about to ask more about this situationship Ana is in when someone taps my shoulder. In the short time we've been next to the bar, I've been bumped a few times, but I can tell this is different.

I turn and find myself face-to-face with a wall of muscle in a tight black T-shirt. I look up and find a pair of sea-green eyes watching me. "I don't mean to startle you, but there is an enormous bug on your shoulder."

It takes me a moment to register what this handsome man has said. *Did he ask me to run away with him? Did he tell me that he just stepped off Mount Olympus?*

"What?" I follow where he is pointing to with his finger, craning my neck to see A HUGE FUCKING BUG ON MY SHOULDER!

It has wings and big eyes and it could possibly devour me. Slowly, but it could.

I am about to scream when he reaches forwards and picks the demonic being off my body. I hadn't even sensed it there. "They're harmless but terrifying," he says as the bug flies up and away to go bother someone else in the bar. I'm officially against open-air bars now.

I let out a sigh of relief. "Thank you," I say to my rescuer. The bar smells like a mix of every perfume and cologne covering a musk of sweat and spilled liquor. Right next to me, he smells familiar, though. Something woodsy I can't quite place, incongruous with the other scents. Not being able to identify it piques my interest.

"No worries. I didn't want you to freak out if I took him off without telling you. I didn't want to be that guy who just walks up and starts touching a beautiful woman." The man before me blushes and it accentuates his smile perfectly. His cleft chin is adorable. His light blond hair is cropped short and I am momentarily tempted to run my hands through it.

"I mean, you were being chivalrous, so . . ." I trail off, suddenly forgetting how to put words together.

Ana reaches round me and extends a hand to my mystery helper. "Hi, I'm Ana. Charlie is going to help me out for a quick sec, so I need you to stop flirting with her until after the bartender takes our order."

"I'm Blaed," he says, and shakes Ana's hand. Which is silly. I must have misheard him over the noise.

"Blade? Like Wesley Snipes's vampire Blade?" Ana heard the same thing I did.

I shake my head in disbelief. "I bet no one ever tried to steal your lunch money as a kid," I breathe, and then check that I'm not literally drooling over this man. Figuratively, I'm drool city. I need one of those dentist suction straws. But I don't want to actually salivate; it's not a good look.

"B-L-A-E-D. It's a family name. And, technically, Blade is a human-vampire hybrid," he responds. "Charlie?" He turns his attention to me and offers me a hand. His grip is strong and warm. He has to be at least 6' 3", has the build of a pro-wrestler with his thick bulky muscles, and his mesmerizing eyes are locked on mine. Thick eyelashes frame his eyes, keeping my attention, forcing me not to look away.

"Hi," is all I can manage to say, because I have no charisma.

"Can I get you ladies something to drink?" Blaed asks as Ana's ex walks up to take our orders. Blaed asks for a beer, Ana orders a margarita, and I know I have to say something. I was hoping to discreetly order a mocktail, but now I'm super insecure about it. It's for my health, but I've been healthy for years. A low-inflammation diet doesn't necessarily mean no inflammation ever. Stressing over it is probably going to cause more trouble for me than one teeny little drink.

"Bourbon and Coke," I utter, borrowing my dad's go-to order, because nothing else came to mind except Shirley Temple.

Blaed turns to talk to the guy next to him and Ana pulls me closer. "He is delicious," she whispers in my ear.

I blush because I was thinking the same exact thing. "Did we ruin your plans with your ex?" I ask.

"Nah," Ana says as she glances back at the woman mixing our drinks. "She probably feels pity now that I'm the third wheel. I can work with pity."

Ana's ex slides our drinks over. I take one hesitant sip and let the sweet and sharp taste wash over my tongue. I'm going to have to limit myself; my liver is not going to know what hit it.

I think of something that will work for me and Ana. "Well, I never play easy to get, so how about we stick to our plan to have fun and leave together to keep both of them guessing and hungry for more."

Ana gasps. "You're a genius! Nice and nerdy but a little calculated." She holds up her glass for a cheers.

I take another sip and remind myself to go slow. And research rheumatologists on my new health insurance. If I'm going to start pushing my limits, I'm going to need a doctor I can call if I push too far.

Blaed leans over and grabs his beer and his hand grazes my shoulder as he does this. I beam at him and we clink glasses as well.

One week down at a new job, a solid lead on a new friend, and a cute guy flirted with me, not so bad after all.

8

CHARLIE

BIG SKY, BIG MILES, BIG SMILES!

The sign over the finish-line arch for our weekend of races in Kalispell, Montana, is cheesy and dorky – and absolutely perfect.

It's a whole weekend of events. The marquee event is today, fifty miles. Tomorrow, on Sunday, the marathon and the half start bright and early, then we pack up and leave town.

The shorter distances are new this year. FIRE already paid to shut down the roads in and out of town, so we got our permits extended and added two more distances to maximize the number of participants (and race entry fees).

"I'm going on a coffee run; you want anything?" Ana asks. We both had to get up before dawn and we look it.

"Yes!" I yawn out and hand her some cash before relaying my very specific order. "Half-caf, iced latte with almond milk."

"No syrups, no sugars?" Ana asks, not even batting an eye.

"Nope," I respond, once again surprised that the small details of my life that are so specific and altered by my condition aren't as big of a deal to others. I've been building it up too much in my own mind.

We arrived on site an hour before the fifty-mile ultra-marathon began. The start of a race always feels ritualistic. The different elements of the religious ceremony that is a run of this length. Praise for the earth and the joints. Also questioning why. Why do this? Why am I putting myself through this? Who am I trying to prove it to? And then the triumphant celebration, the dopamine hit to end all others, the crash and then: when is the next one?

My pangs of longing, of missing the thrill of a finish-line chute, were quickly erased by the long list of tasks to handle while the race was underway. I've been Oliver's shadow all day. Snapping photos of him doing the iconic start-line speech and sending them to our social media manager back in Tampa. Meeting with local officials for the city and state, reconnecting with top run coaches.

"Oh, you're Tom's daughter," most of them said as they shook my hand, eyeing my feet, confirming I am indeed wearing shoes and not barefoot like my father is famous for. Oliver was quick to jump in and sing my praises, even though I've only been on the team for two weeks.

I'm proud to be Tom Ross's daughter. I was his assistant coach for four years. But I want to be my own person too.

The finish line is anything but quiet as the runners are out on the fifty-mile ultra-marathon course. Most won't finish for several hours, but family and friends are camped out with signs for their loved ones, huddled close to the Wi-Fi router to be able to track their runner on our app. It's the same scene at every race. Someone finds reliable Wi-Fi and everyone gloms on.

Ana returns with our coffees and I find a table to lean against in the merchandise tent. Some of our coworkers are milling around here and throughout the race expo area. A few of the other team members from merchandise, expo, and operations are doing a relay for the half-marathon. Trey from travel is on site this weekend too, which seems a little odd. Apparently, before his days working a desk job, he used to haul the frames and arches and set up the expo. He's chatting with Ahmed, who is a six-foot wall of muscle. If he didn't have an infectious laugh and smile, he would be super intimidating. They're chatting nearby, trying to come up with a punny team name.

"Are you doing the relay tomorrow?" Ana asks while checking her phone.

"Nah, I've got to shadow Oliver," I reply, happy for the excuse that has nothing to do with my condition.

"I'm sure he can spare you for thirty minutes," Ahmed says, clearly eavesdropping. He's younger than me and fit and muscular. He definitely looks like a guy who can lift two pop tents and haul them to the box trucks without breaking a sweat.

"Nope. Besides, I just got these sneakers." I point to my fresh shoes. I was told I needed to wear the brand that sponsors our events. "If I ran in these, it would be blister city." *There, now I have two solid reasons that can't be resolved.* I'm grateful that none of my coworkers know about my condition, but I also wish they knew not to ask at all. It's not that I hate running. I love it. *Loved it.* Too much. "Maybe next time." I shrug and turn my attention back to Ana. Trey and Ahmed refocus their attention on which team name will be the most "epic." "The kids' race goes off in thirty minutes. I have five minutes before I need to round up the emcee and PR so they can get the images they need to promote it," I remind her.

"Oh my goodness! The kids are so cute. The parents are so . . . insufferable. Like, it's a two-hundred-meter dash, calm down." Ana rolls her eyes.

I know exactly what she is talking about. It will be approximately three minutes of cute overload as kids from two to seven run in oversized FIRE Kalispell T-shirts and do their own variation of celebration dances when they cross the finish line. The only thing possibly cuter will be the doggy-dash during tomorrow's races.

"I've got to *fetch* Celine," I say with a sigh. "She's supposed to gather the local press for the dash, but she's been hanging with Raj, our 'celebrity guest' all day." Most runners doing the fifty-miler will tackle it solo. But we have an option for a team relay. Three to four friends can all switch off and conquer the course together. Raj Reddy, Mr. 300 Million YouTube Subscribers, also known as King Cool, is running our event with his friends. And recording a video for the channel. This is a big win for Celine. I have to give it to her.

"Ugh, of course she is. I get that she's PR, but she acts so superior because she works directly with 'celebrities.'" Ana sneers as she says this.

I agree. Raj is mega famous, yes. But he's also just a guy.

"Better than the third-place finisher on last season's *Bachelorette* who did the ultra-tri in Wisconsin and threw a diva fit in transition and stormed off course. At least Raj seems nice."

"No way!" I shake my head in disbelief. I guess diva celebrities do exist. I thought it was a bad stereotype.

"Yup, I saw the whole thing. Almost posted about it but didn't want to start a social media meltdown. Besides, Celine is playing nice with the network. I guess they want Oliver to do *The Golden Bachelor*," Ana explains.

The thought of Uncle Ollie on a reality show to find a partner is hilarious to me. *And also, ew, that's my uncle. I don't want to see that.*

"OK, I need to go boil my brain to erase the thought of my boss dating a harem of women on national TV," I say and pretend to retch before I set off for where Celine and Raj are standing near a line of trees on the relay path.

I try to politely interrupt her conversation with Raj and not appear starstruck.

"Hey, Celine, Oliver needs the local press for the children's race," I tell her.

Celine looks like she just stepped out of a catalog for running gear. Her hair is in a perfect ponytail, no bumps or knots in sight. Her black tights have mesh cutouts running down her legs, her sneakers don't have a single scuff or smudge on them, and she is cover-worthy even without any makeup on.

Celine eyes me as if I am one of the many gnats buzzing around the park, mutters "Ah yes," and walks away without introducing me to Raj.

I decide to say hello, because even though he is four years younger than me, he is kind of my hero. "Hi, Raj, I'm Charlie. I'm Oliver's assistant. If you or your team need anything, let me know."

Raj was once a rail-thin teenager with glasses and a smattering of acne on his face. He has evolved as much as his business has and now he has muscles and clear brown skin.

"I don't want to be a fangirl, but I love your low-inflammation-diet-friendly snacks," I tell him, because, in truth, his videos and his recipes saved me from the dark spiral I was in a few years ago.

Raj shakes my hand. "That's awesome. You a sickie too?" he asks, referring to the loving nickname he has given himself and other autoimmune sufferers.

"Yep," I say, pretending my condition is a badge of honor. Raj is outspoken about his experience with lupus and his recent second autoimmune diagnosis of psoriatic arthritis. How he manages to run multiple YouTube channels, a snack company, and global philanthropy without going into a flare is so impressive.

"Oh yeah, what you got?" he asks, as one of his friends who is a regular on his channel runs by in a chicken costume. Of course the hook for Raj's relay video is that he is making his friends run it in ridiculous outfits. One a chicken, another has $10,000 taped to his chest, a third is wearing beer-bottle-opener flip-flops. Not recommended footwear, but Celine was willing to let it slide for the sake of the exposure we'll get on his channel.

"Eosinophilic fasciitis," I tell him, expecting his eyes to glaze over.

Instead, he smiles and gives me a nod of approval. "Ooh, a rarity, aren't we?" His sarcastic praise encourages me to do a twirl and bow. In the few times I've interacted with other autoimmune suffers my age, we tend to commiserate by sharing diagnoses, medicines, and food restrictions like trading cards.

"Hey, I've got to go help with the kids' race. Want to come watch? I know so many of them are going to freak when they see you!" It's true. Raj is a hero to so many kids who started watching him play and review video games and fantasy chapter books. Now he gives away money to schools and they view him as a real-life Batman or Superman.

Raj is excited and waves for one of his cameramen to follow him. The kids' race start is about a quarter-mile from where we are standing, so I take my chance to keep chatting with Raj. *I mean, how cool is this?!*

"How was the trip out here?" I ask, assuming Raj took a private jet with his friends and equipment.

"Well, our bags got lost and my medicine was stolen off my front porch two days before we had to leave, so I had to have an emergency prescription called in." I'm shocked by all of this. That Raj flies commercial even with his vast wealth. And, also, the audacity of someone stealing medicine. I've avoided going back on a prescription for three years now. The damage my last medicine did to my liver was enough to convince me that diet and lifestyle management was my route to health. I can't imagine the stress of replacing (and re-paying for) medicine.

"That's so horrible. I'm glad you found your bags and got your meds. And still, you're here filming and tomorrow you'll help others. It's admirable that you're doing it all."

"I like helping people." He shrugs. "I also hate that more people aren't doing something. The heads of these big tech companies or other billionaires, they don't help. If the richest one percent, or point one percent, are hoarding their wealth and doing the bare minimum or keeping things as is, then it's time to shake it up. To show what real wealth *can* and *should* do." Once again I'm inspired by him. I remind myself that in a small way I'm helping too. By putting on events that bring out the best in people.

We get to the start line of the kids' race. Celine is at the finish line with Oliver and the local press. The emcee for our race has a microphone in hand and is ready to count the kids down. He spots Raj and gives him a big welcome. The kids jump up and down and cheer for his camera. Raj walks over to our emcee and asks to borrow the microphone.

"This is a fun and friendly competition. No pushing or shoving. Help each other out," Raj says before adding an impromptu incentive. "Also, first to the finish line gets fifty thousand dollars for their college fund."

The parents' eyes go wide. The kids squeal with delight. And then our emcee counts down: "Three, two, one! Have fun!"

The cutest two hundred meters in sports goes off as expected. With smiles, stumbles, and at least two kids who stand at the start line unsure of what to do.

9

DECLAN

"*Hola, señor*. Are you dining alone?" the waiter asks, transitioning from his native Spanish to flawless English without an accent. It's Saturday night in Mexico City and the streets are alive with tourists and locals heading out for the evening. The music from the band on the second floor is lively and energetic, like a Saturday evening should be.

"No, I'm expecting someone. Is the terrace available?" I enquire, passing up the chance to sit in front of the social-media-worthy wall of potted plants or study the various neon signs positioned through the first and second floors.

"Yes, sir." He nods. "A romantic table for two, this way." And I follow him. Let him assume it is a date, that's the cover I'm trying to project. Fitted jeans and a black T-shirt. My hair is slicked back.

This *pulqueria* is popular and busy. It is filled with American expats and tourists. All of Roma Norte is. If I were here for fun, for a vacation, I'd stay elsewhere in Mexico City. Explore the real parts of the city, not just what has been gentrified for American visitors. But tonight I need to blend in. No place better than here.

"Can I get you something to drink while you wait?" the waiter asks as he hands me a menu.

"Water is fine," I say and check my watch. I'm early. As planned.

From the terrace, I can see the sidewalk. When Monique walks up, I'll be able to wave her over right away. Outside, the noise of the restaurant and bar carries, masking our conversation without overpowering our voices. She'll be able to slip back into the night without anyone noticing our handoff.

My phone rings. "Ian?" I say as I answer it.

"Have you made contact with Monique yet?" Impatient as always.

While I'm here in person, Ian is following me with a GPS tracking dot on my shoulder. It's more reliable than tracking my phone location, although he has that too. Phones can get stolen or tossed. My body is always with me.

It's how he found me after X.C. and I were left for dead. We think X.C.'s was blown off of him in the explosion. His dot must have attached to one of the pylons after we were catapulted from the dock.

"Not yet, still early."

“Why did it have to be this weekend?” Ian laments. He is busy. FIRE has four events happening across the Northern Hemisphere, which means our website and app are getting heavy volume. Ian and his team are working all weekend to make sure nothing crashes. And now Ian is staying even later to be remote support for this drop-off.

“I know. But Monique always comes through for us.”

Monique Yeats is one of the primary photographers FIRE hires for our marquee events. She is a premier photographer; her work focuses on extreme athletes and intense weather. She was easy to recruit for our clandestine cause. Monique has every excuse to go where she needs to with a camera and press credentials. She has every style of recording device.

Last weekend, she was in Buenos Aires covering a multi-day ultra-marathon. She told me she was able to photograph a potential exchange that happened adjacent to the course.

Frank Castillo, the head of tech giant Vallus, was running the race. As was known arms dealer Stasko Hynds. Hynds is part of the Order, and we believe Castillo is trying to prove his loyalty for an initiation. We’ve picked up chatter about a massive arms deal and a high-visibility target. If Monique caught anything on film, this could be a huge break.

“Still, a full week to sit on this? Why didn’t she send the images to you via encryption?” Ian asks the question that occurred to me earlier. Perhaps she doesn’t trust our digital communication after the issues we’ve been having these past few months.

"I'll ask her when she arrives," is all I feel comfortable saying on the phone. I can speculate with Ian when I'm back in the office. I hang up as the waiter approaches with my water.

"She is running late?" he asks.

"You know how it is," is all I say before he walks away. I take in my surroundings. Most people around me are in groups, moving through the night together. I spot a man across the street on his cell phone, leaning against a tree. I turn my head slightly to see behind me. The bar is filling up.

Toward the back, my waiter is speaking with someone. Could be the restauranteur. *Or.* Is this one of the Order's new agents?

Monique is never late.

If she has the photos she claimed to when she communicated with me earlier in the week, then two incredibly powerful groups would be after her. And could be after me as well. Arms dealers don't stay in business by playing nice. Frank Castillo didn't become the youngest self-made billionaire without burying a few secrets. Rumors have it some bodies have been buried too.

The waiter turns and heads my way.

I have some choices. I can assume he is coming out to ask about appetizers while I wait. I can assume Monique is running behind. In traffic. Nothing harmful.

Or I can speculate that she has been caught. That the Order is on to her and has taken her captive, or worse. That Stasko Hynds and his ilk have captured her. That someone is about to intercept me as well.

Sometimes it feels like X.C. is still here. Like I could just call him up and get his take on things. Like he is giving me advice from wherever he is. Maybe it is my instinct that is telling me to make a quick exit, or maybe it's his voice in my head.

Whatever it is, my gut says something is wrong.

For a split second, I think back to when I locked Charlie outside in the heat. Her sweet smile and pleading expression. One I should have found convincing. My gut said not to trust her, and it seems I was wrong. Maybe my gut is wrong now.

"No," I whisper and shake my head. Something *is* off and I don't intend to stick around and find out the extent of it.

I pull out my wallet and drop a generous tip on the table. An apology for wasting the waiter's time. Just in case he isn't about to apprehend me. Just in case he wasn't speaking with someone from the Order.

I stride through the terrace gate and walk down the sidewalk, passing people heading out for a fun evening. I spot my rental car and keep going past it. Whoever delayed Monique could very well be trying to come and get me too. I can't risk it. I palm my phone and type out a message to Ian.

Declan Davidson

BURN.

Once it sends, I break it apart with my hands. Sliding out the battery and cracking the screen. I put the international SIM card in my left pocket. From my right, I grab a small detonator and throw the remnants of my phone with it into a metal trash can.

The voices of passersby swirl around me, English and Spanish dancing in the air, rising past the beautiful murals and terrace plants into the night sky. The explosion of the trash can, now a good twenty paces behind me, silences them before they call out for help.

Where is Monique? Has she been harmed? Or worse? I shake that thought away. *No, I don't want to believe it.*

But the Order has already demonstrated that they are willing to kill. They took out X.C. and presumed I'd drowned too. The image haunts my dreams. The memory taunts me and my once precious trust.

They have no regard for life. The members of the Order are all multibillionaires. When you have nine billion dollars and there are nearly nine billion people on the planet, you stop caring about them. They value each person's life at less than a dollar; it's not worth their time to worry over when their business development plans eradicate a village or kill people. They don't bother to bend down to pick up a dollar. They don't sweat destroying a life.

I walk into the night. I'll take the last Metro to the airport and be at the ticket desk in less than twenty minutes. I'm sure Trey won't be happy with the last-minute travel expense, but I don't care. With my FIRE corporate card and passport in my back pocket, I'll be on a flight back to Florida in no time.

10

CHARLIE

No one is happy. Everyone is cold. This is a disaster.

Kalispell was hit by a late-season snowstorm overnight. Six inches of fresh snow cover the ground. And our run course.

"I can handle a little cold!"

"I flew all the way from Texas for this event!"

"Well, I flew in from Ireland!"

"Let m-m-me out there. I trained all y-y-y-year for this marathon!"

Yesterday's ultra-marathon had beautiful weather, but today's races are cancelled. Most of the athletes are understanding; a vocal few are not. As a company, we can't risk someone getting hypothermia on course. Oliver made the right call to cancel, but it's a tough one.

The race operations team is zipping around on golf carts to get barricades and signage from the course and break it down. The expo and finish line are still up; they'll be the last to close. Some families are still milling through the race village, stopping at sponsor tents for freebies or information on their products. The mood is sour.

"Raj, I apologize for this terrible mess," Celine pleads behind me.

"You didn't make it snow. It's all good. We got tons of footage yesterday," Raj reassures her.

I'm guessing Celine is nervous about how FIRE will be portrayed in the video he will post to his millions of followers. I turn round to see if I can help.

"Raj, do you and your team need any help rescheduling your travel? Has the snow impacted any flights?"

Celine shoots me a sharp glare. I can't understand how she is mad at me right now. I'm trying to help. She, of course, has flawless makeup and styled hair that looks perfect under a knit FIRE beanie. How did she even think to bring one?!

Raj responds with his casual nonchalance. "Eh, we're good. Hey, what are you guys doing with the finishers' T-shirts?"

"No finishers for these distances, so no one gets a shirt. We usually work with a charity to donate them to children in need around the world." Just like the losing team shirts at the end of the Superbowl.

"We're doing a big project in Côte d'Ivoire in a month. Think you can get the shirts to us by then?" Raj asks, seizing the opportunity. “The shirts still get donated, and then I can do a callback to my video about this race.”

“Raj, that would be wonderful. You are so thoughtful to make this offer,” Celine says as she touches her hand to her heart. “Please give the details to Charlie,” she instructs and then turns to me, as if waiting for me to write down the shipping information.

I hand Raj my fresh business card. “Have your team send the details over this week,” I say, as Raj smiles and pockets my card.

Ahmed walks up, a rolled-up tarp slung over his shoulder. “Hey, man, I can route the shirts to go on the truck that’s heading back to Tampa. They’ll get back to the depot much faster than if they stay on the regional truck.”

Raj nods and responds with, “Cool.”

“That’s perfect, thank you!” I say to Ahmed so he can stash the bulky load on his shoulders in the proper crate.

I’m surprised by how well everyone is working together this morning. A freak snowstorm has thrown everything into chaos, but our crew is business as usual. I look around to see where I can pitch in and help, knowing I can’t go off on course and be too far from Oliver in case he needs something. Our travel team is already adjusting our flights. We’ll leave the park in two hours to head back to our hotels and check out.

As I scan the snowy park, I spot a man running. I assume he’s a local who is braving the cold for his regular morning run, but then I spot a FIRE race bib pinned to his chest. I turn to Ana. "Oh no, we have a rogue runner," I tell her. He's not a race bandit; he paid for his entry. But he is running the course even though we've cancelled the event.

"Good luck with that," Ana says before returning to the merchandise tents to help pack away everything that didn't get wet with snow.

I approach the man hesitantly. He isn't moving particularly fast. "Sir, we cancelled this morning's race. I'm so sorry, I have to ask you to stop."

At first, I think he doesn't hear me, so I start again. "Sir, the race officials have deemed it unsafe to run in these conditions."

My fingers and toes are numb from the cold; my thin layers are barely enough to keep my teeth from chattering. I can only imagine that he is feeling the same, although his movement must be giving him some warmth.

He pauses and catches his breath. "I'm not leaving without crossing that finish line," he tells me. The man is about my height with deep brown skin, and he has about one hundred and fifty pounds on me.

He wheezes and I start to worry he is having trouble breathing, but it could just be the cold. I reach for the walkie-talkie on my hip. "I'll radio for a medic," I start to say.

He shakes his head. "I had a heart attack last year," he begins.

My eyes widen and my own heart rate accelerates. I need to get him help immediately!

He shakes his head and smiles at me, his breath normalizing. "I'm not having one now. It scared my wife, my daughter. I told them I was going to run a half-marathon while I was still in the hospital. I said I would lose the weight and get moving a hundred times before. But the heart attack scared me to action." He lifts his hands from his hips and wipes his nose, which is running from the cold.

"You did the hard work to get here," I remind him.

"My daughter, she's only ten, she got up with me every morning to help me train. She had water bottles ready before I left. Had a smoothie ready when I got back. I'm not about to show her what quitting looks like. What a broken promise looks like. She's going to see me cross that finish line." His eyes meet mine and I see his resolve. I can hear it in his voice too. The peaks and valleys of the journey he has been on. Fighting for his health, for more time with his family. How the weather and snow on course is one more challenge in his way. The last of many. Nothing I can do is going to stop that kind of willpower. It's one I recognize, like for like. A drive I once had, one I had to abandon. "Run, walk, or crawl, right?" he says.

That sells me on it. I nod with my head, indicating for him to keep going. Once he has gone ten feet, I reach for the radio again.

"We have a guy trying to finish the half on his own. He is about two miles out. Is the finish arch down yet?"

The radio squawks. "No, that comes down last. Want me to pull him?" I recognize the race director's voice.

"You ever seen a running back make it to the endzone with three defenders trying to pull him down?" I ask, trying to give him a visual of what I expect would happen. "He's trying to finish for his daughter; he made her a promise to get back in good health. Let's get some of our team to the finish line to give him a real FIRE ending."

"You're pulling on my heartstrings here," the race director quips back. He's got two kids at home too and I know he's thinking what I am. FIRE is all about endurance, pushing limits, and challenging fixed mindsets. It's about changing lives and inspiring others.

"See you at the finish," I say, and I pocket the walkie before dashing over to the merchandise tent and telling them my hasty plan.

Twenty minutes later, the staff and even some of the sponsors from expo are lining what is left of the finish chute. I'm standing closest to the chute when the man rounds the final corner and the thirty of us erupt in applause. You'd think we were at Exponential Endurance – the FIRE World Championships – with the energy we are bringing. My colleagues are cheering and clapping.

"You got this!"

"Almost there!"

"Endure to the end!"

It may be the cold wind, or perhaps the rush of emotions at the sight of the finish line, but I spot some moisture on the runner's face. He is running at a speed that is barely faster than a walk, but he is making progress. He scans the faces at the finish line. I know he is searching for his family.

They were easy enough for me to find. They were the only group huddled near the finish with a neon-green sign that read Go, Daddy, Go!

He's in the chute, and I can tell the second he sees his family on the other side of the finish line. His face erupts with a wide smile. Usually, only VIPs who pay extra receive a medal from their loved ones. It's a security risk and also super inefficient. But we're already breaking the rules, so we might as well make it the best experience. I pulled one finisher medal and shirt before we loaded them onto the truck.

He crosses the line and his girls envelop him. The whole family is crying. Happy tears. Bittersweet tears because of the health journey he's been on.

A hand lands on my shoulder. I turn to see Oliver smiling down at me, a twinkle of a tear in his eye. He gives me a nod and then heads over to the family. They break up their hug and Oliver extends a hand. The runner brings him in for a bear hug instead.

Raj and his cameraman capture the moment. The footage will be gold, and this is a wonderful keepsake for this family.

Celine is beaming at Raj. No doubt she'll take the credit, but I don't care.

For the first time all day, I'm not thinking about how cold I am. How much fallout there will be from the cancelled races. The logistical nightmare. Instead, I'm smiling, crying too. And I remember the unquestionable joy that running brings to people.

11

CHARLIE

"Good morning, Declan!" I chirp as my surly office neighbor strolls into the office on Thursday. I've thawed out from Montana and already find the Florida heat infuriating. The quiet sounds of the office are punctuated with the regular arrivals of the staff. Greetings, computer start chimes, conversations over cubicles that are just out of range.

Every morning, I say hello, or hi, or try to engage in some positive manner with Declan Davidson. I get silence back. I guess strategic operations is too serious and all-consuming to offer basic niceties in return. At least Ian, our CTO, seems to have warmed to me. After Oliver explained who I was, Ian has been very helpful and kind.

Earning Declan's approval feels impossible, like he's already made his mind up about me. I never had a fair chance. I'm running a deficit. Always one step behind at FIRE or saying the wrong thing in a meeting. Or I forgot my security badge! I have never not been the top achiever, the ideal employee. I know I need to prove myself. If I can win Declan Davidson's approval, then maybe I'll feel like I really belong here.

"Hi," Declan grumbles in response, which is better than the silent treatment I've received up until today. At this point, I know it's just who he is. Since attending last weekend's race, I've become more familiar with many of my other coworkers and I'm getting along with almost everyone in the office. The legal team even invited me to join their Hangman games. The only two who continue to give me the cold shoulder are Celine and Declan. I don't have to see Celine too often. But Declan's office is right across from my desk.

"I know you just got in, but I need your slides for the fiscal year budget meeting," I say with a smile. *You catch more flies with sugar and all that.*

I can't spend too much time thinking about how to impress my surly neighbor, how to get him to flash any kind of smile on his handsome face. I have a slide deck to review and proof before Friday's quarterly finance meeting. Each department has submitted a full spreadsheet with requested budgets for the new fiscal year, which starts in July. But they only have two slides to summarize what they need to provide to our finance team for approval. And Declan's are still MIA.

"Right, coming up," he says with a nod, actually looking at me this time. *Oh my gosh, I exist. He looked at me, so I must therefore exist, right?* My sarcastic inner voice is in full gear this morning.

Declan has ignored my previous reminders about this slide deck. He was in Mexico City over the weekend, which is very interesting since our closest competitor had a staged mountain bike race there at the same time. *Perhaps Declan is the person sharing company secrets?*

My inbox chimes and I see a wordless email with no title from Declan. Attached are the slides. He must have already had them done but forgot to hit send. I regret thinking the worst of him, but first impressions are hard to beat.

I add his slides to the deck so they match the formatting and style. After a quick glance, I catch his numbers. The budget for the current fiscal year and the requested budget for next are close. He is only asking for a slight increase to match inflation. That's fair. What makes my eyes pop is the amount he has to work with. The sum nearly equals the total operating budget for the rest of the company.

This can't be right. I jot down the numbers on a bright green sticky note and walk the five paces over to Declan's office. His door is ajar. I tap on it lightly to catch his attention.

"Declan?" I say, hoping to avoid getting snarled at.

He glances up from his computer and levels his dark brown eyes at me, waiting for me to say something.

"I think there's an error on the numbers you sent me, maybe a wrong decimal place, but in the budget you sent, the entire strategic ops line item is more than the rest of the business." I throw in a laugh to show how funny this little mistake is. *See, no biggie.*

Declan adjusts his jaw, chewing on the words he is planning to say to me. Perhaps fighting to bite back more snark.

"I know what my budget is," he says, returning his attention to his computer screen.

Honestly, I'm sick of this guy's attitude. People make mistakes sometimes. It's fine. Just fix it. My tactic of attracting more flies with sugar is not working with this one. Time for some vinegar. I roll my shoulders back, erase my smile, and slip into competitor mode.

"Please submit your revised numbers by close of business so I can update the deck for tomorrow's meeting," I say with a firm tone, then turn and walk away. I've dealt with his type before. People who treat me like nothing I do will ever be good enough. People who doubted my skill and speed, assumed I earned a spot on varsity track and field because my dad was the coach. Well, I smoked those assholes in practice and meets, and I'll show this guy too.

I sit back down at my desk and finish the other slides. I mark Declan's with a bright yellow digital highlight. I'll get back to those later.

"Good morning, Charlie," Ian Turner says as he passes by my desk, leaving Oliver's office. *See, being nice costs nothing.*

"Hi, Ian," I chime back. I watch as Ian raps on Declan's door and then closes it behind him. They chat for a bit, and I don't even notice when Ian leaves. The presentation has my full attention.

I'm about to head out to pick up lunches for the executive team when Declan exits his office. I expect him to brush by without acknowledging me again. Instead, he walks right up to my desk, pocketing his cell phone. A new one, I might add. I can tell it's brand new; I've seen the latest ads for this model all over the place.

"Hi, Charlie," Declan says. This is the first time there isn't a hint of venom in his voice. "Why don't you send me the deck? I'll correct my numbers."

I'm sorry, did hell just freeze? I may need to run to the window to see if pigs are flying around. "Are you sure?"

Declan smiles at me. Actually smiles. I see perfectly straight teeth and dimples. My goodness. Now I get why he reserves this weapon of mass attraction and uses it sparingly. Why does he have to be so good-looking? "Yeah, it was my error, I should fix it." He runs his hand through his hair. He is definitely dialing up his charm. Maybe he is trying to make nice after nearly three weeks of being a jerk.

I stare back into his eyes, the color of fresh hot coffee. "OK, that would be great," I say, accepting this olive branch. I save the deck and send it to him. Maybe things are turning round?

12

DECLAN

What genius decided to have this meeting at the end of the day on a Friday?

Every department head is seated at the massive conference table for the Friday-afternoon finance meeting. And we have a lot of departments and divisions. The heads of regional offices in London, Frankfurt, Adelaide, and Tokyo have dialed in. Our counterparts on the other side of the world are calling in at an ungodly hour. Such is life as an international operation. Someone has a bum time zone.

The head of North American marketing drones on. "The race registration melt numbers may hold steady next year . . ." Trey has already explained the need for an increased travel budget, with flight and hotel costs skyrocketing.

Occasionally, Finn, our CFO, interrupts with a question.

After Ms. Nepo-hire Charlie Ross sent me the slide deck yesterday, I forwarded it over to Finn. My numbers are fine. I didn't need her asking any more questions about matters she knows nothing about – *should* know nothing about.

I didn't expect her to be in the meeting, though. *Oh well.* She'll either see my numbers on screen, pipe up, and make a fool of herself for asking questions above her pay grade. Or she'll learn to stop putting her nose into matters that don't concern her. Either is a win.

When the slides turn over to my department, I straighten in my seat and clear my throat.

"Strategic operations is running on schedule even with recent personnel changes." That is all I have to say. I'm in constant contact with Oliver. I let Finn know when we need additional resources to complete a mission.

Finn moves on to Ian for his budget.

Across from me, Charlie fidgets in her chair. She is looking back and forth between Oliver and the screen as if there is a tennis rally going on in her mind.

She finally levels her gaze on me. I look across at her. There is a hint of pink on her neck. Scowl lines form on her forehead, her eyebrows growing closer and closer. She is holding on to the pen in her hand like it is a lifeline. Her note-taking has ceased for this staring contest.

And I know how to not blink.

* * *

The meeting adjourns and I leave with everyone else. Charlie stays back for a beat, perhaps licking her wounds. I'm already in my office when I hear her get to her desk. Her little heels do their best to announce her entrance, the carpet muffles her steps. No wonder she's unsteady in her heels, the Barefoot Running Princess probably didn't get much practice in them before this job.

She doesn't come to my office to confront me. I'm grateful since I have a slew of emails to handle before I can even think of signing out for the weekend.

I get lost in my inbox and look up to see it is already well past 6 p.m. Charlie is still tapping away at her keyboard, though.

"It's after-hours – you should go," I call out to her. I can see her from where I am sitting.

Most of the staff have cleared out. Half the team is on site at this weekend's events, so the rest were able to cut out early, get a jump on their weekend. Everyone except our little quadrant of the office. Oliver is still meeting with Ian. He found an encrypted message and is asking me to work through it. It's running on my computer while I work on filing my expense report from last weekend's botched rendezvous.

Charlie glances over at me, the cobalt daggers in her deep blue eyes from today's meeting still present. "If Oliver is still here, I'm here. Besides, I want to read through the race reports." I'm impressed by the dedication and effort she is putting in to learn everything. The lingo, the stats, what distinguishes a great event from a mediocre one. I'm about to tell her as much when she speaks up again. "Probably need to rerun those budget reports too," she adds.

She's goading me. I know it. "The numbers are fine. Drop it, Ross," I command, aware of how hard my tone is. Hoping it will work.

It doesn't. Charlie is up out of her chair, stomping over to my office in her black heels. "I know something is up. There's some kind of fraud or embezzlement going on for that much money to be allocated."

Her indignation is admirable, and the way her eyebrows are stitched together over her glasses is cute. Her lips are pursed. Mad looks good on her. It makes me want to cross the room to taste those lips. To feel the fire behind that glare. To silence her.

I have never once been aroused in the office. That would be a totally inappropriate response to this matter and I remind myself to focus. "You have no idea what you're talking about," I tell her, willing her to drop the topic.

Charlie crosses her arms, focusing all her attitude at me. "You're right. I don't. But I know something is up. Something isn't right. And I'm going to figure it out one way or another." She storms off, logs out of her computer, and gathers her things.

"Highly doubt that," I mumble, knowing she can't hear me. There is no way she'll figure out the covert side of the business unless someone tells her about it.

I check my computer and see it will take another hour for this message encryption to crack. A heavy exhaustion settles into my shoulders and my back. Charlie leaving reminds me that I too can go home and finish my work there, so I pack up my laptop and turn off the lights in my office.

I'm a few minutes behind Charlie, so I'm surprised she's still waiting for the elevator when I exit. She rolls her eyes at me; her right foot begins to tap. Her frustration keeps a perfect beat as we wait.

I'm not interested in continuing this argument. I'm resolved to not say anything. Let her stew and feel righteous in calling out the accounting numbers. The elevator doors open and we both enter.

The silence in the elevator car only heightens the other sensory input. For one, the heat and anger rolling off Charlie's body. She is pissed. Out of the corner of my eye, I look at her. Arms crossed, one hip popped out. Next, her aroma. The last vapors of her perfume settle into the car, a pleasant fruity smell.

Don't look over at her, don't make eye contact.

I'm impressed by how quickly she is starting to notice that FIRE is not what it seems. Her smarts, her indignation, that hip pop. All capture my attention.

She glances over at me.

Oh shit. She caught me watching her. I look back at the closed elevator doors, but I still see her roll her eyes at me peripherally. She huffs out a frustrated exhale and shakes her head. *Man, I bet fighting and making up with her is fun.*

We exit the elevator in silence. Charlie scoffs when I hold the front door open for her as we exit the building. *OK, I can't blame her for that one.*

“Have a nice weekend,” she grumbles before picking up her speed, her low heels pounding into the cement of the parking garage.

The evening air is humid and carries a charge. Not of an impending lightning storm, the kind you can set your watch by around here.

No, something else.

I can sense it; something is about to go down and it is not going to be good.

13

CHARLIE

I knew I shouldn't have stopped for a little cry in the bathroom. I'm so mad, so of course my tear ducts are betraying me. But I fixed my face, told myself to toughen up. On Monday, I'm telling Oliver everything. Declan's numbers. His trip to Mexico City when our competitor had an event there. Oliver thinks someone is giving our business details to another race operator. *It has to be Declan.*

And then he rides the elevator down with me. No apology. No explanation. Just that smug face of his, handsome and haughty. And he was wearing some cologne that smells like sandalwood and leather, and his big broad body is distracting me from the fact that I find him odious. It took every fiber of my being to not resume our argument. To not tell him exactly what I think is going on. To push my index finger into his chest and call him out.

Declan's footsteps are close behind me as I walk through the parking lot. *Where are my keys?!* I'm too distracted, still thinking about this man.

My keys rattle at the bottom of my bag.

Somewhere in the garage, a motorcycle revs its engine. It sounds like it is a few floors away. I remind myself not to let my anger get the best of me. I still need to use basic common sense and look both ways before I cross to the stairs. I parked on the far side of the garage this morning, so I have to go up a half-level to get to my car. *Please, please, please, let Declan have parked far, far away from me.*

My fingers close round the keys. Declan is now two feet behind me. I'm so ready to get more distance from this guy. The motorcycle revs again, only this time it is much louder, much closer.

I look up to see it rushing down the middle lane of the parking garage, speeding toward the exit. The motorcyclist's leather outfit is striking, with an all-black full-face helmet and tinted visor. The overhead lights reflect off the helmet. But what really catches my attention is the swift motion they use to draw a gun from inside their jacket and point it at me.

I take a half-step back, but my body moves much further. As I register this, I assume I tripped over my own heels. But, no, it is something else. I'm falling, being pulled down.

A symphony of fear blares through the garage. A shower of tempered glass rains down, some of the bullets striking car windows. The ping of a bullet on steel or aluminum. A resounding thud of pierced cement. Loud pops echo off the pillars and few remaining cars. Lights flash as the motorcycle passes by, speeding away. I land, hard, on top of Declan.

His arm is round my waist, pinning me to him, down and away from the bullets that whizzed overhead. I fall against his body, hard and warm. Before I can take a breath, I am on the ground. Declan's body covers mine, protective, as the last bullet echoes through the garage. He is shielding me, putting himself at the most risk of being shot. To protect *me*. Coworker from hell to human shield in an instant.

His breath is all I can hear now; his cologne is all I can smell. We're in the narrow space between two indistinguishable sedans, one tan and the other a faded red. There is no space between us, his body completely covering mine. Even though we were just shot at, even though the gunman could be coming back this very instant to finish us off, I feel safe. I know, deep down – *I know* – Declan will keep me safe.

"Charlie?" Declan's voice is calm, trying to get my attention.

My mind catches up. Someone shot at us. At me. At Declan. I see a perfect hole in the cement pillar above us. A bullet hole.

I'm too shocked to scream, to call out. And Declan, of all people, is above me.

"Charlie, are you hit? Are you OK?" The urgency in his voice intensifies; that's what startles me the most.

My eyes finally focus on Declan, whose eyebrows are gathered with worry. His eyes scan my face, reading me for some kind of sign. I don't feel any pain, just the cold of the cement below me and the heat of Declan's hand cradling my head. His face is so close to mine, only an inch or two above me. In another context, the way he is holding me would be a lover's embrace. It feels like the most natural alignment of our bodies. The closeness. The way he thought nothing of his own safety and protected me instinctively.

The end-of-day stubble on his chin is so close I could reach my face to his and nuzzle into it. I could close the gap between us and press my mouth to his. I guess life-and-death situations make you think senseless thoughts.

"No, I'm not OK," is all I can say before I actually and truly faint.

14

DECLAN

Charlie's eyelids close and I know I have to act quickly. My trauma field training kicks in. I check her pulse and gently set her down on the ground, careful that her head doesn't hit the concrete.

I pull out my phone and dial Oliver's secure line. He answers after two rings. "Shots fired in the parking garage. Send down the operations team. We have repairs to make."

Immediately, Oliver relays the message; I assume Ian is still in his office.

I stand and survey the area. The motorcycle is long gone. I spot a few holes in the concrete. "We need to patch this up." Oliver has yet to directly ask me for details. We're both in tactical mode. Time for explanations and theorizing will come soon.

"Most of the ops team is gone for the weekend; we'll send down who is left in the office," Oliver tells me.

All the remaining cars are FIRE employees. I recognize them. Thankfully, the other offices in our building do summer Fridays. They've all been gone since midday. Still, we need to contain this.

This wasn't an attempted hit. A real hitman wouldn't have sped by like that. They would have stopped and taken the clean shot. They wanted to cause damage; they wanted to make a headache for FIRE. To attract the wrong kind of attention, have us answering questions.

"I'm coming back up. Grab an ice pack for Charlie," I tell Oliver.

At this, Oliver begins to rattle off questions, dropping his tactical mode to focus on Charlie. "She's there? Is she injured? Is she shot?"

"I asked for an ice pack, not an ambulance," I growl back at him. I should be more understanding. He's just concerned. I'm still dealing with the adrenaline in my system. This anger is my fight-or-flight response telling me to fight. And I'm fighting the only person I can right now, Oliver.

I disconnect the line and pocket my phone.

"Charlie," I say as I crouch next to her, "I'm carrying you back into the office." I narrate my actions so she won't panic. Her eyelids move; she must be coming to.

I lift her up, my arms under her shoulders and her knees. I grab her huge purse and let it fall to the crook of my elbow.

She rouses as I walk and her arms wrap round my neck. I can't help but smell her perfume and her shampoo. The hints of strawberry and vanilla calm me, pushing back at the adrenaline that's been coursing through my system since those first shots rang out.

I glance down at the headstrong woman in my arms. For weeks, all she has done is press my buttons. This horrible attack has forced me to wake up, to see that she is still one of the people I've promised to protect. She knows nothing of this world and has been exposed to the worst of it. The ice block of frustration I feel toward her is thawing.

That's when a fresh wave of grief hits me. X.C. and I were all alone in Osaka. I couldn't pull him back from the blast. Couldn't find him in the water after diving back down several times. I couldn't save him. But today, when it mattered, I did protect Charlie. *I'm sorry, X.C.*, I say to his memory in my mind.

The operations team starts out the office front door; one of the guys holds the door for me. They silently head to the garage to do what they do best. To put things back as best as they can. I give them a nod as they head out. "Garage is empty. You'll need to tow a few cars for new windows."

I make my way to the elevator bank and nudge the button with my elbow, careful to not jolt Charlie with the motion.

We enter the elevator together once more. This time, she isn't willfully ignoring me. She is in my arms. Her strong body is light, easy to hold. Her smooth cheek is pressed against my neck. I could move my head an inch and plant a kiss on her forehead, tell her everything will be alright, but both are too familiar, too intimate. She's barely conscious; my thoughts should be on my first-aid training.

The elevator dings and the doors open. Ahead of us, Oliver is waiting at the front of the FIRE offices. His face is stricken with worry.

He opens the door for us and immediately I know what he needs to hear. "It's shock. She wasn't hit."

Charlie mumbles something, as Oliver follows us down the hall to his office. I place her as smoothly as I can into her desk chair. I let the purse fall to the ground and some of her things spill out. But that is the least of my worries.

I turn to Oliver as Ian walks up to report. "Ops should have this cleaned up within the hour. They have cones blocking off the entrance to the garage. The two cars that lost their windows belong to Oliver and one of my guys."

His quick assessment of the damage is helpful. It answers the easy questions.

Now for the one I have wanted to ask since the motorcycle took aim at me: "Who the hell did this?"

15

CHARLIE

"Let's go over what happened one more time," Uncle Ollie asks Declan. It all happened so fast – not even ten seconds. It feels like an eternity has passed since Declan scooped me up and carried me back inside. I only lost consciousness for a second or two, but my body was still in shock.

Next thing I know, Ian, Declan, Uncle Ollie, and I are all in his office. Someone got me an ice pack for my hip. I suspect a bruise the size of Declan's forearms is forming right now. My mind is turning over details that can't be right.

We were shot at.

Almost run over.

I swear Ahmed, Trey, and some of the other operations guys passed us on the way back in with toolboxes. Declan is explaining everything with a practiced calm. Like this is par for the course.

"I didn't get the tags; we may need to hack into building security to get the parking garage feeds," Declan states.

"Probably stolen plates, but worth a shot," Ian responds.

I'm sitting in the middle of this, wondering how I found myself here. Wondering what the adrenaline and cortisol in my veins right now will do to my muscles. I used to thrive on those two chemicals. Once I was diagnosed with a rare autoimmune condition, I knew I had to cut both out of my life as much as possible. I had my spot on the US team for the World Games and everything, and then bam. My muscles stopped working. Or, more specifically, the fascia. The layer between my skin and muscles became inflamed and angry. I can picture it fighting me again right now. Because this situation is stressful. I figured this job would have run-of-the-mill office stress or meeting-deadlines kind of stress. Not mortal danger levels of it.

Mentally, I'm back in a doctor's office, one of a dozen. The final doctor who was actually able to give me a diagnosis. Eosinophilic fasciitis. After a year of medicines that wrecked my skin and my liver, I had a choice. Continue the medicine whose side effects were worse than the symptoms they were treating. Or never run again, at least not competitively.

"Charlie!" Uncle Ollie's voice breaks through my thought spiral. My uncle's face is close to mine, his eyes probing, full of concern. He turns to Ian and Declan and offers his assessment. "She's still in shock."

"You can say that again," I mutter.

"Got her sense of humor," Ian responds with a nervous chuckle.

I want to snap and tell them to stop talking about me like I'm not there. To stop acting like this is just another day of business. *Why aren't they more panicked? Why aren't they fawning over Declan who was* also *shot at? Why aren't the police here yet?*

"Charlie?" Declan addresses me.

I gaze up into his eyes and he looks scared. *Why is he scared?*

"What happened?" I ask.

"She doesn't remember." Declan looks over to Uncle Ollie, fear written clear across his face.

I shake my head. "No, I know we were shot at. I was there," I snap at him. "What caused this? Why did this happen?" I clarify my question.

Declan and Ian remain silent, their mouths sealed, their eyes fixed on Oliver.

I turn to the man I've known my whole life. "Uncle Ollie?" I say, wanting someone to just tell me already. I can see he's holding something back. His eyes track from me to Ian, to Declan. A silent conversation, an internal debate, warring in his mind. He hangs his head and fixes his hands to his hips before letting out a sigh.

"Everyone, take a seat," he instructs Declan and Ian.

I know that look. Whatever it is, he just decided something.

"Charlie, what I'm about to tell you is privileged under the company NDA you signed on your first day here." I get that funny feeling. The one where my stomach is hollow and the tiny hairs on my skin all stick up at once. Like when my parents explained my childhood dog had to be put down. Or when the first doctor told me, "I'm sorry. I can't help. I have to refer you to someone else."

I give a nod and brace myself for what is about to be revealed. My hand squeezes the ice pack, a stress response, and cold condensation spreads across my shirt. I wiggle, the wetness only reminding me this is very, very real.

"As a spectator, you've experienced the front-facing operations of FIRE for years, and as a team member this past weekend. Over the past few weeks, you've seen how the back office runs, with marketing, accounting. I'm impressed by how quickly you've been learning the ropes about the business side, but it isn't the full story."

Declan clears his throat and I peer over at him. He is rubbing his brow. Was Declan hurt too?

Uncle Ollie's next words call my attention back to him. "About a decade ago, we recognized the name of a notorious crime boss on our registration list. Sound familiar?" I think back to the conversation I had with him about a sleazy senator but not a mafioso. "We knew he could be a liability, so one of the team –" Oliver nods to Ian – "got on course and trailed him. He looked like any other athlete."

Ian takes over the story. "I saw him veer off course and photographed him making a deal. Literally exchanging funds and handing it off to one of his associates." Ian appears lost in memory, as if he were watching this crime unfold before his eyes again.

Oliver tells me the rest. "Then he finished the race. We handed over the evidence and he was convicted. When the mayor of Palma saw the headline and asked us to keep an eye on the comptroller who was planning to do our triathlon in Mallorca, I knew we could do this again. We could help. We go into these communities, bring tourist dollars, and do charity projects on race weekend. But these missions, for lack of a better word, could bring actual change."

I take this all in. This sounds outlandish. But it fits with all I've seen and heard so far. Everything that just happened in the parking lot. "So you're telling me that you're all spies?"

Declan finally chimes in. "Not everyone."

I look him in the eye, trying to see if he is mocking me or simply relaying information.

"A few critical team members work on both sides of the business. Strategic operations," Oliver says, gesturing to Declan, "is our corporate-sounding name for this division."

I take a deep breath. I can't decide what to ask first.

Oliver keeps talking. "I know we discussed a very different job. That your role would be an entry point into the business side of sports. Give you experience so you could work your way up the corporate ladder here or elsewhere. But, Charlie, you're too smart."

I start to shake my head.

"Yes, you are," Oliver pushes on. "You've caught on to so many details already. Identified Titus Kilbride as a potential mark. Noticed the budget discrepancies – yes, Declan filled me in. You'd be great at this. Working in secret intelligence is something you could excel at. It's a lot of listening, taking in all the information, recognizing habits and routine so you can spot when the pattern breaks. You're already doing that. You're already an asset to the team in your current role. You're sharp, you're ambitious, and you know right from wrong. You could join us on this side of the business too."

I stand up because I need to walk, to get some space, to get out of this room and the information within it. I drop the ice pack and wince at the sudden motion of my hip. *So when Uncle Ollie said he thought someone was sharing company information, he was really saying there could be a double agent.* I connect our earlier conversation with this new information.

"I need to get home; I need to think." I rush out and grab my purse.

"Charlie." Declan stands behind me in the empty hallway. "I'll get you a ride share." He is already tapping on his phone.

"My car wasn't damaged; I'm not leaving it here all weekend." I'm firm, but I can hear in my voice that I'm too exhausted to fight.

"Fair point," Declan says, putting his phone away. I think I'm about to be rid of him when he says what I least expected. "I'll drive you home." His voice is steady, even. The sound of it calms me down; it's amazing what a difference there is when he isn't snarky with me, even if I still don't like what he is saying.

I brush off his offer. "I'll be fine."

"No offense, but you are not fine. You're in shock and you passed out. It would be irresponsible for you to operate a vehicle." There is a finality to his voice.

I don't really have a choice. I roll my eyes and start walking to the elevators. *Again.*

"You know the last time we were here, we got shot. So maybe I'm safer getting home on my own," I tell him, trying to lighten the mood. To alleviate the weight of this knowledge.

Declan laughs as we exit the elevator, actually laughs. He runs a hand through his hair and I see a dark purple bruise splayed across his wrist and forearm.

"Declan, you need to get that checked out!" I say, my voice too high, as I grab for his arm instinctively. As if I could provide any kind of first aid.

Declan shrugs off my concern. "Eh, I've had worse." His skin is warm beneath my fingers and I realize that *I'm touching Declan Davidson*! That reminder alone should have me dropping his hand like it's hot, but I don't. I glance over the ghastly bruise and wonder how much he is trying to look brave and tough. Is he impervious to pain? Or is it all for show?

I release his hand and he flexes it, moving it this way and that. The taut muscles and tendons of his hand and forearm are on display.

"Maybe *you* shouldn't be driving either," I point out to him.

His thick eyebrows knit together, as if he is considering that my words might have merit. I decide to not roll my eyes at him and continue toward the parking garage.

We remain silent for the rest of the walk to my car. My plain, ordinary sedan waits for me on the far side of the parking garage, completely unaware of the excitement and chaos from the half-floor below.

I unlock the car and Declan swoops in front of me. He opens the driver's-side door, pops the trunk, and then inspects below the steering column. Satisfied, he moves round the vehicle, looking for what, I don't know. He roots around in the trunk and then slams it shut.

Declan moves with precision and purpose. The way he deftly puts his hands on my car reminds me of the strength he displayed earlier. He could pin me down and keep me from harm but also carefully lift me and carry me inside.

"All clear," he announces, setting his hands on his hips, his inspection of my car complete. A fire inside my belly screams for him to continue his inspection. To check me with his thorough hands. If rude Declan was attractive, then focused and protective Declan is on a whole other level.

He is being a decent person. He is doing his job, I remind myself.

I mutter my thanks and hold my car keys tight. "I'm fine, really," I assert once more.

Declan scrutinizes me, his eyes tracking from my eyes down to my hands. "I'll follow you home in my car," he says.

I open my mouth to object and he holds up a hand. "Final offer. Take it or hand over the keys." He holds out an open palm, waiting for my decision.

I get in the car. Before I can close the door, Declan stops it. I look over at him, at his arm casually on top of the door. His chocolate eyes are searching, his cologne still fresh and alluring. Declan assesses me like I might faint again.

"I'm letting you follow me." My words are a little cold.

He gives one nod, accepting this. "We'll talk more on Monday," he tells me. "Oh, and I know you and Ana are getting close," he starts, "but she doesn't know about the covert side of things. So if you need to talk to someone about everything . . ." He trails off and reaches into his pocket and pulls out his wallet and a pen. Quickly, he scribbles something and hands it to me.

Don't look at his hands. Don't look at his forearms. Eyes forward.

His FIRE business card. On the back is another number. *His number.*

If I need to talk to someone about getting shot at and finding out I am working for a bunch of spies I have to talk to . . . *Declan?!*

I shake my head; the unbelievable nature of this situation continues to escalate. "Got it," I say and pull the door closed.

Driving away, I can't help but wonder, *What have I gotten myself into?*

16

DECLAN

Weekends when I'm not traveling for work follow a thorough routine: Training rides. Sauna at the gym. Muscle recovery.

This past weekend was anything but routine. Certainly not relaxing. Instead of training, I ran through hours of security footage on my laptop while I staked out Charlie's apartment.

You need to be more trusting. Oliver's parting words to me on Friday evening played over and over in my mind.

It's not lost on me that no one was shooting at me *before* Charlie Ross arrived.

But if I take Oliver at his word and we *can* trust Charlie, then she is in a shitty position. She didn't know what she was signing on for. Like it or not, she's one of us now. I need to assume she's going to help our team, but I'll keep my guard up for a double cross.

I am the kind of person who helps, who protects. And Charlie needs someone – *me* – to watch out for her. *That's why I'm here. I'm working.* I won't let us lose another team member, not on my watch.

Walking into the office on Monday morning with a crick in my neck, my eyes catch on the fresh patches on the cement pillars in the parking garage. I needed rest to be able to focus, to be able to get to the bottom of what is going on. I didn't get that, but work still demands my attention.

I let out a yawn as I walk past Charlie's desk. "Good morning," I call out before I set my bag down and dock my laptop. In the hours of footage I watched from the driver's seat of my parked car, I couldn't get a clear shot of the motorcyclist's plates. It's like they knew where the cameras were.

I don't hear Charlie respond. *Did something happen between when I saw her leave for work this morning and arriving?* But she is there, steadfastly ignoring me.

At nine thirty, everyone heads to the lobby for an all-company town hall. Oliver does this once a quarter and the atrium of our building is the only space large enough to fit us all. The lobby has a few couches and ledges where people can sit. Many opt to stand.

I spot Charlie at the far end, sitting near the lobby fountain, chatting with Trey and one of the paralegals. I make my way over and sit next to her. She does a double take and then unlocks her phone and makes every attempt to ignore me.

"You OK?" I ask.

She gives one nod and sets her phone aside. "How is your wrist?" she counters, finally looking at me.

I move my right hand, the one with a receding bruise, and show her. "It'll be fine. How's your hip?"

Charlie has her arms wrapped round her waist. Her salmon-colored T-shirt dress and navy-blue blazer are professional. Her hair is down and neatly straightened. Nothing about her appearance would give away any trace of the trauma from Friday night. "I'll live," she says, once again avoiding my gaze.

"You on board?" I ask. The cat is well and truly out of the bag. She's involved in this now, whether she likes it or not. It would be nice to start briefing her on the mountain of information for her to catch up on.

Her dark blue eyes connect with mine through her glasses. I think she is about to say yes or to ask for more time. Instead, she looks away and shrugs. Not the enthusiastic sign-on I was hoping for. Charlie waves Ana over. She moves to the side so her friend can sit between us.

This tells me two things: 1. Charlie thinks I will give up because someone is sitting between us, but she has no idea how focused I can be. 2. She hasn't told Ana about what happened on Friday. Otherwise there is no way Ana would smile and sit next to me.

I pull out my phone and send a text message to Charlie. I could have pulled her number from her file, but instead I asked Oliver for it. He was more than happy to give it to me if it means more protection for Charlie.

Declan Davidson

It's Declan.

Are you going to help us, like your uncle suggested?

I try to push on the familial obligation.

I see Charlie check her phone out of the corner of my eye. She dismisses the notification.

I try to get her attention with the financial benefit.

Declan Davidson

The pay is better on the strategic operations side.

She picks up her phone again. This time she taps out a response.

Charlie Ross

Don't care about the pay.

Declan Davidson

Good answer.

Charlie leans forwards to make eye contact with me again. Ana hasn't noticed yet. Then Charlie pointedly puts her phone face down on her lap. Conversation over.

Oliver steps to the middle of the crowd and delivers a fifteen-minute company-wide update. The new race in

Finland. Our annual championship event on the horizon. "A delegation from our office will be going to the World Games in Rome – keep an eye out for an email from Charlie." Our colleagues all look her way. She gives a sheepish grin and nervous wave.

Oliver dismisses us and Shauna from HR chimes in that there are complimentary bagels, donuts, and coffee in the break room. Our hardworking and hungry coworkers jump up and make for the elevators. Ana and Charlie stand up together.

"Charlie?" I call out. "Can you stay back for a second?"

Charlie looks annoyed. Ana appears confused but gives a small wave and heads upstairs with the rest of the staff.

"Let's go for a walk to Caffeine Corner," I suggest. It's a little off-brand café that serves most of this office park, about a five-minute walk on the other side of the complex. "My treat," I add. "We need to talk."

To her credit, Charlie may very well be as stubborn as I am. "I'm too keyed up for caffeine."

"Tea then."

"I'm allergic," she counters.

"Will you just go for a walk with me?" I am exasperated and running on too little sleep for these games.

Her stoic expression breaks and a small smile sneaks up her lips. It's a slight shift, a playful adjustment in her demeanor. It feels like a win, a small victory. I can't help but mirror it and my own lips curl too.

"Let's go," Charlie says and leads the way.

The morning sun has relented behind a dense arrangement of clouds, threatening to let loose their cargo of rain any moment. We're halfway to Caffeine Corner when Charlie stops on the sidewalk. I pause and face her.

"Who was shooting at us and why?" she asks. I guess she's finally fed up with not knowing.

"Can we get coffee first?" I ask. My head is starting to ache; my muscles are sore. I am in need of serious caffeine.

"I thought that was a ruse so we could talk without anyone overhearing?" Charlie is much sharper than I ever gave her credit for. I'm suddenly realizing that all of my first impressions of her were wrong. Well, except that she is beautiful, that is undeniable. Even sweating in the midday sun that first day, she was a stunner.

"It was," I confirm. "But I'm also exhausted. I was on a stakeout all weekend," I confess.

"Were you tracking the guy who shot at us?" she asks.

"No," I tell her. "I was making sure he didn't show up at your place." She takes a half-step back and wraps her arms round her body again. Charlie's blue eyes dart to the ground, her face sober. Her lips disappear, as she pulls them into a tight line, biting back some comment.

I thought it would have been obvious that whoever shot at us would have tried to come back. It seems Charlie hadn't considered this at all. I didn't mean to scare her, but maybe a little fear will help her understand how serious this is. How committed the Order is to their precious plans.

I continue walking and she follows in silence.

I have a hot coffee in hand. Charlie finally caved and ordered a decaf iced latte. We find a seat in the back of this small café. It's empty, except for a few of the staff changing out the morning breakfast for their lunch set. No one else is here, and with the clouds pouring their deluge outside, I don't expect anyone will arrive any time soon.

"Start talking," Charlie commands before taking a sip of her drink.

"What Oliver said was true. Endurance events are where these nefarious plans can often go down. In the aide tents, jogging alongside each other on course. No wires, no eavesdroppers, just open road and an alibi. 'I was running an ultra-marathon.'" I watch Charlie's reaction, how she fidgets. Her worldview of happy finish lines tarnished. "These heads of crime syndicates, arms dealers, they aren't lazy thugs sitting around. While they may not be the muscle of their group, they want to show how strong they are. How powerful they are. *And* how rich they are. How better to do that than rolling up to a cycling event with a ten-thousand-dollar bike, another couple thousand for the bike fit. Show off their muscles, flex on their splits, intimidate their potential buyers into giving them asking price. International sports events are the best opportunity for sharing intelligence, brokering peace, and occasionally running down a bad guy or three."

Charlie considers my words. "So why are they after you? Shooting at you?"

"Ian, Oliver, and I came to the consensus that this wasn't a botched hit. It was a warning, a shot across the bow. Telling us to stop meddling, to stand down. We had another incident at one of our events a few months back. A bomb. Left somewhere it would be found, easy enough for us to intercept and disarm. But the threat was clear. That they can get to us."

"Who is '*they*'?" Charlie asks. She's leaning forwards now, curious.

"We think *this* attack came from a group that calls themselves the Order." Charlie rolls her eyes at this. "Yes, they think highly of themselves." I lean in too, trying to keep this information close. "It's a group of some of the wealthiest people in the world. Massive corporate titans who still want more. Even though the age of colonialism is over, in some ways it has just shifted. It isn't countries trying to conquer the underdeveloped world but corporations. They think if they can disrupt the status quo enough they can remake the world."

"How so?" Charlie asks. We are leaning in so close, I can smell her perfume again. The fruity aroma I've been thinking about on and off since Friday afternoon. Breathing it in is so much better than my memory led me to believe. The hints of strawberry and vanilla are so subtle yet tantalizing.

"The nations without infrastructure need roads, power lines, solar-powered internet, you name it. And these tycoons want it to be *their* steel, cable, pipelines used. They want to create peace by first causing chaos. It's a backward logic, but that is what corrupt people do. They call themselves the Order as in the 'new world order,' the world made for them and by them."

Charlie's eyes widen. When I first learned about this, the magnitude of it, I was shocked too. "So you're trying to stop them?" she clarifies.

"Little by little. We believe a massive cache of arms was exchanged recently. We don't know what they'll be used for," I begin, and Charlie finishes my thought.

"But it can't be anything good."

"Exactly, and the person who was previously in charge of strategic operations on our side, Xander Caruso –" I watch as recognition flits across her face – "was killed on a mission six months ago in Osaka. Someone knew we were going to be there and rigged the dock to explode. We think someone within FIRE is leaking information about our plans to stop the Order."

Charlie sits back in her chair and takes a sip of her imposter coffee drink.

"We never had anyone actively working against us before. But now we do. It's a shadow war between two agencies that aren't supposed to exist, taking on missions that never happened," I continue.

Charlie is silent, still processing. I wouldn't need to think about it. I'd jump in and ask, where do I sign up? How do I help? Since I was a kid, I wanted to be the hero. To stop the bad guys. I grew up and went to Annapolis and served in the military and learned that there isn't always one clear bad guy or good guy. The villains are telling themselves a different story, one in which *they* are right.

Helping to stop illegal arms deals and broker peace, I'm living out my childhood dream. Mostly.

Charlie seems more hesitant.

I press her for an answer. "Now that you know, what are you going to do? Go back to being an assistant and pretend you don't know about the bad things in the world? Let someone else take care of it?" She meets my gaze, her blue eyes curious and probing. I finish my question: "Or are you going to do something about it?"

17

CHARLIE

"Hello, Charlie," Celine says as she waltzes into the break room behind me. I was spacing out and letting my mind spiral in the peaceful empty room. My thoughts are circling around the attack on Friday and everything Declan just told me. It can't be real, but somehow it was. Celine jolts me back to the here and now. "My, aren't you the caffeine fiend? Another coffee?" she enquires.

"This is for the executive finance meeting," I explain.

Oliver and Finn are meeting to review the proposed budgets in twenty minutes. Which means I need to have Oliver's mushroom coffee and Finn's decaf brew ready and in the conference room soon.

My conversation with Declan lasted longer than expected. He patiently answered all my questions. Patience and Declan were two words I never thought could co-exist in the same breath. But then again, I also never thought I would dream of his hands on me. Of him holding me close. Protecting me. Touching me.

My impression of Declan is shifting, the ground unsteady beneath my feet. His fierce loyalty and protectiveness put me on the defense. Being on the other side of his protection, I can't help but rethink every interaction we've had.

"Congratulations on the King Cool video," I tell Celine. Raj and his team posted their recap of the Kalispell race over the weekend. It was number two on trending for all of YouTube within hours. Apparently, our registration site is near crashing from all the people racing to sign up for one of our events. It was a big win for Celine and FIRE.

"*Merci*," Celine responds with a demure look away as she grabs an energy drink from the refrigerator. This brand sponsors our entire global race series and they stock the fridge weekly. While most of the employees here live, eat, and breathe endurance sports, they also embrace quick energy hits and caffeine.

I take this interaction with Celine as a win, as I watch her pour her energy drink into a glass and then mix in a vitamin C booster pack. As she stirs the pink powder into the highlighter-yellow fluid, she addresses me again, her French accent playing with the vowels. "You know, Charlie, with so much to learn here at FIRE, I wanted to make sure someone reminded you of several key company policies."

I turn to her, confused. "Which policies?"

"Well, the dress code is fairly relaxed, but, of course, if you couldn't pass a fingertips inspection in grade school, best not to wear it here," she says as she eyes my outfit. This T-shirt jersey dress hits me mid-thigh. And my thighs are kind of massive. Which is a point of pride for me. These pistons used to propel me to win after win after win. I keep them in shape now with yoga, Pilates, and long walks. I'm not ashamed of them, but I'm not flaunting them in the office either. As for the test she is referring to, my fingertips are at least two inches from my hem.

"OK, thanks," I mutter as I turn my attention to the coffees for Oliver and Finn.

"And there is the no-fraternization policy as well," Celine adds.

I bristle at this. "I don't think that's going to be a problem," I tell her, my tone making it clear that her "friendly reminders" are anything but. I highly doubt that anyone in this office would want to spend their time dating me. I haven't run a mile in years. My body let me down so completely, so how could I expect it to be good enough for any of the fit people working for FIRE?

"Well, I wouldn't want to see you get in trouble," Celine adds, taking her drink with her. *With who?* is all I can think. Then her greeting replays in my mind. *Another coffee?* Did Celine spot me walking to Caffeine Corner with Declan? Is that who she thinks I'm breaking the rules with?

I have whiplash from the sharp turn in that conversation. But I don't have time to focus on it. I carefully walk Oliver's and Finn's drinks to the conference room. Then I erase the whiteboard, check that the markers and pens in there all work, and head back to my desk.

Oliver passes me on the way to his meeting. "How are you feeling today?" he asks, his voice laced with concern and – I tell myself to ignore it – pity. Yes, my initial plan was to get a low-stress job, but at heart I wanted two things: new opportunities in sports and to shed the persona of the girl who had to quit when her body stopped working.

No one could see a reason for me to quit racing, to step down from the World Games team. No limp. No surgical scars. No mobility devices. But my body wasn't working as designed anymore. Stress – physical stress – was causing my immune system to attack as if my own muscles were an infection. But people couldn't see that, so they assumed I was mentally weak, too afraid. I don't need my boss to start viewing me that way because of what happened on Friday.

"I'm good," I tell my uncle, who patiently followed my medical saga with my mom and dad. "Everything is all set for your meeting with Finn." I hesitate to relay my next thought but muster my long-dormant courage. "I had a productive conversation with Declan this morning about my helping with strategic operations."

I have an opportunity staring me in the face to do something meaningful and brave. I might as well take it and see where it leads.

"That is excellent news," he says just as Declan exits his office. "I'm looking forward to an update for this weekend's mission now that Charlie is on board," Oliver tells Declan.

Declan appears confused, as he should be. I told him I needed to think about it more before committing to the spy side of things. But I guess my mind is made up now. "Yes, sir," is all he says before Oliver walks away.

"Charlie, my office," Declan orders.

If helping the world means working with Declan, who, until I was shot at, treated me like gum on the heel of his shoe, then so be it. At least his surly demeanor is helping me to remember that in spite of his good looks he is not for me. I am shoving this work crush into a file titled "don't go there."

"Here is a dossier on our mission this weekend," he says before giving me a once-over. "You're going to need to dress accordingly." *Cool, another dress code to manage.*

18

DECLAN

Since X.C. and I were burned in Osaka, I've been flying solo. This weekend will be different – we need all hands on deck.

"Charlie, you sure you're ready for this?" Oliver asks for the third time in the back seat of the limo. On the short drive from FIRE headquarters to the marina, he drilled Charlie on details. It would stress me out if Charlie weren't acing every question.

"The plan is to get whatever intel we can on Frank Castillo. Where he has been, where he is going, and where he might hide a massive cache of illegal arms on his yacht," Charlie recites, clearly trying to ease Oliver's worries. "We have no concrete evidence that he has been initiated into the Order, but we believe this arms shipment from Hynds is his 'audition,' as it were. He is trusting us enough to give us a ride, so we have to assume he doesn't have access to the Order's intelligence on

FIRE's clandestine activities." Charlie recites nearly word for word from the file I gave her on Monday.

She nods to Oliver. "Your role is to chat up Frank, talk like old times, get information, and keep him distracted. I will act like the wide-eyed inquisitive one and ask the captain of the boat for a tour of the bridge. In essence, we're acting like our normal selves, but with a specific purpose."

"She's got this," I tell Oliver, ready for his coaching to be at an end.

My boss turns to me without a hint of humor on his face. "Don't you forget it." His pop quiz was as much for me as it was for Charlie. For me to see that she is ready. He picked up on my stubborn resistance to her joining FIRE. For the past week, I've been prepping her for this mission. She's one of us now, for better or worse.

Charlie, ignoring this back and forth, stares out the window. I'm guessing she's never been in a limo before. Her fingertips hover over the various buttons and controls as if she is tempted to toy with them but restrains herself.

"Whoa, is that the boat?" she asks.

"Yacht," I remind her, and slide forwards to catch an early glimpse myself. Once we all exit the limo, we need to act like this is business as usual. *Sure, another weekend, another yacht.* I've never stepped foot on one, but I can't act like a newbie. Not now.

"Places, everyone," Oliver reminds us as he types out a message on his phone and lets Ian know we're at the dock.

Cell phones don't work aboard boats unless you use the onboard satellite connections. We've agreed it's too risky to use the onboard system and risk Castillo intercepting our intel. Charlie, Oliver, and I all have means of recording and communicating with Ian back in headquarters. All discreet and hidden.

My device is in my watch. I'm guessing Charlie's is in her glasses. Today her frames are all black, no hint of blue to accent her eyes.

I step out of the limo first, then Oliver follows. He waits to hold out a hand for Charlie. She wobbles on her heels but steadies herself for the short walk up the gangplank.

The Waves of Time is a superb vessel. Frank Castillo, the CEO and founder of Vallus, has one of the best fleet of ships in the world. He is waiting for us when we board the ship. Castillo is a few inches shorter than Oliver, which makes him a full half-foot shorter than me. This titan of technology has ditched his glasses (thanks to laser surgery) and added a single diamond stud to one of his ears. With his brown hair slicked back into a low ponytail, he looks like the modern Silicon Valley It guy.

The staff are ready with flutes of champagne and snacks. The vessel has the white hull and teak flooring you would expect. There are multiple lounge decks, an inset couch, two hot tubs, and a support vessel. It screams wealth, privilege, and spoils.

"Oliver! Welcome aboard!" Castillo calls out. He is wearing a casual suit and his previously pale skin is now tan. Castillo, once the world's richest geek, has transformed his image over the past few years. Outwardly, he went through a midlife crisis: cheated on his wife, divorced, and started dating a string of starlets and models. What I know, what everyone on the FIRE strategic operations side knows, is that Castillo has courted the Order. Like so many in his income bracket, he believes he is too big to ever get caught or be held accountable for his actions.

Oliver introduces both me and Charlie. I've met Castillo before and he recognizes me. "Declan, how are you? Still training for Athens?" I'm impressed he remembers.

"Yes, but not getting as many miles in as I'd like. Can you talk my boss into giving me better hours?" I joke as Castillo leads us over to a seating area next to a bar.

Oliver and Castillo chuckle at this. "Thank you for the ride down to our event. I can't believe the private airline cancelled our flight without any help rebooking to another carrier. Never using them again, let me tell you." This is our cover. Really, we wanted a chance to stake out Castillo's vessel. He may be hiding the black-market arms here. Or we may be able to see where the boat has been or where it is headed to. Any evidence we can find. Oliver called in a favor.

"Of course. Happy to help an old friend," Frank Castillo says as he takes the final sip of champagne in his glass. Vallus, Castillo's company, is a major sponsor for FIRE. And for any major sporting event. Depending on the demographic, they either promote the front-facing e-commerce platform, or, for high-earning athletes that race with FIRE, they promote Vallus web hosting and servers.

When Charlie read through the dossier, she immediately asked the obvious question. *Why are we allowing Castillo to sponsor our events if he is a bad guy?* I reminded her that he wasn't always a prick and that it's best to keep your friends close and your enemies closer. Also, we *highly suspect* he is a bad guy. No damning evidence *yet*.

"Charlie, have you ever been to Key West before?" Castillo turns his attention to her fully, using all his billionaire charm. Charlie sets down her champagne and doesn't notice as Frank Castillo's eyes travel up her arms, down her chest, to her hips, and waist.

His leering is troublesome. Charlie is artwork, meant to be admired, not eyed up and down.

There is a constellation of freckles on Charlie's arms. She is certainly showing a lot more skin on this yacht than she ever does in the office. Her professional attire has been swapped for a remarkably chic bathing suit and wrap. Her arms, shoulders, and legs are on display. The bright red fabric is clinging to her hips as well, demanding attention. And her other . . . assets . . . are also accentuated, her cleavage visible. I have to remind myself that this is a job and we have to work together on Monday. Also, I don't want my boss – her uncle – to catch me *noticing*. Castillo is ogling enough as is.

"No, I'm so excited to go. Hopefully I can sneak away and do a little sightseeing. I'd love to visit Hemingway's House. And T. S. Eliot had a place there too, though it's supposed to be more off the beaten path." Charlie is giving Castillo every breadcrumb he needs. I'm not sure how much is genuinely her or how much is a show for the mission.

"Do you like to read? You know books are where it all started for me." Castillo begins to wax poetic about the origins of his company as the yacht sails through Tampa Bay and out into the open gulf waters. The day is bright, the reflection of the sun on the water dazzling and blinding. The salt spray of the waves hisses as we fly over the water.

A man in a crisp uniform with sea-battered wrinkles and a Caribbean accent approaches and introduces himself as Captain John. After shaking hands, he offers to give Oliver a tour of the bridge.

This is the first wrinkle in our plan. With Charlie being so new, we wanted her to get the tour of the bridge with the captain and the ship's crew. Chances are none of them know the depths of Castillo's involvement with the Order, but they would know where the ship has been and where it is going. Oliver was supposed to keep Castillo talking and distract him while I search for information.

"Sure thing," Oliver says, taking a sip of his champagne.

We agreed before the mission to go with the flow and let the plan be fluid. Charlie doesn't jump in and ask to join. Oliver doesn't decline the captain's offer. *I guess this is our new plan.*

"Fair warning, I've been thinking of investing in my own ship, so I have a lot of questions," Oliver jokes and the captain offers a good-natured chuckle as the two walk away.

We'll all be thinking on our feet from here on out. I do my best to avoid eye contact with Charlie, not wanting Frank Castillo to pick up on any signals.

We hit one wave, then two, as the yacht speeds along. This is my cue to excuse myself and check out the interior of the vessel.

I stand and set down my champagne, which I haven't touched. "I'm so sorry. I'm feeling a little seasick. Where is your nearest restroom?"

Castillo points me in the right direction without a second thought; he's too busy chatting up Charlie. Given the switch-up, she'll have to take over Oliver's role: keep Castillo talking on the deck. Distract him.

I'm not comfortable leaving her alone with a man who may have purchased millions of dollars' worth of black-market weapons. But we have a mission to stick to.

I head into the interior hallway and see the bathroom, but I don't go in.

I spent eight years in the navy; of course I'm not seasick. But Castillo doesn't know or doesn't remember.

Now is my time to snoop around and see what I can find.

I can only hope Charlie can hold her own out there.

19

CHARLIE

I hate to admit it, but I spent all last night scouring my wardrobe, thinking, *What does one wear on a yacht? A flipping yacht?!*

When nothing appeared to be good enough to wear, I thought, *What would Celine do?* Because, surely, she has some kind of yacht attire. That led me to Ana, who helped me out with this black one-piece bathing suit with cut-outs and a red wrap halter dress. The pineapple bun updo was her idea too. So are the wedge sandals that make me feel like I'm on stilts. I told Ana a half-truth, only as much as she needed to know.

"Charlie, why don't I give you a tour?" Frank Castillo offers.

His gaze is not meeting my eyes. It is on my cleavage. The plunging neckline of this bathing suit gives me no way to hide the girls. They're on display.

With the captain giving Oliver a tour of the bridge, I'm now responsible for distracting Castillo. While no one expressly stated that distracting Castillo would require me to flirt with him, it doesn't take a rocket scientist to figure out his greatest motivating factors: power and ego. Letting him flirt with me plays into both. I'm glad Uncle Ollie is on the bridge, otherwise this would be even more awkward and cringey than it already is.

"That would be lovely," I purr. And this isn't really a lie. One, I know I need to be checking for anything suspicious. Two, I've never been on a yacht before. Castillo walks a few steps ahead of me, so I discreetly tap the side of my surveillance frames to start recording and transmitting to Ian.

As Castillo leads me into the interior of the boat, my chest tightens. That sense that danger is not just near; it is here. This man could discover our purpose and dispose of us. After all, someone in the Order shot at me and Declan only last week. Who is to say Frank Castillo wouldn't finish the job to protect their nefarious plans? Courage finds me quickly, steadying my nerves and my hands. If flirting with Castillo helps me find information to stop the Order, so be it. I can do that. So people aren't hurt. And, more selfishly, so I'm not shot at again. I can care for the world at large and also act in my own best interests at the same time.

As he leads me through the first hallway, I make sure to take in every detail. Not just for my own curiosity but so the recording picks up anything I might miss. The interior hallways are lined with artwork. I can't imagine the additional insurance costs for that on a boat. On the doorways, I catch small details monogrammed with "F. C." in case anyone ever forgot who owned the vessel. The dark paneling offsets the carpet flooring, the color exactly matching the tangerine Vallus logo.

"My navigation team has an office. There are so many sophisticated systems nowadays, but I want them to have what they need to navigate by the stars if necessary." He points to an open doorway. Inside is a wall of monitors. In the center is our current route to Key West. On the other screens, I notice other destinations. Madeira. Sicily. *Hmm, navigate by the stars, or intentionally go off grid to evade the authorities?*

"Where are you headed after you drop us off in Key West?" I enquire, a totally normal question. If I weren't in these high heels, I would be the same height as Frank Castillo. But with the shoes Ana sent me with, I am taller, putting my collarbone directly in his eyeline.

"To the Mediterranean. Have you ever been?" Castillo gestures for me to follow him.

I continue to chat back and forth, looking for more opportunities to ask about his plans.

He leads us down a spiral staircase to the deck below. "This is where we have a gym, a spa, and four suites." Castillo points to each in turn.

This ship is huge! But I can still feel the motion of the vessel, the speed and the chop knocking us accordingly. I envy

Declan's diversion of being seasick, because I may actually be if I keep walking on these heels throughout this boat.

"Our masseuse isn't on board today, but I'd be happy to give you a massage if you'd like?" Castillo offers as he points to the frosted-glass door that leads to the spa. The way he eyes me as he says this makes my skin crawl. His cologne is too strong for this short hallway. His fingers stroke down my exposed arm, while his other hand moves to the small of my back, guiding me to the room I have no desire to enter ever, let alone with this guy.

I freeze instead of flinch. I'm supposed to get information from this guy, but I have limits as to how far I'll go for this mission.

Just then, one of the doors further down the hallway opens. Castillo puts his hands away as Declan stumbles out. My colleague's left hand covers his stomach; his right is to his mouth. *Wow, maybe he really is seasick.* Or a phenomenal actor.

"Are you OK?" I ask reflexively.

Declan nods, his fist covering his mouth. "The steward suggested I go lay down. Frank, does your team keep any ginger ale stocked?"

"Yes, let me go find you something," Castillo says, trying to stand back from Declan as if motion sickness were contagious. "Charlie, I'll be right back to finish our tour."

Our host hurries up the spiral steps.

I turn back to Declan, who is now standing tall, his eyes alight with fury, staring at the staircase Castillo ascended. "I bet he will."

"Declan, are you actually OK?" I whisper.

He gives me a single nod, a reminder to keep our conversation to a minimum, in case the hallways are being recorded.

"That guy giving you any trouble?"

"Nothing I can't handle," I respond. The muscles in Declan's jaw tighten. "Nothing I haven't had to handle before," I remind him.

As a female in the world, I have had to deal with slimy guys who think my eyes are in my cleavage. I can handle myself. Besides, I know nothing bad can happen to me with Uncle Ollie on board. Or Declan. That thought both surprises me and doesn't at all. I know Declan won't let anyone hurt me. He's already proven that when he shielded me from bullets last week.

Right now, Declan is a little too protective, though. Like he thinks I can't take care of myself. I need to show him I can handle myself on these missions.

Declan keeps his eyes on the stairs, ready to slip back into his ruse at the first sign of Castillo. "Well, you shouldn't have to." He finally moves his eyes and locks them with mine. With these heels, I'm much closer to his height. I can hear his breath, see how his chest moves up and down beneath his pressed polo. Declan looks so natural in this element, dressed up for a day of boating. His calves and forearms, my kryptonite, are on display. I am doing my best to *not* notice, but I'm not blind either.

Remember he's only making sure you don't ruin this mission. My brain gives me the reminder I need so I can stop ogling and say something. "Finally, something we can both agree on."

The ship tilts and these traitorous shoes give me no room to balance. I knock into Declan, who grabs my waist to keep me from falling further with deft precision. His leather and sandalwood cologne surrounds me again, a welcome aroma. This embrace lasts a second, maybe two, before he helps me back to my feet. He removes his hands quickly, but the spot where his hands touched my skin is still warm. I miss his touch instantly.

At first, I think he is mad at me for being clumsy. But then I catch the pink on his cheeks, his eyes refocused on the stairs. *Is Declan Davidson blushing? Because he touched me?*

I feel them again. Those butterflies that only ever made themselves known in my stomach when I was crossing a finish line, when I knew I had that podium in my sights. They choose this moment to resurface.

Castillo's footsteps *tap-tap-tap* down the stairs and I step back from Declan. On cue, he grabs his stomach with one hand and braces the other against the wall.

Our host returns with a can of ginger ale in his hand and a sick bag in the other. "Why don't you head to the lounge, some fresh air may help," he instructs Declan.

My teammate makes his way up the stairs, his tall frame wobbling as he disappears.

"So where did we leave off?" Castillo says and he puts his hand on my upper back. His palms are damp, sweaty. My skin does not react anywhere near the same way it did for Declan. "Ah, the primary suite is ahead." He starts to lead us down the hallway.

"You know, I probably should check in with Uncle Ollie too. Make sure we have everything sorted for when we arrive." I turn and put on my charming smile; this motion also causes his hand to fall.

"Uncle Ollie? I didn't realize Oliver had any family." Castillo is now appraising me with a different set of eyes. Less lascivious, more suspicious.

"Well, he does," I say brightly and turn to head back down the hallway, up the stairs, and away from this guy and his bedroom.

Frank Castillo is silent for a beat before redoubling his efforts. "You know, Charlie, I'm sure working for your uncle has its perks, but you would be a great fit with my team. I'm sure I could find a *position* for you." The way he says it makes me want to barf, but I keep my face stoic.

This man is as old as my uncle, as old as my father! Also, the whole "buying illegal arms and trying to recreate the world for his own profit" thing – huge turnoff.

"Sure," I say, not sure how else to lead with this. "Especially if it would mean travel. I love that I get to travel in my current role."

"Well, I'll be based out of Italy for most of the summer. Working with me would ensure you'd see all the best places. Lake Como. Milan. Rome, of course."

I nod my head as we climb the stairs. Making a mental log of his itinerary now. Oliver and Declan are out in the lounge. I do my best to keep my pace even as we walk toward them, trying not to run to the safety that I know they offer.

The rest of the cruise down to Key West is uneventful. Oliver keeps Castillo busy with conversation. They talk about business and potential new tariffs that could impact both enterprises. Declan keeps up his charade and sneaks below deck a few more times and each time I know he is gathering more data. I turn off the camera embedded in my glasses and wait for us to arrive in Key West.

We disembark in darkness; we'll all have to get some rest before our early morning for the swim start.

"Thank you again for the ride. The next time you have your eye on one of our finish lines, let me know. We'll arrange everything on our end." Oliver shakes Castillo's hand and beelines for the limo, checking his phone.

Frank offers to carry my bag to the car that is waiting for us. Declan is a few steps ahead of us and I catch him roll his eyes.

"Charlie, it was such a wonderful accident we were able to meet this afternoon." Frank Castillo grabs my hand and plants a kiss on it. "I hope we'll meet again soon," he says with a twinkle in his eye.

I give a smile, because I know if I open my mouth to say anything, bile will come out. All our bags are in the back of the limo and I slide in next to Declan. The doors are closed and the limo pulls us away from the dock. Not fast enough for me.

"Please tell me you both got something?" Oliver says, his voice tired.

"Yes, but first I need a towel or a wipe or something," I say, cringing, wanting to clean my hand.

"His ship was running slower than max. Which means he either wanted this to be a longer trip or it is running heavy," Declan announces as he hands me a heated towel from one of the side compartments.

"You think the weapons were on board?" Oliver asks.

Declan gives a nod. Could be.

"Alright, next we'll assess any major targets in the Caribbean and potentially the Yucatán. The captain told me they're sticking to this region," Oliver adds.

I correct him politely. "He's spending the summer port-hopping in the Mediterranean."

Both Declan and Oliver glance at me, clearly asking for clarification.

I tell them about the navigation room and Castillo's boasting. "Madeira is a likely port after crossing. He specifically mentioned ports along the west coast of Italy."

"Good work, Charlie." Oliver turns to me as I make a show of rubbing my hand clean. "Please never tell your father I put you in this situation." This makes me furrow my brow at him. Patriarchal bullshit, but I understand what Oliver is trying to say. He's second-hand embarrassed. I don't need him to be.

"Can you be frenemies with less creepy people?" I ask, trying to make light of the situation.

Oliver puts the information together. "We now have an idea of where the weapons may end up. Not a complete waste of time."

I give a nod and feel a sense of accomplishment. One clue at a time, one piece of information at a time. We can stop him.

"Charlie," Oliver says, peering at me over the top of his glasses, "if that guy does another one of our races, I will personally put a hole in his tires and add Ex-Lax to his electrolyte drink."

This makes me smile. I look over at Declan, expecting him to give a laugh as well. Instead, his face is serious, unfeeling. *So much for being a team*, I think to myself as I wiggle out of my sandals.

This is what snaps Mr. Serious from his stare. "We're not at the hotel yet," he states the obvious.

"I would rather walk barefoot over every seashell in Key West right now than spend another minute in these shoes," I shoot back.

This earns me a chuckle from Declan, which is just as much of a win as our intelligence gathering.

20

DECLAN

Having multiple eyes and ears on Frank Castillo's yacht turned out to be necessary. After Oliver, Charlie, and I got off the prop plane back in Tampa on Sunday evening, we found out the photos I took of the ship schematics with my hidden camera and Charlie's eye-glass frame recordings were all scrambled. Ian said the entire system went down on Sunday morning because of the overload from multiple races going on at once. The poor guy worked non-stop to try to recover it. Ian has a work ethic like no one else I know. At least we have a lead on where Castillo is headed thanks to Charlie.

With the extra work hours, I had to get up incredibly early on Monday to get my miles in on the bike. Spending the morning in aero position up and down the Courtney Campbell

Causeway was both beautiful and backbreaking. By 10 a.m. I am dragging. I head to the break room for a third coffee.

The speed of the drip coffee is painful. As I wait, someone calls my name. By the accent, I know who it is before I turn round. "Declan," Celine says with a smile. "How are you?" Her sugar-sweet perfume invades my nostrils as she stands too close. The scent is chemical and reminds me of my grandmother.

"Tired," I respond. I don't mean to be rude, but I learned a long time ago that if I reciprocated pleasantries with Celine, she would take it as an opening. And I have no romantic interest in her.

Yes, she is tall and leggy and beautiful. I'm sure men fall over her all the time. But a bully, even a glamorous one, is never going to be my type.

"Well, a run might help wake you up." Celine grins. It's a fantastic bright smile. But it is such a shame she only uses it with me, with Oliver, with Finn. Come to think of it, she and Frank Castillo might be a perfect match. Although I'm not sure it would be fair to either of them to make that introduction.

Trey, Ahmed, and our athlete development manager enter the room. They're all chatting about the event they'll be at this upcoming weekend. We exchange hellos and I hope their presence will be enough to distract Celine.

It's not.

"The sponsorship team is organizing a friendly race to Sunnyside Brewery after work. It's four miles down the road.

We'll all get a ride back after a few beers," Celine offers, her invitation directed at me.

"Today?" I ask. Because while I am exhausted, I know that a run would be amazing. A chance to think. To cross-train.

"Yeah, man. Last one to arrive has to buy the first round," Trey calls over. The room is small, so it's not unrealistic that he would overhear. But unconcealed eavesdropping never sits well with me.

I pour the fresh coffee into my thermos and turn when I hear another set of heels hit the tile.

It's Charlie. Immediately, my shoulders relax, the tightness in my forehead abates. I don't take the time to analyze how her presence put me at ease. Maybe it's because I now have a buffer for this conversation with Celine.

"Ross, Celine is telling me about a team run this evening. You in?" I ask.

Charlie startles; her blue eyes widen until she stammers out a response. "A run, huh? This afternoon?" she stalls by repeating the information I already told her.

She heads to the cabinet with the mushroom coffee for Oliver. Even though she is wearing her low heels, she pops up on her toes to reach the new box of Sprout on the top shelf. My eyes travel north and it is clear that Charlie does not skip glutes day at the gym. I remind myself to stop checking her out and lean over to help her, ignoring the death glare Celine is shooting me. And Charlie.

"Thanks," Charlie says, averting her eyes. She straightens her white and blue button-down. She looks much more like herself in her work attire, but the image of her in that bathing suit and wrap is something I can't forget.

"What do you say, Charlie?" Celine asks, calling our attention back to her. "Will you run with us?" I can hear the dare in Celine's words.

"Yeah, we gotta see if you hang with us," Ahmed goads her, because daring someone to race by implying they aren't as fast as you is typically effective. He crosses his arms and his biceps pop out. I know what he's doing, but does Charlie see through it?

"Oh, I wish I could, but I have plans tonight. Maybe next time," Charlie says as she busies herself with fixing Oliver's coffee.

Plans? It's Monday. Must be nice to have time to make plans.

"Too bad, we'll have to run again another time," Celine mutters as she stalks to the break room exit. "See you later, Declan." She offers a little wave and disappears. The others file out as well, snacks and beverages in hand.

"What plans do you have?" I ask, not caring how direct or rude I might be.

Charlie double-checks that everyone else has left before turning to me. "Oh, I don't have any plans. I just don't want to go to the run." She grins as she shares this little lie with me.

I'm shocked by her deception. Then again, she did skillfully let Frank Castillo think he was charming her when she told Oliver she didn't like him at all.

"Didn't you used to be some hotshot runner?" I ask, watching Charlie expertly prepare Oliver's drink.

"Yeah, *used* to be," Charlie corrects me.

She finishes her task and we walk back to our corner of the office together.

"Well, I'm sure you can put a few people in this office in their place," I tell her. "They might need it." I picture Charlie running past Celine, giving that woman a dose of humility.

The mental image is clear: Charlie in running shorts and a sports bra, cheeks flush from the run, her stomach bare, her legs tired. She leans down to do a post-run stretch. I might be able to help her aching muscles. I push those thoughts away to focus on Charlie's response.

She shrugs. "Eh, some things are more important than team bonding or sticking it to people on high horses."

I have to bite back a laugh. "Like what?"

"My health." Charlie's answer is sharp; she is trying to cut off this line of questioning.

She seems perfectly healthy to me. I think of what I've seen other runners go through. "ACL, MCL, or meniscus?"

She adjusts her glasses but doesn't answer. We're nearly back at my office.

"Shin splints from hell?"

Charlie is quiet, one of the first times she isn't chattering on. She's on the receiving end of the questioning this time. Maybe because it's her business and she doesn't want to run with us. Or maybe she does have plans to divulge information to someone in the Order.

"Achilles?"

Charlie turns to me, tight-lipped. "Nope." And ducks into Oliver's office with his mushroom coffee. She emerges and sits at her desk, ignoring the fact that I am still standing there.

Turns out Charlie Ross does have secrets. Are they what I think they are? Or something else?

"I'm glad to see you can keep a secret, Charlie," I say, willing her to look up at me. "But sometimes honesty is the best policy. We have to trust each other."

At this, she glances up at me and drops the envelope in her hand to her desk. "That goes both ways," she says.

She's right. I haven't been able to give her that trust. Still, I wait for her to elaborate further.

After a beat, she nods for us to go into my office.

"I'm allowed to not want to run," Charlie begins as soon as the door is closed. "Some people assume being the daughter of Tom Ross, 'legendary running coach' –" she adds air quotes – "would come with a lot of pressure. It did. In a good way . . ." She hesitates before continuing. "Pressure to push myself, to compete against who I was yesterday and the day before. It didn't hurt that I was a natural, or perhaps a lifetime of subtle coaching from Dad turned me into the best runner. A machine. Perfect form. Perfect timing."

Charlie takes a breath. Her cheeks grow pink; she is agitated and trying not to show it. "But I retired from running and from being his assistant coach for a reason. I need you to respect that."

“OK,” I tell her, still turning over her words in my head. I get it, I think. She has her reasons to not want to run. Little Miss Sunshine has some dark and brooding thoughts, some mental block here. My quick judgments, my snap reactions, have led me so wrong.

Charlie leaves my office and returns to her desk. She begins to sort the mail again.

I know I should get to work. Force her from my mind. But now I have a new mystery to solve: Charlie Ross.

21

CHARLIE

Thursday is chaos! I get to work and I have a mountain of stuff on my desk. Crowding out my neon Rubik's cube, array of comical rubber duckies, and a framed photo of my parents is a tower of mail to sort. A shipment of misprinted T-shirts from race ops that they need me to send back to the printer. And that's just the physical items. My email has a barrage of requests. Many of them from Celine.

A famous football star is planning to do one of our triathlons; Celine needs me to help coordinate the entire day and extra-VIP experience for his wife. Trey and Shauna have an email on travel etiquette they want to send to the entire company that I need to proof before I send it from Oliver's email account. Everyone on the marketing team has been subtly hinting that they want an assignment at the Exponential

Endurance Championships because, hello, work trip to Fiji sounds amazing. The Smithsonian wants "something" from FIRE's first year in operation. Oh, and my computer is giving me the blue-screen-of-death. One of Ian's team said he would be over soon to help. Which means I'm left to manage everything from my phone.

"Ugh," I groan as Declan passes by.

"Hello to you too," he says sarcastically.

"Sorry," I reply. "It's not you." *This time.*

"Whatever it is, I know you can overcome any *obstacle*, clear any *hurdle*." Declan looks even taller when he stands at my desk while I am sitting. He towers over me, offering me the same Cheshire-cat smile he did before not changing the numbers on the budget deck. The dimples in his cheeks are inviting and dangerous.

Then the words he used hit. I sit up out of my stress slump, my back ramrod straight.

"You googled me, didn't you?"

"Steeplechase is pretty badass, Ross." Declan throws me another grin before taking a swig of his coffee. He's right. The steeplechase *is* badass. Along with the 10K and 15K, this was my event. I qualified for all three for the World Games four years ago, but I was most excited to clear the massive hurdles and splash in the water reservoir round the track. I think again of the quote behind my back: *Quitters never earn a line in the history books.*

Boy, do I know it.

I don't know what to say next, but Declan changes the topic. I'm grateful for that. "What's on the docket today?"

I'm not sure if I trust him yet, but maybe he's making an effort. I can give him another chance. I tell him about the myriad requests from Celine.

"Isn't a Smithsonian submission branding or PR?" Declan asks.

"It's both and neither, hence it falls to me," I explain. Because anything that doesn't fit neatly into one department usually makes a stop at my desk before it gets resolved.

Declan mulls this over. "I can take you over to storage to find something. Should be easy."

"You would do that?"

"Yeah, I'm one of four people who have the key. You can't get in without me, and anyone without clearance needs to be supervised," he tells me as he starts walking to the exit. *Begrudging assistance, but I'll take it*, I think as I grab my purse and phone.

The storage unit for FIRE isn't fancy. It's a double unit at a local facility. Declan has the key, and I wonder if I should have one too. Thankfully, the A/C is running, but as with most things in Florida in the summer, it is almost too cold. I regret not bringing a sweater, but we shouldn't be in here for too long.

"The further back we go, the older the memorabilia gets," Declan states as we snake our way through a makeshift aisle built between towers of boxes.

I marvel at decades' worth of stuff. That's the fable capitalism has sold us time and time again. This tycoon started from nothing with nothing. Humble beginnings evidenced by a company started in a garage. There are many companies that have the same origin and so few find the path to eternal consumer staples, vertical defining brands. FIRE *did* start out of a garage, though. Finish lines and orange cones piled into a golf cart. The timing equipment was rented until Oliver decided to buy it. The shirts and medals would overflow into the kitchen on race week and then a gaping hole would be left until the next event and the next. Until he needed volunteers, paid helpers. And more space.

I sneeze. The dust in here is thick.

Now the artifacts of Oliver's life's work reside in this storage facility. The memorabilia and legacy items are in one container, the old sponsor signage forgotten in another, the plastic boards doomed to never deteriorate or fade. The sponsor team is secretly hoping the old companies sign back on and we don't have to recreate the posters, I'm sure.

"Hey, these shouldn't be here," I say aloud as I spot the finisher T-shirts from the cancelled Kalispell races. The same ones Raj and the King Cool team need us to deliver so he can donate them on his next philanthropy trip to Côte d'Ivoire.

Declan turns back to see what I'm referring to. But it is dark in here, even with the lights on. Many of the boxes tower high enough to block out the bulbs.

"Can you shine a light over here for me?" I ask him.

I take a photo of the shipping label with my phone and try to send it over to Ahmed. He's in the office this week, before he heads back out to set up several of our events in Central America. I hope he can get them sorted out in time. There's a boat leaving next week for our races in Africa, so we can still get the shirts to Raj in time if we have it in that shipment.

"No service in here," I mutter as the email fails to send. I'll have to remember to send it later.

"Yeah, concrete does that," Declan quips.

OK, so he is being helpful, but he still retains most of his snark.

He leads us further into the unit until we hit the back wall. "Here are the most 'historical' items."

"Let's see if we can find any of the original finish-line banners, shirts, or medals. That could be good for a display." I start working on the boxes to our left, Declan the right. There is one light bulb shining enough that we don't have to use our phones.

We find exactly what we're searching for: a box with leftover shirts from the very first race and a roster, handwritten, for the first FIRE triathlon.

"Alright, let's get out of here," I say as I put the items carefully in my purse, grateful for its obnoxious size.

"What's that?" Declan asks, his attention on something else.

Then I hear it too. It sounds like something scratching at cardboard.

"Do you think it's bugs? Or a rat?" I ask, because, honestly, a storage unit would be a likely place for them to hide.

"It sounds bigger," Declan says, not taking his eyes off the passageway we came down. He moves in front of me, with his hand held back, as if to block me from going round him. This protective stance tells me he does not think it is any kind of vermin but rather something that could actually harm us.

"Are we in danger?" I whisper. I look behind me, even though we are at the back of the unit and the only thing next to us is a concrete wall. This narrow opening in the precariously heaped boxes looks smaller and smaller with each second. *Is this what claustrophobia feels like?*

"Shh," Declan hisses at me.

I want to snap at him for dismissing my very plausible question, but I don't get the chance. I inch forwards and – without meaning to – walk into his hand. His palm touches my stomach and stays there for a second. Two. Three.

"Sorry," he whispers. "Stay behind me." But he still hasn't moved his hand. The tips of his fingers are pinpricks of heat against my shirt, matches about to ignite my body.

It's just the closed space, his cologne, I tell myself.

His hand is gone and I take a half-step back. He's been trained how to protect people; it's not like he *wanted* to touch me.

My ears search for any sound to indicate what could be in here with us, what or who might be coming toward us.

All I hear is Declan's breath. My own. His shoes scuff the concrete floor as he shuffles forwards.

That's when the lights go out and I hear the roar of the front gate to the unit roll closed and clang shut.

22

DECLAN

"So," Charlie says, sighing, "what are you going to do if we ever make it out of here?" Her voice finds me in the darkness. After the lights went out and the door locked closed, she let out a small scream. The complete darkness is unsettling. I'm doing box breaths to help. I guess Charlie copes with nervous humor.

"It's been ten minutes, Ross," I remind her.

We've each found an uncomfortable and cold seat on the cement floor while we wait. We're locked in until help comes.

"No, this is supposed to be a life-affirming moment. Like 'I thought I'd never escape and now I will donate all my possessions to an orphanage,'" she tells me. Even though I can't see her, I can picture her arms gesturing wildly.

"When I get out of here, I'm going back to work. Then I'm going on a training ride. Same as I had planned earlier," I tell

her. My bike, the trail. Where I can trust that the bike is fit, the tires full, the gears clean. When I ride, the worries of work and life slip away. I pedal away from them, faster and faster until I'm flying. The thought of the open skyline puts me at ease in the dark, confined space.

"That's right. You're a *cyclist*," she says, a sarcastic bite to the last word.

Cyclists have a reputation for being . . . less than generous. Perhaps her applying this stereotype to me is apt? I wince thinking of how rude I have been. In the darkness, when no one else can see us or hear us, I find the courage to say something that has been on my mind. "I'm sorry," I tell her.

I can't see her reaction, but I bet those perfect eyebrows are creeping closer together.

"For how I treated you on your first day, your first week. I'm sorry."

I hear Charlie moving and then see the blue glow of her phone. "Hold on, I'm going to record this as a voice memo," she jokes. I guess that's her way of accepting my apology.

"Well, keep recording because –" I pause and take a deep breath before I eat more humble pie – "you're doing a great job. You have great instincts. For the job you were hired for and the other one you're taking on. You pay attention to details. And I heard what you organized in Kalispell. For that runner."

Charlie turns off her phone and we're in the darkness again. "That was a team effort," she says, brushing off my compliment.

"No, that was all you," I remind her.

The darkness makes the silence stretch out longer.

"I guess I never said thank you for saving my life," Charlie admits. "When the shooting happened, you protected me." Her voice sounds smaller, even though she is still only a few feet away. "I guess we're even now. Besides, I know you were trying to protect Oliver and the company. After you explained everything, I understand you were being cautious that first day." We're silent again for a beat before she continues. "And I appreciate your vote of confidence. I have always been the A player, the smartest in the room anywhere I went. Then I start at FIRE and I'm barely pulling a B minus."

Her analogy makes me chuckle.

Charlie sounds exasperated. "It doesn't help that everyone is freakishly fit and cover-model beautiful."

"See, you fit right in," I tell her, knowing that if I had to compare Celine and Charlie, I know who would win for looks, personality, and more. Hands down, Charlie is exactly my type. Bookish. Those sexy librarian glasses. The backside with curves I want to get lost in. At first, my walls were up; spies never trust someone who asks so many questions. Her honesty, her positivity, her kindness. She's someone who goes out of her way to make someone's day, rules be damned. Helping that runner in Kalispell was the right thing to do.

I don't elaborate and she doesn't press any further. I'm grateful, because if I had to tell her she is just as cover-model beautiful as other, less welcoming people in the office, I'm not sure I'd be able to face her again. Maybe this all-encompassing

darkness is loosening something in me, in both of us, but it hasn't made me forget my pride. My own fear of rejection.

"I googled you too," she admits.

"And what did you find?" I ask, knowing full well what the answer will be.

"Nothing. Not one social media profile. No newspaper clippings. You really are a spy, huh?"

Her words amuse me. "That's the easiest term to describe it."

Charlie gasps and I can picture her overreaction. "Is Declan Davidson even your real name?!"

At this, I laugh. "Yes, it is my real name. My parents were super strict when I was in high school about no social media. When I got to Annapolis, it seemed safer to not have an account to avoid infractions. Then I got used to not having a real account. I have a few burner ones I can use to look people up when needed."

"So Annapolis to FIRE?" Charlie asks.

"Yeah?"

"There's a story there. How do you go from a solid career in the military to endurance sports to being a spy?"

I hesitate. "It's a long story."

I hear Charlie moving in the darkness, shifting to find a comfortable position on an unforgiving floor. "We have time."

I tell her about my rebellious streak as a kid. How my dad was in the army, went to West Point. Served all twenty years before retiring with a full pension. "The most defiant thing

I could think to do would be to join the navy. Old rivalries die hard." This earns me a small chuckle from Charlie.

Oliver is also retired navy. While FIRE isn't affiliated with any one branch of the military (or any specific country), the navy trend is strong among the executive team. "Four years at Annapolis in exchange for eight years active duty. Retired two years ago. I was lucky," I continue, "to have great mentors and leaders. Served with a tight unit and had a commanding officer I admired. Was happy to follow him. My CO took a civilian job at a sports company.

"He called me up and said, 'You gotta exit at the end of your current tour. Come work for me. It's more than it seems.' Sounded like every kid's dream, right?" I think back to when I got the call, knowing I had an option to get out of the navy or re-up my commitment. I hadn't even begun to think about life as a civilian. Then a perfect opportunity fell at my feet. "I took the job. I trusted him; he had never steered me wrong. I was deployed with him. I knew his family. And he was right. This is a great job. Both sides. And then . . ." I trail off.

Charlie figures out what I didn't say. "And then you were both on that dock in Osaka, and only you came out of the water?"

"Yeah," I say, not wanting to talk about it anymore.

The guilt, the loss, the feeling that I could *and* should have known what was about to happen and prevented his death. We were on a mission in Japan. It went sideways. I thought we would always save the day, beat the odds, make it out alive together.

Nope.

I stop my train of thought. Ruminating on it is a wasted effort. *Focus, Davidson.*

I hear movement in front of me and then beside me. A pressure on my hand. It's Charlie. She fumbled in the darkness to move next to me, to comfort me. Her touch is light and reassuring.

"I'm sorry," she whispers.

We sit like that, her holding my hand for a moment. The warmth of her body is so close, the fragrance of her perfume so subtle and welcome.

Charlie is the one to break the silence. "So is it too much of a coincidence that *we* are the two people trapped in here? Like, whoever the mole is, probably locked us in here?"

"Could be," I respond, hesitant to jump to any conclusions after my massive flub on her first day.

"Or it could have been an honest mistake," she offers.

"The lights were on; anyone who came in would have surmised someone else was in here and called out. Whoever it was knew we were in here and didn't want us to know."

"And they wanted us trapped," Charlie adds.

"Not a very good trap, though," I tell her.

"Why? We can't get out. I'd say that's a good trap," she counters, as the door rolls open and the lights blink back on.

Charlie is surprised. I'm not.

"Yoo-hoo!" Ian Turner's cheerful voice calls out.

"We're back here," I respond, helping Charlie to her feet before navigating the maze of boxes.

I still feel too exposed, like my thoughts and fears were too close to spilling out of my mind, filling up this storage unit and another.

"Someone locked us in," Charlie says as we approach the front, Ian in sight.

"Huh?" He puts his hands on his hips.

"She's right – there's no way the door closed and the lights shut off on their own."

"Looks like we have another set of security cameras to hack." Ian shakes his head and turns back the way he came.

"How did he know we were in here?" Charlie asks me.

"My tracking dot. I hit the alarm on it as soon as the lights went out," I explain.

"Tracking dot?" Charlie asks.

"Oh right." I haven't told her about this yet. "I have a tracking dot on me at all times." She nods, accepting this. "We should probably get one for you too," I add.

At this, Charlie crosses her arms and scowls at me. "I don't plan on being trapped in any more storage units any time soon," she announces.

Do I have to say the quiet part out loud? That she's in danger because she works for FIRE and by putting any effort into stopping the Order?

Before I can warn her, she is already down the hallway, putting distance between us as quickly as she can. She may not want to heed my warnings, but I think we just had our own team-bonding moment. An escape room without any cheesy prize at the end. We stuck together as a team, didn't argue, and made it out the other side. Charlie is my colleague, an equal – and maybe a friend.

23

CHARLIE

Beep-beep-beep.

My alarm clock reminds me of the poor choice I made yesterday. Or, well, a good choice, I guess. To get up at 6 a.m. and go for a run. I slide into my shorts and sports bra. And my shoes.

They're well worn, these sworn enemies. Stored in a box at the top of my closet, I couldn't leave them behind. They're a part of me. Is this how an addict feels? It's so easy to make the wrong choice, the bad decision. So close to getting that runner's high once more. The action that you know will hurt you. And yet . . .

The irony of my life is that the things everyone else is prescribed, I've been told to avoid.

I guess I've been feeling it for a while. Sensing it was time to try again. Yesterday, being locked in that storage unit made me realize I can't spend the rest of my life being afraid of my own body. Weak and cowering.

I pull the box open and peek inside. There they are: bold blue with pink accents worn from hours in the sun. The smell hits me first. The distinct odor of every puddle of rainwater they've been through, of the mud caked on, dried, and flaked off. My sweat mixed in with each aroma. To me, it's a smell of freedom. Of a defined trail through the woods that demands my presence, my commitment. The tingle at the start line knowing I'm about to push myself again. The dopamine rush when I cross the finish line.

It's a dangerous aroma. Like a grieving ex-girlfriend who breathes in her lover's cologne. The sense-memory too strong.

I slip on my old sneakers and promise myself I won't push it. Won't fall over into my old ways. Just one mile. Just one run. I'm a recovering type-A athlete. *Can I really limit myself?* Only one way to find out.

A text from Ana flashes on my phone.

Ana Alonso

I'm outside.

She graciously agreed to join me after I texted her last night about my plan to run this morning. Thankfully, her apartment is down the block from mine. Very convenient for early-morning runs or emergency outfit sessions.

After so much back and forth with travel, we haven't had a chance to catch up. And if I'm being completely honest with myself, I'm scared. I've always been aware that running alone as a female has inherent risks, but after being shot at and then locked in a storage unit, I'm on edge. Even though these attacks were likely targeting Declan and his operations to thwart the Order, I don't like being in the crosshairs.

I put in my contact lenses and lock the door behind me.

"I'm re-evaluating if I want to be friends with you," Ana grumbles as she hangs sleepily on the railing in front of my building. Her long dark hair is pulled back into a high ponytail, showing off her ripped shoulders from her hours preparing for body-building competitions. Not everyone who works for FIRE does endurance events, but ninety percent of the employees are competitive in some kind of sport or activity. For Ana, it's lifting, flexing, and posing.

"You agreed to join me," I remind her.

Ana rolls her eyes. "Yes, and that version of me was not thinking about how much I would miss sleep this morning."

Even with her protests, we start out with a light jog, keeping in step.

"OK, this is better than the gym," Ana offers as we turn onto Bayshore Boulevard. The bright orange-pink of the sky greets us.

I smile as we run in silence for a moment, our feet tapping out a beat on the sidewalk. The early-morning air is cool, if not muggy. We're nearly twinning, her in a bright pink sports bra and high-waisted black shorts, me in matching shorts with a maroon top. I'm sure our ponytails are swaying to the same rhythm as we settle into our cadence.

There are some universal truths: running hurts, but the feeling of accomplishment afterwards is a drug. Oh, and, total creeps will honk at you. Not even half a mile in and two different trucks honk and catcall us.

Excuse me, it's 6:15 a.m. CALM. DOWN.

Ana mutters some curse words under her breath as they pass. I'm grateful she's with me, to have the two of us against the creeps of the early morning.

My mind switches into deep thought. I have a few things to mull over and a run always helps me clear my head.

For starters, the storage unit. *Who locked Declan and me in? Who even knew we were in there? And what was this person getting into?*

Also, yesterday left me feeling weak. I'm always erring on the side of caution. Forcing myself to hold back. And I've become inept because of it. I have to be able to find a balance between strength and endurance. Between too much physical stress that could wreck my health and throw me into another flare and the need to be able to move my body and be confident I can protect myself. I'm not a damsel.

I force these thoughts from my mind and focus on the view before me. The sunrise is morphing the color of the sky, the bright colors turning to a more subtle yellow, then light blue. Next to me is the Hillsborough River. I peek over and check for the manatees I've heard frequent this stretch of water.

I remind myself of the real puzzle I need to piece together. *Think. Think. Who could be the mole?*

Celine is giving off villain vibes, but maybe she's just a mean girl?

Ahmed is strong and has access to all of our logistics, but he seems like such a teddy bear. Or is that just a well-played disguise?

Trey has access to everyone's personal information to be able to book travel. Date of birth, credit card loyalty member logins. But he'd be more likely to run a scam to get everyone's frequent-flier miles than leak information to the Order. Right?

Ana? I steal a glance at my running partner out of the corner of my eye. She's focused on the turnaround point just ahead. *No way! In the movies the least-suspected person may often be it, but this is real life, and she is way too kind to ever side with the Order.*

Declan? My mind stops at the thought of him being the one to betray his own missions. The footage from the yacht trip was lost. He was there and could have done it. *Hmm, and he was close to Xander. Could he have planted the explosive to take X.C. out? Declan is so obsessed with rooting out the mole – maybe he's trying to throw suspicion off of him?*

Something in my gut tells me that's wrong, though. *The pain in his voice yesterday when he told me about how much of a mentor Xander had been to him; there's no way he could fake that.*

Ana interrupts my thoughts. "So you and Declan were MIA yesterday," she says.

"He took me to the storage unit. I needed to grab some items for Celine," I explain.

"Oh really?" Ana asks, her gasps for air punctuating her words. "Because it was Celine who called it to my attention that she couldn't find you."

"What is her problem?" I mutter, pushing on.

"Hold up." Ana waves her hand. "Let's walk a bit," she requests. I hadn't noticed how much my pace had increased, how I had slipped into my faster gait without even thinking about it. "I only do cardio, like, twice a month," Ana reminds me. She takes a gulp from the water bottle in her hand and I do the same. "Celine's problem is you. She definitely has the hots for Declan."

I'm not following. "And?"

"Remember, this girl does not like competition," Ana reminds me.

I don't know what to make of this comment. *Celine is jealous of me because I spend time with my coworker doing our jobs?* "If she likes him so much, she should ask him out. Or fetch her own items from storage instead of dumping it on my desk." I roll my eyes and stretch my arms.

Ana shrugs.

I change the subject. "Speaking of asking people out, how are things with your ex? Or is Lucy not an ex anymore?"

Ana's grin confirms the latter. We turn and jog back the way we came at a pace that allows Ana to give me the details of their latest exchanges and how this time it might stick. I love to hear her romantic optimism. I can't help but feel a little envious, wanting someone of my own to gush over.

Before I know it, we're back at the entrance to my apartment complex. It was a relatively quick mile, even with our brief stop. I could go another round. I'm no closer to figuring out who the mole is. The facts aren't coalescing the way I would like. But I'm energized by the burn in my muscles right now. The taste of salt on my lips reminds me I'm sweating; my body is tired and exhilarated in equal measure.

Another loop could clear my mind further, but that is a dangerous exception to make on day one.

Ana waves and finishes her water bottle. "See you at the office."

"Coffees are on me," I call out as she walks out of the front gate.

"You know it," she retorts.

I head inside to shower and get dressed for work. I love that no matter what today throws at me, I've already crossed off the hardest thing on my list. I leave my running shoes by the front door and head back out into the beautiful morning before the humidity and my newfound anxiety settle in.

24

CHARLIE

OK, coffee shops are popular on Fridays. It's as though everyone else in Tampa had the same idea this morning.

This café is on the way to work and I've been meaning to try it ever since Ana told me they make "legit Cuban coffee – not just the type for tourists." I owe her for getting up early to run with me, so procuring her favorite coffee in town is the least I can do.

The line is to the door, so I squeeze in as best as I can. A woman hurries past me on her way out, balancing two to-go containers of coffees. She appears frazzled; I hope she makes it to her car without the hot drinks toppling.

As if my thinking it has summoned this outcome, her tower begins to wobble. Those in front of me in line recoil, leaning away from the impending mess. A gentle hand lands on my shoulder and pulls me so I have to step to the side. The drinks fall and steaming coffee pools on the floor right where I was just standing. I look over at whoever it was that just saved me from scalding-hot splatter.

I turn and see Blaed, Blaed-from-the-bar, standing next to me.

"Hi," I manage to breathe even in my state of mild shock. "Thank you," I add quickly, as he removes his hand from my shoulder and smiles. Those green eyes lock on to mine.

My brain seems to catch up to everything that is happening. I look over at the woman who is desperately trying to clean up the coffee mess all by herself. No one else got out of line to help her. I can't believe it! I leave the line and grab a pile of napkins from the stand in the corner.

The woman nods as we both dodge the steady stream of people still entering the café. A barista approaches with a dish towel and offers to refill the order. "Your friend told me you jumped in to help, so your order is on the house," the barista tells me.

I'm confused. Helping doesn't require a reward. And who is my friend?

I look up and see Blaed walking back from the counter. He must have alerted the staff. The woman confirms her order and I give mine before the barista heads back. I debated ordering the gluten-free coffee cake too. It makes me think of my dad, as it's his favorite treat, one my mom and I would bake for him every year on his birthday. He asked for a gluten-free version once I started my low-inflammation diet. But two coffees on the house was enough. I didn't want to abuse the offer.

I look around and spot Blaed at a corner table. He waves me over. "Thank you for getting help," I say. "And for pulling me back."

"And that big bug," he adds with a smile. He gestures for me to sit with him while I wait.

I play along. "Yeah, seems I should just hire you as personal security. I have no known threats, but apparently Florida is full of bugs. Can't be too safe."

"My rates are steep," Blaed counters, and the spark in his eyes tells me that, yes, we are indeed flirting. "The bugs here are out of control."

"They weren't nearly as bad in Eugene."

Blaed is staring at me without blinking. I can't read his expression.

"What? Do I have another bug on me right now?" I quickly check my arms.

"You're from Eugene?" he asks as he cracks a smile, and I nod. "Eugene, Oregon?" he clarifies. I nod once more. "I'm from Portland," he confesses. That specific aroma of his, the one that first night at the bar and again this morning, makes sense now. Sagebrush and lupine. He must have Oregon in his pores. It's so specific, so familiar.

"No way!" I shake my head in disbelief. "How did you end up in Tampa?" And for once it's nice to talk with someone about life. About things that aren't related to finish lines, logistical issues with shipping, or black-market weapons deals.

Hearing Blaed talk about his family back in Oregon, homesickness creeps in. And not just for my home but for my old life. For a time when my biggest problem at work was a few pity stares. Now I have to worry about secret societies, shooters, and overly competitive PR managers.

"Do you come here often?" Blaed asks, turning the conversation back to me.

I shake my head, nervous under his gaze. "No, I'm picking something up for me and a friend before I head into work."

"That same friend from the bar?" Blaed asks.

"Yep, Ana," I confirm. I'm impressed he remembered her too.

"So not a male coworker then?" Blaed clarifies.

And yep, I'm blushing. Because there is a very clear question behind that question. "No," I say. And it's the truth. But Declan's dimples flash in my mind.

Blaed nods. "I haven't seen you around. I went back to the beach bar the last two Fridays hoping to catch you." Blaed is putting on all kinds of charm. He offers a sheepish grin and fiddles with the cardboard wrap of his to-go coffee cup. I remember that when Blaed rescued me from that ginormous bug, I was quite taken by him.

He's classically handsome by anyone's standards. The tan skin offset by light hair and green eyes. The cleft chin. His muscles are bulky, which is usually not my thing. I go for endurance guys: lean muscles and stamina. And there is Declan's face, popping into my mind again.

But I'm new in town. I can count Ana as a friend, for sure, and Declan is becoming more tolerable as a coworker, and after being locked in yesterday, I think we're solid work friends. But outside of work I don't have anyone to hang out with. Being friends with Blaed could be good.

"I had to travel for work. I might be there next week, though."

"That sounds fantastic, I'll see you next week then," Blaed says with a twinkle in his eye.

Oh gosh, I hope he doesn't think it is a date. But would a date be the worst thing? Again, my mind snaps to a picture of Declan. *Whoa, where did that come from?*

I steal a glance at Blaed as he walks over to the napkin and sugar stand. His chiseled triceps are peaking out of his skintight black T-shirt as he jots something on one of the napkins; they move deliciously along with his forearms as he writes.

Blaed seems sweet. It wouldn't be the worst thing to have someone in my life, romantically or platonic, who isn't enmeshed in FIRE.

He walks over with a confident swagger and hands me the napkin. It has his number on it.

"In case plans change again," he tells me.

I can't think of a flirty response, so I say "thanks" and pocket the napkin.

The woman behind the counter calls my name.

"See you next week," I say before I head out, waving to Blaed.

The warm feeling after chatting with Blaed dissipates quickly, fizzling as soon as I exit the café. Outside, the urge to hurry to work kicks in. To the safety of crowds.

Maybe I should have stayed and chatted with Blaed longer. At least he distracted me from this new ever-present anxiety.

Both times I've been in danger recently have been while on the job for FIRE. Rushing to get to work feels counterintuitive. But I know Uncle Ollie, Ian, and Declan will keep me safe.

So far in this job I've been shot at and locked in a storage unit. What's coming next? Will I be able to dodge it in time?

I really need to figure out who this mole is so I can get some peace of mind for myself, my colleagues, and, oh yeah, the free world which is at risk of an impending attack.

25

DECLAN

I enter the office in an uncaffeinated fog. I set my laptop bag down on my chair and grab my FIRE mug without thought, all muscle memory, headed for the break room. When I step back out of my office, something catches my eye. Or someone.

Charlie sits at her desk, focused on whatever she is typing. She is wearing her usual casual business attire instead of the more relaxed Friday dress code most people embrace. We're the only two odd ones out. But that's not what is distracting me. "Your face looks different today," I say to her.

Charlie's placid expression shifts to incredulous. "Happy Friday to you too? Your face looks the same."

As someone who works in intelligence and surveillance, changes must be noted. "What's different? What did you change?" I take a few steps closer to see if I can figure it out.

"Is this supposed to be a compliment?" Charlie asks sarcastically before returning her attention to her work. I don't budge. After a moment, she admits, "I went for a run this morning."

I'm not following how this explains what I'm seeing. "You're not in running clothes."

Charlie rolls her eyes, and I realize what is different as she is speaking. "I wear my contacts when I run. In my rush to get out the door, I forgot to take them out."

"Oh." I pause. That is plausible. *Charlie still looks great without her glasses, but—Wait, what is my brain thinking here?*

"Is this where you pull a Freddie Prinze Jr. and tell me I should stop wearing them because I look better without them?" Charlie asks.

"What? A who? No! Quite the opposite actually." I'm on the defense.

"Um, thanks," Charlie mutters, and it's as though all the progress we've made as teammates is slipping away.

"No, I mean you look better in them." I hesitate, realizing I might as well be the guy who locked her out on day one again. "I have quite a hole to dig myself out of."

"Yes. Are you going to tell me to smile more next?" She cocks an eyebrow, daring me to make another comment.

"No. Just . . . I like the frames. The hint of blue . . ." I gulp before making this final confession, but it may be the only way to salvage this exchange. "It makes your eyes pop."

Charlie glances up at me for the first time this morning without suspicion. Her shoulders lower, her defenses too. "Oh," she responds, training her cobalt irises on me, disarming me as well.

I should offer to grab her some coffee too, I tell myself. But there is already an iced-coffee cup on her desk.

Charlie is assessing me, and I can tell I should say something. *How can I get her to smile? Why am I so concerned about making her smile?*

Celine turns the corner, and Charlie gives her the go-ahead to start her meeting with Oliver. "He's ready for the championship media plan," Charlie tells her. Celine gives her a "hmm" of acknowledgment, flipping her hair over her shoulder as she waltzes into Oliver's office. I barely register this interaction; I certainly don't greet Celine. Not with this awkward silence between myself and Charlie. I head over to the break room, so I don't have to stand there thinking about how to undo my comments.

When I get back to my office, Charlie isn't at her desk. Which is good because I need to get to work. *She's a distraction*, I remind myself.

I dive into my latest intel reports and the hour passes quickly. I'm interrupted by a ping on my phone. One of my contacts in Denmark has spotted Monique, our MIA photographer who no-showed in Mexico City. She hasn't surfaced for weeks. This could be a chance to find out what happened, and whether she sold those images to someone else, someone who wants them to disappear.

It's the piece I keep puzzling over. I can understand how a mole in our organization was recruited. Money. It's always the money. But Monique is an artist. While she has to fund her life somehow, she has prioritized art over financial gain for years. Her award-winning photos have allowed her to buy what she needs and the rest she spends on gear or trekking to remote areas for the best shot. She has integrity. *How did the Order get to her?*

I reread the message and respond:

Declan Davidson

> Any signs of distress? Bruising, cuts, extreme weight loss?

I need to know what we might be up against.

My contact sends an image. When it loads, I spot no visible injuries. Monique appears the same. Like any woman casually strolling down the streets. *Perhaps she sold out to them willingly?*

I shake my head, thinking about how easy it is to prey on someone's integrity nowadays. Anyone can spin up a social media campaign calling for a need to save a very worthy group – children, refugees, animals, souls in need of aid, people worthy of help. But so often fraudsters can manipulate the urge to help and warp it into donations for shadow charities. Or pit people against the genuine article, distorting their views so that suddenly they're siding with terrorists or calling for violence in the name of peace. It's all one well-placed hashtag away. Could this be how the Order got to Monique?

Or is there a plausible explanation? I recall how quickly I misjudged Charlie, how embarrassed I was when she turned out to be Oliver's new assistant.

I peer out my office and catch Charlie at her desk. "Hey," I call out. She looks over at me and I wave her in.

"What's up?" she asks. Her navy-blue blouse and white dress pants look elegant today. And, of course, the blue draws more attention to her eyes. Her perfume starts to waft my way. It's sweet and makes me want to lick my lips. I fight the urge and motion for her to close the door before I fill her in on the information I've just received.

"I'll book you a flight," Charlie says without preamble.

Outside, Oliver's office door opens. His booming voice carries, even through closed doors. Through the frosted-glass wall of my office, I see him and Celine file out of their meeting.

Oliver knocks at my door and opens it without waiting for the all-clear. "Hey, Declan," Oliver begins as he enters my now cramped office. "Oh, hi, Charlie," he says, not surprised to find her here. "Declan, can we talk about the Finland registration opening date?"

"We've got other matters," I say and nod to the office door.

Oliver shuts it and takes a seat next to Charlie.

I review the information again, as Oliver nods his head, following along. "Great, you'll go right away." Then he gestures to Charlie. "This would be a good opportunity for Charlie to get some field experience."

Charlie perks up in her chair.

I do not mirror this action. If anything, I want to challenge Oliver.

Copenhagen with Charlie in tow. A flight, taxis, all with her never-ending stream of questions and curiosity. A rendezvous with my contact to not mess up. A cover to not blow. Another team member I'd be responsible for protecting, bringing home alive.

At least at the end of the day I'd get a break when we go back to the hotel. My mind catches on that word. "Hotel." Keys. Locked doors. Perfectly made beds with plush duvets. Charlie's piercing eyes. Her hand finds mine in the darkness . . .

26

CHARLIE

"*Hej. Velkommen til København*," the concierge at the hotel says, greeting us as Declan and I approach the desk. I'm exhausted, but I can't stay still. My eyes are wide, taking in the glimmering details around me. The hotel we booked is distinct and refined. Not a chain. The lobby has gilded mirrors and a marble entryway.

But my excitement for travel is dampened by the very real danger of this assignment. We need to find Monique, Declan's mysteriously disappearing photographer. Sure, work is stressful right now, but I like the job itself. And I'm not going to quit just because the job's tough. I don't quit things when they get hard, only when it is medically necessary.

Declan slept for the entirety of the flight over, which left me to read case files and stay hopped up on ginger ale.

Now he responds to the concierge in what sounds to my ear as perfect Danish. "*Tak, der er en reservation til Davidson.*"

The concierge hands us an antique skeleton key with a tassel on the end. Very social-media-worthy, but a pain to keep on us. I hold it awkwardly as we head to the birdcage elevator, one of those old-fashioned kinds with the door and the fence.

"They're bulky but no one can hack the room lock," Declan says when he catches me admiring the key.

Great, now I'll definitely be able to sleep well tonight, I think and roll my eyes. This is the most he has said to me since we landed. "Wait, where is your key?" I ask him. He must have pocketed it already.

"That's it." He points to the key in my hand.

One key? One room?!

"Uhh." I try to think what to say.

The elevator stops on our floor and we both shuffle out. The walls are hung with artwork, the carpet plush.

Declan checks the hallway before whispering. "Our cover" are the two words he offers me.

I look back at him confused. This does not explain why we are sharing a room.

"Couple on a romantic holiday," he states matter-of-factly. As if this should have been obvious. He nods his head, indicating we should move on and finish this conversation in our room. *Our room!*

We find the correct door and I unlock it.

I gasp. This is not a room. This is a well-appointed suite. The midday sun is pouring through the white curtains, the gilded accents on the antique couch sparkle. There are two doors on the far end of the living room. *This suite is so big it has a living room!*

I place my bags on the floor and resolve not to let the pretty decorations distract me for a moment longer.

"Why can't we just be coworkers? Wouldn't that be easier, since it's the truth?" My brain has the priorities straight. My stomach is dancing, flipping, doing eccentric jumping jacks at the idea of sharing this room with Declan Davidson.

Declan indulges my question. "Oh, you're on a work trip. What type of work do you do? What company do you work for? Why are you here on a weekend and not a weekday?" He pauses and drops his impression voice, one that sounds a little too familiar to me. "It invites too many questions," he explains. "Besides, any spy worth their salt could check the registration log and see if we stayed in separate rooms."

I don't want him to have the last word here, but his reasoning makes sense. "OK, but I don't need another reason for Celine to hate me."

Out of the corner of my eye, Declan smirks. "I do. Can we somehow get her to back off?"

As I move further into the room, I see an incongruous modern sofa that looks infinitely more comfortable than the antique couch.

"So one of us on the couch?" I point to it, assuming that will be mine.

"Yep, you can take the bed," Declan offers. Which is nice, but he is too tall for the couch. Also, I have yet to find the bed. I turn round, hoping I missed it. Declan indicates the doors on the far wall.

I open one and find a clean and updated bathroom. The second door leads to the bedroom. An ornate four-poster bed fills most of the small room. But at least I'll have some privacy in here.

"Let's get some rest and we'll head out in an hour to establish our cover," Declan states as he makes himself comfortable on the newer couch. His robotic non-answers remind me of my first week on the job. I know he's focused on the mission. But how serious he is, is making me more anxious about this operation. I don't want to mess up. And I really, *really* don't want to be shot at again.

"Should we synchronize our watches?" I ask, putting on an air of sarcasm. I'm trying to lighten the mood.

Declan shoots me a look that says he is not amused.

I grab my bag and move it into the bedroom. Even if we're only here for a weekend, I want everything in its place. I set an alarm and let myself sleep. I hadn't realized how exhausted I was until my body hit the bed.

And "hit" is indeed an apt word. Not "bounce," not "flop." Because this mattress is as hard as a rock. I realize now that Declan opted for the modern couch not out of some kind of chivalry but because he knew which option would be more comfortable. I roll my eyes, accept my torture, and fall asleep.

When I wake, a few moments before my alarm, I remind myself of where I am. That this is an opportunity to prove myself in this new job. More than that: a woman's life is on the line. And potentially the lives of whoever will be on the wrong end of these weapons. This isn't about sightseeing. It's about keeping people safe.

Declan Davidson

In the lobby.

It's a text from Declan.

I change out of my plane clothes for our outing. The weather here is cooler than Florida, but it is still summertime. I have on a butter-yellow sundress and a blue cardigan. I look like a tourist, which was my only instructions when packing for the trip. I hurry out of the room to find Declan.

He stands up from one of the richly upholstered couches when he sees me cross the lobby toward him. He's in well-worn jeans and a fitted black Henley shirt, his lean muscles visible. I'm grateful for the prescription sunglasses I brought so he can't see me checking him out.

Declan indicates with his head that we should move outside. He holds the front door open for me, while he does a visual sweep of the street. Scanning for someone, something. Or just keeping an eye out. He dons the baseball cap that was in his hands, TAMPA BAY embroidered on the front.

He wordlessly navigates us down the sidewalk; he must have an idea of where we are going. The temperature outside is perfect, the afternoon buzz of the city giving me all the jet-lag-fighting energy I could hope for.

As we cross the street, Declan moves his hand protectively, reflexively, to my lower back. I look over at him, but his gaze is focused ahead of us. It dawns on me for the first time that I am massively complicating this mission for him. Because of me he has an unfamiliar cover, which I have to help maintain. He has to watch both his back and mine. I remind myself to stay sharp. If we get trapped somewhere, Ian can't come and let us out. It's only the two of us.

This should make me more nervous. Before we left, I was on edge. Like I was being watched. I haven't been able to shake that feeling ever since the shooting. But in a foreign city on a secret mission with Declan, I'm relaxed. I think maybe it's Declan whose presence is soothing me.

"Well, *honey*," I say with emphasis, "let's get something to eat."

I'm hoping that sitting at a café where he has a view of the entrance and the street will put him at ease. Instead, he leads us into an open-air market.

"Way ahead of you, *sweetheart*," Declan says. His voice is lighter.

This place is amazing. Food, flowers, drinks. The aromas from various stalls create a mouthwatering medley in the summer air. But to a spy, even a novice like me, this is a nightmare. Faces, people everywhere. Lots of areas operatives could hide, the buildings that surround the square could be the ideal cover for a sniper. I may never view the world the same way again.

We head to a stall and order sandwiches. My body hums with excitement and a tinge of anxiety.

"I thought you were gluten-free?" Declan asks as he hands me the food.

I take a bite and let the flavor hit my tongue. Four years without gluten. FOUR! "Shhh, I'm going to enjoy this." I let out a moan that my body has never created before, never. Not even with my college boyfriend.

I chew slowly and open my eyes to find Declan studying my face, curiosity dancing across his eyebrows.

He is ruining my vibe, but I don't mind explaining. "I'm gluten-free because it can cause inflammation." I decide not to tell him that inflammation can exacerbate my condition. Because he'll ask what my condition is. "A lot of travel forums I'm on mention that people who have issues with gluten, dairy, or meat in the US can usually enjoy them symptom-free abroad," I lie. It wasn't a travel forum. It was an autoimmune support group. But the anecdotes were plentiful enough to have me enjoying this sandwich guilt-free. I take another bite, and I can't help it. I do a little hop.

"Do you need a moment alone with your sandwich?" Declan asks.

"You said we're a couple on a romantic trip, well, this sandwich is now part of our throuple," I say between bites.

Declan's eyebrows raise before he barks out a laugh. "Should we get you some *brunsviger* too?"

I nod enthusiastically. "YES!"

With our stomachs full and a few hours to burn before our planned intercept of Monique, we stroll through the city. Declan explains that his contact in Denmark – who we will not meet in person so that their cover is not compromised – was able to confirm that Monique is meeting someone at a bar not far from our hotel this evening.

"You think she's going to sell the evidence?" I ask.

"I hope not," Declan says.

It's the first time I've heard him say the word "hope." Maybe he's thought it, but he's never expressed it aloud. I wonder at how much losing X.C. messed with his head.

We arrive at the most photographed place in the entire city. The famous statue of the Little Mermaid. If I was visiting this city for fun, I'd be doing all the Hans Christian Andersen book-nerd things. But this is work, and I'll take the opportunity to see the iconic statue since we're here anyways.

You're not supposed to touch the statue, so Declan and I stake out a good spot to watch her as tourists continue to clump and break away for photos.

"Are you supposed to make a wish when you see her?" I ask. And then I realize that the man standing next to me is the last person who would care about such things.

"I don't know. I guess you can, though. I won't stop you," he answers and crosses his arms. His sleeves are pushed up, revealing his forearms. They're tanned from hours in the sun riding his bike, his dark arm hair, his lean muscles, all inviting mental images that I should not be thinking about.

"Alright," I say and squeeze my eyes shut. I let my wish run through my mind and open my eyes. I peer up at Declan, and his eyes are closed too. "What did you wish for?" I ask before I can stop my invasive question.

"Haven't you heard that if you share your wish, it won't come true?" He shakes his head. "I guess I'll risk it," he says. "I wished for us to find these weapons, get the Order behind bars, and put an end to this madness."

"That's a hefty wish," I say, guilty for my much more selfish desires.

"You?" he asks, glancing over at me.

The stubble on his face is darker than I've ever seen it before and his brown eyes are probing mine. Is he trying to guess? His nearness is making me feel things. His attention is confusing my body. He can't be attracted to me, right? I need my body to calm down and stop acting like I have a schoolgirl crush. I have a grown-woman workplace crush that will never come to anything. Very big difference.

"I wished for what she wanted." I nod to the statue. "I wished for my legs," I say, my voice low so I won't start to cry. I might explode in tears because my wish was selfish, especially compared to Declan's. But, also, because I never really thought about *her* pain before. The mermaid's woes. Her longing for a body that would allow her to live on land. And now that I compare it to my own desire, it's like I'm experiencing my pain all over again.

My body is totally different now. I'm weaker. I'm at the same weight but with much less muscle and suddenly I have hips and curves. I like how my body looks now, but I loved how I *felt* in my body then. Now it feels like something foreign, something I can't fully trust. I keep telling myself that white-knuckling this condition is working, but the anxiety of it, always wondering when it will flare up again, is exhausting.

Declan is watching me. *Can he tell what I'm thinking?*

I explain myself a bit. "I miss the drive and the pain and the adrenaline of finishing first. Of pushing and pushing, pumping my legs, pounding my feet. Giving it everything I have until I crossed the finish line. It was a beautiful rhythm. Push. Pump. Pound." I look up into his eyes and see something. An appreciation from a fellow athlete. And something else.

Because *ohmygod!* I think back on what I just said and it sounded so incredibly dirty. My neck and cheeks are suddenly ablaze; I'd guess they're as red as the Danish flag. Declan bites down on his lips, fighting a smile.

I try to recover. "I liked being in my element. Running was my thing. Now." I pause, realizing I've officially launched into a pity party.

"This can be your thing," Declan says, finishing my sentence, saving me from more embarrassing rambling. "Travel the world. Put on badass endurance events. Do what you can to save innocent people."

A swell of appreciation builds in my chest. That he could sense I was veering into a topic that I'm not comfortable talking about. That he is inviting me into this world with him. That he didn't dismiss anything I said or try to lecture me on keeping my head in the game for this mission.

The sun is setting and the sky is moving between yellow and orange to pink. It's time to head back to our hotel and prepare for the real reason we're here.

All I need to do now is prove myself.

27

DECLAN

The lounge is upscale. The bespoke drinks and low lighting are reminiscent of a bygone era. It's as if we've entered a speakeasy in Prohibition-era Chicago. I'm not sure whether that was the aim for this cocktail lounge in the middle of Copenhagen, but that's what it is.

Per my contact, Monique should be here in thirty minutes. I don't like to take chances, hence we're early.

Charlie slides into a booth near the back. It has enough of a sight line to the bar that we'll be able to keep an eye out for Monique, but it's removed, giving us some cover. It's also close to the bathrooms and the exit. Did Charlie think all of those details through when she picked it? Or was it beginner's luck?

We prepped briefly this afternoon. She read the file on Monique on the plane and knows what she looks like from intel photos. I don't fully know what to expect on this mission, so I told Charlie to follow my lead. She did well on the Castillo mission. I have no doubt she'll shine here too.

Charlie stays in the booth while I order two whiskey sodas from the bartender and bring our drinks to the table. Charlie smiles as she accepts hers. We both let the drinks sit in front of us, untouched. No drinking on the job.

Charlie and I both changed in the hotel before coming here. We're supposed to look like a couple on vacation. I dressed up, putting some gel in my hair, changing to a nicer button-down. Charlie has on one of those sequin tops that demands attention. I gave her my blazer to help cover the shine. I told her it was part of the cover. She didn't question it. Before our next mission together, I'll advise her that she needs to have options to blend in, as well as stand out.

Charlie pulls the blazer closer round her. I don't know much about fashion, but I know she is pulling it off. The sight of her in my blazer is starting to distract me. I check my watch; we still have time.

"So why do you trust this contact but not anyone else?" Charlie dives in.

The question is fair. After Mexico City, I began to doubt each of my contacts. All of them could be vulnerable to the right offer from the Order, or any other nefarious organizations.

"We worked together. My first year with FIRE, I was stationed here in Copenhagen. Spent a year learning the race operations side of things while building contacts across

Europe," I explain, as Charlie nods, following along. "I guess I needed to trust someone. To have some solid ground." I stare down into my untouched glass. "Those weeks after Osaka, when I was healing and trying to process what went wrong on that mission, I didn't trust anyone. Anything. But I took a leap and trusted Oliver. Trusted Ian. I realized I had to trust at least a few people, otherwise everything was unstable, like sand beneath my feet."

"But not too many people?" Charlie asks. There's a playful hint to her voice. I look over and she gives me a knowing wink. She's referring to our first encounter, trying to lighten the mood.

"Right. Can never be too careful about runners in executive assistants' clothing," I quip while I do a quick visual sweep.

"What about Monique?" Charlie asks. She is twirling the tiny black straw in her drink.

"Well, I obviously can't trust her anymore. Not unless she has a *really* good explanation," I say, wondering what excuse might redeem her.

"So, you two . . ." Charlie starts to ask a question and then lets the words hang in the air. I glance over at her; her curious blue eyes are watching me, waiting for a response. The implied question dawns on me. *Were we ever together?*

"No," I say with finality. "For starters, Monique is a lesbian, so I'm not her type. And secondly, I don't date. Or do relationships." I avert my eyes as I say this last part, unsure if I want to see Charlie's response. Will she be shocked, disappointed, or worse – unfazed? I'd never second-guessed or been embarrassed to admit my self-imposed dating ban, but saying it aloud to Charlie feels wrong. I wish I could pull back those words.

"Oh," is her response.

I need to explain, to justify my decision. "I can't risk liking someone, or even falling in love with someone, only for the Order, or whoever else, to come along and put them in danger so they can get to me. Not happening. I respected X.C. and losing him has been hard enough to handle." I hazard a glance at Charlie, who is nodding along. Her face is expressionless, as if she is trying to hide something. Maybe reminding her of the critical stakes was a little much. "Also, the hours and travel schedule I'm on barely leave enough time for training. No way could I manage dates in between covert ops." I've never been one for casual hook-ups. That leaves one logical option: no romance of any kind.

"That's very practical," Charlie responds.

I wish I could read her mind right now. What is she really thinking?

I don't have time to dwell on that, though, as I look up and see Monique heading for the bar. She either hasn't spotted us or is willfully ignoring our presence. Her dark brown skin appears healthy, her clothing fits and is fashionable. No signs of any stress or trauma. Not held against her will.

I glance over at Charlie and motion with my head for her to turn and see Monique as well.

Monique places an order with the bartender and when she has her drink, she fiddles with the coaster. *Is she nervous about whoever she is meeting?*

I'm about to stand up to intercept her when Monique tilts her head back and knocks back her drink in one gulp. She pulls out some krone and drops it on the bar before leaving out the front.

She left something under the coaster, I think.

Instinct takes over. I'm moving to stand up and grab whatever she left when someone passes our booth. A white man, maybe my age and height, walks up to the bar. He sits at the same stool Monique vacated and orders a drink. He has short brown hair and a full beard, but it's kempt.

This guy is familiar. I can't place him right now and I don't have time to think on it.

I stand and discreetly motion for Charlie to stand up and follow me. She sees the man at the bar and does a double take. When she looks back at me, her expression is confused.

I start down the hallway next to our booth, the one that leads to both the bathrooms and the side exit. The same hallway the man at the bar just came through. I'd bet that was who Monique was meeting. They must have arranged to enter and leave using different exits. If my hunch is correct, the man at the bar will be leaving via the back exit in a minute, maybe less.

Behind me, Charlie hisses, "What's going on? Is that guy the buyer? Or is he a rando?"

I keep moving and open the back door for Charlie to walk through ahead of me. I'm not sure if this guy has any backup, but there's a fair chance he might. A cursory glance shows no one in the alleyway, but there could be someone waiting for him on the street at the front or in a car. The alley doesn't smell atrocious, but it isn't clean either. Slick puddles and wet bricks on the wall shimmer in the moonlight that is trying to pierce the backstreet.

"Declan, what is going on?" Charlie asks at full volume once we are outside. "Are we in danger? What's happening?"

I can hear the panic in her voice, but I can also sense it within me. She is talking too much, too loudly. She'll draw attention. She also just used my first name. This is a very different mission from Castillo's yacht. Charlie is not acting like the polished operative she was on that mission; she is acting scared. Or maybe not acting at all. This kind of uncontrolled fear is a liability to us both.

I need to get us out of here. Now.

I turn round and do my best to silence her with my index finger to my lips.

This only eggs her on, creating the opposite of the desired effect.

"If we're going to work together, you have to talk to me and tell me what is going on. I can't help if I'm in the dark. This is ridiculous," she continues to rant. I couldn't explain anything to her if I tried. "Are we in danger right now?" she asks again.

I've been leading us down the alleyway as she continues her less than subtle litany of questions. They're valid, but this is not the time to discuss them.

We need to get out of here.

My hopes of intercepting this guy are all but dashed. We'll have to regroup back at the hotel. If we make it out of here, that is.

"Declan, what the hell? This is not OK!" Her voice hits a new pitch as a loud *thud* echoes through the alleyway. I turn quickly to see the source.

The door to the lounge opens and closes, as the man with the beard walks through. He has his hand to his face; I'm assuming he's calling someone to confirm receipt of the evidence. I can't hear a thing he's saying, though, over Charlie. And, of course, we're both in this alleyway with him. If he's a trained operative, he'll suspect first, attack second, and verify later.

I need to silence her.

I need to conceal our faces.

I need to be able to hear what he is saying.

I need to rely on our cover and hope we get out of here unscathed.

Only one action will allow me to achieve all of these things.

I turn and face Charlie, close the space between us with one step, place my hands on her cheeks, and plant my lips on hers.

28

CHARLIE

Declan's lips are against mine, at first like a vice. His hands are on both sides of my face, urgent and firm. But in seconds, not even, the kiss relaxes. It goes from something desperate and necessary to something powerful and soft and, oh, *this is necessary too*.

The last words on my tongue dissolve. I can't even remember what I was about to say. I whimper as my lips part. Declan reacts to this moan; he lets out a ragged breath before his lips connect with mine more firmly again.

His hands shift and move. One hand cradles my head, the other wraps round me as tight as he can. Without even realizing it, my own hands are on his back, holding him just as tight as he is gripping me.

His tongue finds mine and the whole world is this embrace and his mouth. I can hear someone walk by, but it doesn't even matter. I was already enveloped in his scent with his blazer round me, now I am getting the full sensory experience. The light, ticklish scratch of his stubble on my chin. His fingertips activating every nerve in my body with just a gentle touch. His tongue, soft and delicious. His breath fresh from cleaning up before we arrived. The sound in his throat is somewhere between a growl and a moan; it sends my hormones racing.

My body is the first light of flame on a candle wick: initially timid and unsure, but with a spark I am alight for Declan. My body pushes against his, closer. No, even closer. I move one of my hands to touch his hair. Something I've longed to do for a month now.

Declan's lips leave mine for a second, long enough for us to make eye contact. To confirm that this is real. There are other sounds in the alley that should demand my attention. They don't. His eyes are half closed, focused entirely on me. He glances at my lips again, then back to my eyes.

Declan says something that sounds like "more," but I can't be sure because I think my brain has stopped working.

His mouth meets mine again and our bodies are still pressed together. I'm grateful he is holding me instead of pushing me back into the grimy alley wall.

I know he didn't lead us out into this alley for this. *I know that*. But I still can't help but melt, letting the wildest thoughts in my head run loose. That Declan is attracted to me. That he wants me. That he might even break his no-dating rule for me. Yes, I'm a grown woman, but in his arms I'm a foolish, romantic girl.

His arms and aroma surround me, blocking out the less than pleasant scent of this alleyway.

As our bodies connect, his rigid length presses against my belly. Heat rushes to my center, desire pooling for him. I want to remind him of our hotel, not even a block away, but my body is a magnet locked on to Declan, savoring every swipe of his tongue on mine, each motion as his hands start to roam from my neck to my lower back. I move my hips to invite him to continue his survey, to grab my ass and lift me up so I can wrap my legs round him.

This is the most passionate kiss I've ever experienced – and then his lips are gone again. I tilt my head forwards, searching for them. Only the night air greets me.

I'm in the void.

I open my eyes and Declan is a foot away, two feet away. Out of reach.

"I . . . uh." Declan stumbles for words. "The contact was coming. I didn't want to blow our cover." He isn't looking me in the eye as he runs his hands through his hair.

"Oh." So it wasn't some mind-blowing kiss for him then? He goes around kissing people like that and it's business as usual? "Right. Of course," is all I can manage to say, while my lips and hands and arms are suddenly cold, longing for the warmth of his body and mouth again. I find the will to snap into professional mode. "It's our cover. I should have expected," I mutter while he still isn't looking at me. I turn my attention to the ground as well. Perhaps it holds some fascinating details.

"No, I crossed a line. It'll never happen again."

I stay still and silent, unable to agree. Sure, we are coworkers, and we didn't discuss the physical element of our cover on this mission, but inside my heart, on my lips, my neck, I'm disappointed at his vow to never kiss me again.

Never? I wasn't imagining that he was into that kiss, right? Or is he just that good at being a spy that he can fool me so easily?

I get back to business. "Did you hear what that guy said as he passed by?"

Declan curses under his breath. "No."

Shit is all I can think. I didn't catch anything either. I was so off my guard because of the kiss. Did it knock Declan's world off-kilter too? Is that why he didn't hear anything?

"It's my fault. I should have followed your lead," I admit. The depth of the implications settles on me.

The evidence of Castillo's arms deal is gone. Which means FIRE will have to directly find the munitions *before* they are used. This was a huge misstep.

Declan doesn't acknowledge my words. "I think I might have recognized him, but I can't place his face yet." Declan stares out at the open street, a few paces to the side.

I nod, unsure what to say or do.

"Let's go," Declan says with a nod of his head. I follow, silently.

* * *

The whole way back to the hotel, we said nothing. I could only surmise that Declan was fuming over my fumbles, mistakes that cost us information, a chance to expose the arms deal that Castillo made. To prevent violence. This was a huge step back for me. All that work I'd done trying to prove myself to Declan, Ian, and the team. I messed up, big time.

I lay awake most of the night, vacillating between self-loathing at my failure to follow Declan's instincts and the lives that could be lost because of it. Not to mention the shattered hope of a woman who had the man of her dreams in her arms, on her lips. But now that hope is dead.

Declan didn't speak to me when we checked out of the hotel. When we rode to the airport. We barely exchanged a few short words on the flight home.

My mistakes on this mission haunt me.

And so does that kiss. It was the sweetest promise of what could be, sandwiched by such crippling rejection.

He doesn't date.

And if he did, it certainly wouldn't be me – someone who blew her chance to help. Who ruined this operation.

He'll never kiss me again.

29

DECLAN

The multiple long-haul flights are getting to me. I can't get any quality sleep. And I have the aftermath of this botched mission to deal with.

I do not handle failure well, and that's what this mission was. A complete failure. One with dire consequences if we can't stop these weapons from being used against innocent people.

I hate that the Order is winning. That they are one step ahead of us.

I wake up early on Monday with a plan.

First, I ping Oliver directly and ask to speak with him as soon as possible to brief him on the mission. I need to take full responsibility. I don't want him to think Charlie messed up; it was only her second assignment. I won't mention how

I silenced her in a moment of panic. I get the sense he would not approve.

Then, on the way into work, I get two large coffees and a gluten-free crumb cake.

As I head to my office, I stop at Charlie's desk. I saw her only ten hours ago when we parted ways at the airport. We didn't say much on the flight home. There wasn't much I could say.

The mission was a bust. There is no way round it. No silver lining. Monique sold key evidence to an unknown entity. We have no way to get the evidence to the authorities so they can seize Castillo's yacht and search it for the weapons. Which means we need to intercept somehow before they are used or resold.

I'm exhausted. I'm cranky. And the kiss with Charlie keeps replaying in my mind. Of all the ways I've pictured kissing her – I can admit that now – in a dark alley in Copenhagen just so I could shut her up was not one of them.

It doesn't matter; there is no way she will let me kiss her again. I'm an executive here. She isn't *my* assistant, but we were on a job together. I crossed a line. Another loss from this weekend.

"This is for you," I say as I stand next to her desk, decorated with bright colorful tchotchkes and a floral-print calendar. *Very Charlie*, I think.

Her blue eyes shine behind her glasses as she peers up at me. I can see she's also exhausted. And the awkward grin she gives me, polite and distant, is like a slap. Like she would rather forget the kiss too.

I put the coffee and the crumb cake on her desk. "Gotta beat the jet lag, Ross," I offer as an explanation for my gift.

I'm not sure what made me think of her while I was in line. To plead with her to not report me to HR. To show her that the kiss did mean something, but I can't explore those pesky emotions right now. That I care for her, about her, but that, as I suspected, romantic entanglements would be a distraction.

She eyes the coffee cup and brown bag. "It's half-caf," I say, "and gluten-free," I add. *I know what you like.*

Charlie nods. "Thank you," she says as she reaches for the coffee. I'm not sure what response would have been enough to calm the storm inside me, but that wasn't it.

But this is the response I needed. Professional. Removed. Detached. I cannot risk innocent lives because of a crush. I cannot risk *her* life, should someone within the Order find out.

I trust Charlie now. She is one of the few people in this world who have that. But though I feel more than that for her, it's too late to claim anything else. This means I will hurt. If not today, then tomorrow. Because I cannot pursue Charlie, and eventually she'll find someone else and I'll be unhappy and jealous. Every rotten part of me will bubble up to the surface again. She deserves better than that.

I head to my office and wait for Oliver's schedule to open up. Outside my door, I spot Charlie working. Ana stops by and they chat before heading out.

Pro: with Charlie not at her desk I can stop being distracted.

Con: now I have to worry what Charlie might be saying to Ana. Even if Charlie doesn't disclose the mission, what if she and Ana discuss *the kiss*. Women do that, right?

Focus, Davidson.

I ping Ian and ask for access to our database of known associates for every member of the Order. I still can't place the guy from the bar and I'm hoping he'll turn up in the photo index.

I'm digging into my inbox when I hear my door open. I pop my head up and look out to the hall. Charlie's desk is still empty as Oliver walks in. He closes the door and sits down immediately. He leans forwards, his hands steepled, waiting for me to talk.

I tell him about the lounge. Monique's discreet drop. My movement to intercept and the appearance of an as yet unidentified male who beat me to it. I detail my logic in using the back exit, assuming they had pre-planned on it.

"And did you catch him as he left? Did you overhear anything?" Oliver asks, his gaze unflinching.

The touch of Charlie's lips on mine, the brush of her cheek, her hair under my palms. The excitement and arousal flash before my mind in an instant.

"No," I tell him. I offer no explanation as to why. Mercifully, he doesn't press me.

"Well, on my end, I met with the head of the World Games Organizing Committee this weekend. Based on their security team, they think there is a potential attack lined up for the World Games in Rome," Oliver discloses.

I nod as the pieces start to fit together in my mind. "Could fit, given Castillo's planned route on the Italian coast."

"But it could also be a distraction," Oliver cautions. "The Order isn't one for flash-and-bang attacks. There could be a separate group targeting the World Games and it just happens that key members of the Order would be there. Or maybe the Order is switching up their MO."

"The World Games has excellent security. Chances are an attack could be stopped by local law enforcement or the added security for an event," I remind Oliver.

"Exactly." He nods his head. "We can't dismiss the potential threat. This was a huge arms sale. If you hear a thunder of hooves, you think horses, not zebras, right? We have someone with a cache of arms and a credible threat at a marquee event. Logic says they are somehow linked." Oliver leans back in his chair.

He waves his hand as if swiping away at that theory. "I think, if anything, Castillo is there to re-sell the arms to some mercenaries working in Lagos. He wants Vallus to be the only internet provider in sub-Saharan Africa. If those weapons are used to blow up any existing infrastructure, Vallus can come in and look like the good guy, even when they provide expensive internet."

"Sounds very on-brand for him," I agree. "We need to know for sure. Let's monitor Castillo at the World Games to see who he's re-selling to," I say, listing the first item that comes to mind.

"You'll be part of our team going to Rome later this summer. Charlie will be there too," Oliver tells me. "Maybe Castillo will slip up and tell her something helpful," he mutters. I can tell he doesn't like this idea. I *hate* it. My fists clench beneath my desk. The idea of that man being near her again flash-boils my blood. "Let's hope we discover the real target before we get there." Anything to get this solved sooner and spare Charlie another minute with Castillo. "I'll see if there's any chatter on another target in Rome."

Oliver nods but remains seated. His gaze is focused ahead of him, lost in thought. I wait for him to share whatever theory is forming in his mind. "You know, we've been focused on Frank Castillo. But he may just be joining the Order. The real kingpin is Holden Ambrose."

I nod to show I'm following. Holden Ambrose is the man who invented social media. People either love him for his tech ingenuity or they hate him for the addictive all-consuming media he invented. "You think Ambrose could have something planned?"

"He's always talked the talk of a pacifist, but his earnings have been in decline. Social media lives and breathes advertising dollars. But as people find ways to avoid ads, his bottom line is hurt. The algorithms know so much about us. Where we go, who we like and don't. They start serving up baby-registry ads before people even realize they're pregnant." Oliver pauses, his thoughts still forming.

"So what do the arms have to do with that?"

"I'm not sure." Oliver shakes his head. "But Ambrose has been meeting in DC a lot. The potential for the data he owns to be used to apprehend enemies of the state, however that is defined, could be lucrative to Ambrose. A defense contract to mine data will always pay way more than banner ads."

"Huh," I say, catching on to his logic. "You think Ambrose could trigger an attack that would push through his pending contracts?"

Oliver equivocates. "It's a lot of *coulds* and *mights*. It's a weak theory."

"Don't discount your gut and I'll keep an ear out for any chatter," I assure my boss.

Oliver nods and stands up. "That's good, but let's cast a wider net just in case."

A wider net. There is always more to do. Another riddle to solve, some hidden game. We make progress at making the world safer, and then someone else decides to mess it up. I don't feel expendable like I did in the navy, but the missions, once thrilling, are starting to feel a little like whack-a-mole.

I jot down my next steps from Oliver and there is a knock at my office door.

"Come in," I say a little too forcefully, hoping it's Charlie.

Ian pops in and closes the door behind him. "I printed out the images of those in the database that most closely matched your description. Even those without facial hair, in case the beard is new."

I nod and take the stack from Ian. This will save me combing through the server myself.

Oliver catches Ian up on our new focus: Rome and the upcoming World Games. Oliver doesn't mention his theory about the Rome threat being a decoy or about Ambrose and his contracts, but I'm sure Ian can riddle that out for himself.

"Alright, I'll refocus my searches," Ian says.

We have a plan.

Oliver opens the door to my office; the conversation is over. "Good work, team," he says and heads back to his office.

I hazard a glance at Charlie's desk; she still isn't there. Damn. I have to admit that so much of my angst about Charlie is actually about my growing attraction. My defenses are buckling under what I'm trying to hold back.

I haven't tried to romance anyone in a while. And it doesn't even matter. If I decided I cared about Charlie and wanted something romantic, that's reason enough to never try. She would be a liability, a weakness any enemy could use as leverage. And if they hurt her, I'd never forgive myself.

Best to focus on her faults, reasons to not want to be with her. I'm going to have to dig to find something, anything, to stop these longings from jeopardizing our mission, FIRE, or her safety.

30

DECLAN

Knock knock knock.

I tell myself this will be quick. A short mission and then back to work.

Knock knock knock.

I've never been one to tap on someone's door. If I need to get in, I'm going to demand attention; I'm not some polite Amazon delivery-man. My hands are already sweaty in the sterile gloves, which pinch at my wrists. I can't wait to take them off.

"I'm coming," a soft voice calls from the other side of the door.

Good.

Through the door, I hear the chain slide and the bolt unlatches. She opens the door and I act quickly. I reach into my jacket. I grip the handle, my finger resting on the trigger. I'm careful not to squeeze too soon.

Charlie Ross stands before me in her doorway.

I aim for her forehead and pull the trigger.

Doot doot doot.

A pleasant chime indicates that the handheld thermometer has given her a passing temperature. She rolls her beautiful blue eyes at me, but I can't be too safe.

"You don't have a fever," I announce, my words muffled by the mask. "Is it intestinal?" Involuntarily, I move backwards. Only a slight lean just in case.

Charlie crosses her arms and shakes her head.

"So you aren't sick," I respond.

"I am," she corrects.

I remove my mask and gloves and enter her apartment, brushing past Charlie. I don't mean to, but the soft fabric of her blue pajama set caresses my knuckles as I pass. When she opened the door, I could tell she wasn't prepared for company. Still in pajamas at 10 a.m. Her long hair is piled high in a bun on top of her head.

"Why are you here?" she asks, as she closes and relocks the apartment door, a weariness to her voice.

"I wanted to make sure you were actually sick. Not being intimidated by members of the Order or that you didn't lock yourself in." The last option was meant to be a joke. Sort of.

I do a quick scan of her apartment. Charlie has her curtains closed; the midmorning light that filters through them casts a soft pink glow over her living area. There is a bookshelf next to her entertainment center bursting with books, the spines arranged in rainbow order. Her place is tidy and warm, with bright pops of color here and there. The furniture isn't just the standard post-college cheap stuff everyone buys because it's all they can afford. There are some stylish pieces that give her place a level of sophistication I hadn't expected. It's welcoming; it looks like a home.

"No, I'm just too tired to function. And I'm in pain, but I can only take Tylenol. And, by the way, Tylenol is the shittiest pain reliever ever." Charlie isn't one to complain so I'm shocked by her rant.

"So that's why you're out today?" I'm tired too. I'm sore from my training ride and I still clocked in. I didn't take Charlie for the type to use her sick days unless absolutely necessary.

"I didn't call out. I'm working from home," she says, sauntering over to the side table, shuffling in her fuzzy slippers. I take a seat on her couch, which is deep and comfortable. "Besides, I told Oliver."

"No, you *texted* Oliver," I correct her. "Charlie, anyone can incapacitate you, unlock your phone, and send a text."

Charlie looks at me, fear in her eyes. I can't believe I have to continue to explain these things to her. She turns away, her expression uneasy.

"Charlie, you have access to the schedule, personal and business, for the entire executive team. Of course the Order would be keenly interested in you," I remind her.

She shakes her head, as if that could keep my warning from settling in her mind. "I'm not much in the mood for company," she says, abruptly changing topics.

"Well, can you tell me what's going on?" I ask. I came all this way to make sure she was OK. I expect some answers.

"I'm sick, Declan," she says.

"We've already ruled out a fever. Did you take a COVID test?" I regret removing my mask before confirming.

Charlie lets out a sigh and turns to face me again. "No, Declan. I have a chronic illness. I have an autoimmune condition." She shakes her head again and continues her slow shuffle to the far corner of her apartment.

Oh. I didn't expect that. Autoimmune? I don't know much about this class of illnesses, but my aunt has psoriasis. I think that's one. I do another sweep of the room. There's a heating pad next to me on the couch, warming one side of my body. There are balms and creams on the coffee table. "I know people with autoimmune conditions, which one?"

Charlie bends down to get something. I realize I should offer to help, but before I can, she stands and in one quick motion takes aim at me. "I could tell you, but I'd have to kill you," she says before pulling the trigger.

BUUZZZZZZ.

A massage gun. I let out a huff of laughter. She moves the device to her left shoulder, her face relaxing as the motion eases her muscles.

"Try me," I say.

Charlie raises her eyebrows in warning. "Eosinophilic fasciitis," she says with the practiced pronunciation of someone who has had to explain this many times before.

"*Gesundheit*," I respond, hoping a small stupid joke will lighten the mood. She gives me a pity laugh. I process this new information along with everything else I know about Charlie. "What does that mean?"

Charlie removes the massage gun from her shoulder and begins to explain. "The fascia is the layer between the skin and the muscle. My immune system attacks it like it's an infection."

I nod my head, following along, realizing this has to be the reason she quit running. This is why Oliver said she wanted a low-stress job.

"When it flares up," she continues, "it's like I have a sunburn on the inside of my skin. If I keep ignoring it, it can lead to my limbs not working altogether." Her expression is blank as she delivers this explanation.

I wince at the thought of it. "Ouch."

She resumes her massage gun and works on her right shoulder as she walks over to the couch. When she sits next to me, her sweet, fruity aroma surrounds me. I long to comfort her. My fingertips itch to caress her skin, to alleviate whatever stress she is feeling.

She pauses the massage gun. "You know that ache? That pain that comes after a great workout?"

"Mmm." I nod and my hand reflexively reaches for my bicep, sore from yesterday's lifting session.

"There's nothing like it," she says wistfully. "Or I thought there wasn't. That soreness you wear like a badge of honor. The sign that your muscles are growing; you can feel them getting stronger."

I wait for her to continue; I can tell she has more to say. In my line of work, listening is an asset, but Charlie isn't a witness I'm trying to extract information from. She's someone who deserves my patience and attention.

She lays the massage gun in her lap and sighs. "I had that burn, all the time. All over. Even when I hadn't been particularly pushing it in the weight room. I thought it was a sign I was doing my job. I was pushing myself but in the wrong direction."

The pain in her voice, the disappointment, is clear. "You couldn't have known," I remind her.

"That's what scares me the most," she snaps, and then she softens her tone. "That I didn't know what was going on in my own body. That it betrayed me so completely. No one knew. The first three doctors assured me the 'fainting,' as they called it, wouldn't happen again. I was a perfectly healthy athlete. But it wasn't fainting. I was fully conscious, aware that my limbs had given out on me."

I give into my instincts, ignoring the part of my brain telling me to refrain, that I should be professional. That I should keep my distance. Because Charlie is hurting in more than one way. I reach for her hand and she welcomes mine, interlacing our fingers. I give her a reassuring squeeze. *You're not alone.*

"When they did more tests and more scans and finally learned that muscle pain was actually my body having an allergic reaction to itself, I stopped working out. Stopped eating anything inflammatory. Started one medicine, then another. The first morning when I woke up and the pain was gone was the morning I saw one of my former teammates win the gold in the steeplechase. I got my health back." She says this as if it was the worst outcome. As if fighting for her health wasn't the ultimate goal.

I realize why and finish her thought. "But it cost you your dream."

I won't say it aloud because this moment is about Charlie, but I picture myself in her shoes. If I had been forced to take a medical discharge from the navy before I was ready to separate. If I had been told to walk away, to give up on what I'd worked for. The frustration, the weight of the what-ifs must be infuriating.

"Yeah," she says, and I give her hand another squeeze. I want to pull her to me, to wrap my arms round her. I promised myself after Copenhagen that I would keep my distance. Now I'm dangerously close to breaking my own rules.

Because I cannot and should not say what is on my mind, I switch back to practicalities.

"What does your doctor say?" I prop my free elbow on the side of the couch, getting comfortable. Still not removing my hand from hers.

"I have an appointment with who I hope will be my new rheumatologist next week. My doctor back home recommended him."

"Could you do an online consultation with the old one?" I ask before realizing she probably already considered this.

She shakes her head. "This is the protocol we decided on. Once I got out of the last flare and we saw the damage the medicine did, we decided to manage with lifestyle and diet. There is no long-term medicine for this condition. The big-name autoimmune diseases have some, but often people have to switch out after a few years. My trigger for this condition is exercise-based. If I get into a flare, we decided I'd do a short round of steroids to reduce the inflammation and then discuss if it needs more monitoring."

I'm starting to understand. "You're hoping you're better by the appointment next week?"

Charlie's eyes open wide. "Yes!" She nods her head with emphasis. "I'm desperately hoping this muscle pain is the good kind. Not the bad kind. Because I need to be able to maintain muscle if I want quality of life now and into my golden years. It will just take longer and there will be some setbacks."

This is heavy. I can't imagine what the pressure of this must feel like. To have to question every action, every piece of food, to avoid losing her delicate grip on her health. I want to console her, though I'm not sure my preferred method would be appreciated at this moment. I chastise myself for thinking naughty thoughts when Charlie is in pain.

I break our hands and reach for the massage gun in her lap. My fingers graze her thighs and I have to tamp down the excitement in my blood. I examine the device carefully. "You had me going there for a second that this was going to be a very different conversation."

"You pointed a thermometer at me before you even walked in," she reminds me. "Besides, this is for muscle release."

I raise my eyebrows and give her a wolfish grin. Because there is one set of muscles I would specifically like to help Charlie release. "Oh, I mean, that is a muscle too, so that's fair."

It takes Charlie a second to riddle out what I am implying. I can tell when she does because that smart mouth of hers drops and forms a shocked "o." Her cheeks turn a beautiful shade of pink.

"It specifically says on the instructions to *not* use it for that," she rushes to correct me. The mortified look on her face is priceless.

"Oh, so you were thinking about that use, then? Had to check?" The idea that Charlie would ever think about that is hot as hell. I want to know more. I'm walking a fine line between flirting and trying to lighten the mood.

For once, Ms. Chatty seems too stunned to speak. I wonder if she is going to think about this conversation the next time she uses this, or another device, on herself.

"I'm giving you a hard time," I say, and then look back at the device in my hands. The double meaning isn't lost on me. In my periphery, Charlie licks her lips, debating what to say next. I give her an out. "Also, you need a better massage gun. For starters, this isn't the brand that sponsors FIRE, and this has only five settings."

She grabs it back from me. "I don't use it much."

"You need a better one," I repeat.

She rolls her beautiful eyes at me and I know I've pulled her out of her darkest thoughts.

"It was your shoulder that was bothering you?" I ask.

She nods and I gesture for her to turn round.

"Let me try to help," I say.

As my hands get to work on her shoulders, I can tell I'm falling for Charlie. I'm going to need some serious restraint to keep myself from losing control.

31

CHARLIE

Declan is in my apartment. And his hands are kneading my shoulder muscles. The leathery scent of his cologne is going to leave traces of itself on my couch cushions so I will still smell him after he leaves. And he just asked me if I use my massage gun as a vibrator?! Is this really happening?

My head is telling me that I am losing ground professionally. That I am showing every facet of my weakness to someone who was hard to impress in the first place. Now he is seeing me at my worst, only a few days after I fumbled our mission. I should act like everything is fine. I should put on a professional face and refuse this massage.

My heart and my sore muscles tell my brain to shut up. I close my eyes and relax under his touch.

Gently, his hands pinch and knead my shoulders. His grip is perfect; it's the right amount of pressure. My muscles are grateful. But beyond this my skin hums under his touch. My arms and lower back and neck are all crying out, wanting his hands there as well. My thighs clench at the thought of his hands working over other parts of my body.

"That's good," I breathe. My voice is deeper than I expected, a seductive tone I wasn't aiming for. The soreness he is working on is deep in my bones. The run the other week. Lifting equipment on site in Kalispell and Key West, because that's what you do at a new job. You pitch in. Traveling to Copenhagen and back in one weekend. And the gluten. All that delicious, delicious gluten. It was one too many drops in the bucket. One too many "it's just this one little thing" on the scale. And now my body hates me, I think.

I'm mad at myself. I know better. Yet I gave in to my temptations. And, like a hopeless fool, part of my brain is still wondering if this is normal muscle fatigue and tiredness.

"We're a team. I'm happy to help." Declan's hands stop for a second as he says this.

I turn my head. Our faces are so close. He could close the distance between our mouths. I could too.

"If the massage is helping, then it probably is the good kind of muscle ache," I offer with a smile. I move my gaze from his lips; his eyes are serious, focused. And I'm a chicken. Because if

I said nothing, he would have kissed me again. *Maybe*. Instead, I finish the thought. "I hate that I can't tell. That I couldn't tell before. It's like I can't trust myself."

Declan sits back, putting more space between us, breaking whatever spell we were just under. "If it makes you feel any better, I trust you."

"Oh wow. We need to call the *New York Times*. Stop the presses. This is headline news," I say as I playfully reach for my phone. I have it in my hand when Declan's arms circle my waist and pull me back toward the couch. The casual touch, the way I am longing for the next and the next and the next, has me smiling. I'm fully leaning back onto him, his hard muscles flat against my back.

I look down and see a notification. I hadn't heard my phone chime. I sit up to check it.

Ana Alonso

> Do you happen to know where Declan is?
> Celine has stopped by twice asking me.
> I'm not his keeper.

I pull my lips tight together and turn the screen for Declan to see it. He gives a grunt and releases his arms from my waist.

I tap out a response:

Charlie Ross

> I can neither confirm nor deny
> that he is here checking on me.

I put my phone face down on the coffee table and look over at Declan. I want to resume the exact moment we were just sharing. His arms on me. Our bodies close. I realize what I've told him about my condition is the ultimate test. We aren't a couple. We aren't dating – Declan doesn't do that. We kissed. It was fantastic. But if he can hear all this and still think he would want to kiss me again, then maybe my crush isn't hopeless. I chide myself for allowing any glimmer of optimism. Who would want to be with me? Who would want to sign on for this?

"Well, I guess I need to get back," he says. The disappointment in his voice has me thinking wildly optimistic thoughts. "Or –" his tone turns mischievous – "I can pull up the live feed for the Tour and I can stay to help you and watch for a bit?"

This is a surprising, if not unwelcome, suggestion. Declan, being a cyclist nerd, is clearly eager to watch the Tour. But he has two monitors in his office; he could watch it while working at his desk. My foolish longings are going to read too much into this. "Is it to help me or to watch the Tour?"

"Can it be both?" He stands to take off his blazer and then sits back down, unbuttoning the cuffs of his shirt and rolling them up.

"Mr. Work and Responsibility slacking off to hang?" I ask playfully.

"Don't tell anyone and ruin my street cred," he says with a twitch of his eyebrow.

"I wouldn't dare. Now I have leverage over you. Isn't that what spies do?" I turn back to my phone.

I have a new message from Ana. It is a long string of exclamation points and question marks.

I send Ana back the shrugging-shoulders emoji. I'll have to fill her in on everything soon. I didn't know how to tell her about the kiss with Declan without disclosing the mission. But the kiss and then this impromptu house call and hangout session is *something. Right?* I need some girl talk to sort it all out.

Declan stands and finds his way into the kitchen before returning with two ice waters and snacks. I set up the livestream of the Tour to play on my TV. After a few moments of quiet snacking, Declan glances over at me.

"Is it hard to watch this? Or to think about watching the World Games?" He is very insightful.

I consider his question. The answer used to be a clear yes. I didn't want to watch any endurance sports. But it's faded over time. "Not so much anymore," I tell him.

And it's true. The year I had to give up my spot at the World Games, I couldn't watch. When the day came to make the announcement, I was numb emotionally. All those hours in the hospital describing my symptoms didn't prepare me for emotionally dissociating from the call. My dad dialed; I was on speaker. Talking to the head of the US track and field committee for the World Games. Saying the necessary words in order to quit and give my spot to the next runner in line. My dad took over the logistics. And then it was done. A lifetime striving for a dream, a magnificent record-setting race to earn it, and one call to end it.

"The pain was worth it," I say. Something I've always known deep down. I turn and look at Declan, his deep chocolate eyes meeting mine. "It was worth all of it."

"Glory always is," Declan adds. And I know he gets it. He gets why I kept pushing, why I ignored the warnings from my body, why I was willing to risk it again. Because he's an athlete too.

"So you know you're probably not supposed to run, but you did it anyways?" Declan asks, recalling the morning run I mentioned last week.

"Yeah," I admit sheepishly.

"That's a good kind of stubborn, though, right?" Declan asks.

I smile at him, a man who knows a thing or two about being stubborn.

My brain is spinning up a fantasy that he will lean in and kiss me, giving me more of what we sampled on Saturday. Giving me a rush of endorphins and the touch I so desperately need right now. "Yeah," I say with a nod, and we both turn our attention back to the screen.

After thirty minutes of watching lean men in a tight peloton race through the hills of France, Declan gets a call from Oliver.

"Time to go back in, I guess." He stands to leave. "Can I heat you up anything to eat before I go?"

I stand and shake my head. "Nah, but thank you for making sure I wasn't locked in my own home." I pause. "And for listening." I get the idea Declan doesn't have many people open up to him like I did. I don't want to take it for granted.

"That's what friends are for," he says and walks out my front door. My health and the ongoing missing weapons were freaking me out. Being with Declan helped me forget about that fear, that worry. Even just for a short while.

I close the door and I'm both heartened and crestfallen.

Declan, who used to be a thorn in my side, who seemed to give no one any patience or care, came over to check on me. He is watching out for me. He is a *friend*.

I'm still new in town. Having another friend is a good thing.

It also hurts. Because I know – I have known – that I like him as more than a friend. That kiss in Copenhagen sealed it for me. And now I have to either pine away for him in this interminable friend zone or find someone who thinks of me that way. After telling him about my medical issues, there is no way he would ever consider me romantically. Who would? My personality may be low maintenance but my body is the opposite.

So long, friend. See you at work tomorrow.

Yeah. *Friend.*

32

CHARLIE

It's not a date, I tell myself as I pack up my desk promptly at 5 p.m. on Friday afternoon. If it was a date, I would be nervous and there would be expectations.

I plop my phone into my purse, push in my chair, and quietly tiptoe away from my desk. Oliver, Declan, and Finn are all meeting in Oliver's office to review budget numbers.

I don't want to make a big announcement about leaving on time. Thursday and Friday were markedly better in terms of my muscle pain and fatigue. Maybe it really was just jet lag and the new level of physical exertion. Still, I made meticulous notes for my next appointment.

Oliver asked me on Thursday if I needed another work-from-home day and I declined. Ian dropped a box of vitamin C mix on my desk. Misguided, but it's nice to know the team is looking out for me.

I tried to thank Declan again for stopping by, but he cut me off, instead focusing on potential targets within Rome that could be hit before, during, or immediately following the World Games. I tried not to show it, but the idea of an attack there has me terrified. My dad is coaching Team USA again. He'll be there. It's selfish. I don't want anyone to be a victim. But I really, really don't want my dad to be one.

Declan has kept a professional distance. Which tells me what I need to know. The kiss in Copenhagen truly was a mistake, or at least he sees it that way. His coming over the other day was him checking on my safety. Nothing more.

It's not a date, I tell myself again, as I make it to my car and crank up the A/C so I don't sweat on my drive over.

Mercifully, the green lights are timed in my favor and I arrive a little early. The gravel and seashells that cover the parking lot crunch beneath the tires of my car. I cut the engine and flip the visor down to check my face.

In the tiny mirror, I pinch at my eyebrows and assess their shape. "It's not a date," I remind myself aloud as I reach into my purse for my lipgloss.

I've dreamed of Declan each night since his visit. That he burst back into my apartment, throwing caution to the wind. That he would surrender his control and rules and lose himself in me. His ability to read a situation, to master a mission, to be steadfast and reliable is absolutely why I'm longing for him. And those hands: strong and protective.

Bury it, I tell myself. *Put it up in the closet where the running shoes used to be.*

I add a fresh layer of lipgloss and smooth my hair as best as I can.

"It's not a date," I say again to my reflection. I snap the visor shut and get out of the car.

I'm wearing my white jeans and a dark green silk button-down. Casual but dressy for a Friday. Not completely boring for going to the bar either. I'm hedging my bets. I still look nice, but I'm not going out of my way to change. Just in case Blaed doesn't show. *Because it's not a date. We're just hanging out.*

Ana left this morning to work one of our ultra-marathons in Europe. I'm bummed she won't be here as my buffer.

I enter the bar, remembering the last time I was there. My first week at FIRE. I was blissfully unaware of the other side of the business, of how serious things would become. I also knew my neighbor at work was a grump. Now I know that he's guarded and that he let that guard down ever so slightly for me. Even if he won't ever want anything more from me, I know I'll hold on to those few moments between us.

I make my way up to the bar and order a club soda with lime. The bartender, a different one, not Ana's girlfriend, gives me a wink and a nod. I'm always grateful for bartenders who don't think twice when I order a non-alcoholic drink.

I take a refreshing sip and there is a light tap on my shoulder. I turn and there is Blaed. Handsome as ever.

"I'm glad you didn't stand me up," Blaed says by way of greeting. That familiar sagebrush and lupine scent cuts through the smells of the bar. I feel my eyebrows relax; I hadn't realized I'd been stress-scowling while I waited.

"I would never," I respond, and turn on my flirting. It's a little forced, a little rusty. I've been too tongue-tied around Declan to flirt back much. If he was even flirting with me at all.

"How was your week? Put out any *fires* lately?" Blaed leans against the bar, his biceps popping out with the motion. His green eyes are fixed on me. The other women around me shoot daggers; they're envious that I have his attention. I should be flattered, but my mind is playing tricks on me, picturing Declan making the same move, saying the same thing.

I shake my head. "You could say that," I mutter, not picking up on the emphasis at first.

He orders his drink and we toast to the weekend. I ask about his plans and he tells me about a kayaking route he wants to try. I let the worries of work fade away. Even if I only get a few hours' reprieve from worrying about weapons and evil billionaires, I'll take it.

I finish my drink and Blaed offers to get me a refill. "Sure," I give a hesitant answer.

"And maybe something to snack on?" he adds. Okay, this is quickly veering into date territory. *But, is that so bad?* I give a nod and he hands me the bar menu. Not much looks like it would fit with my gluten-free diet. I point to the flight of tacos and hope they use corn tortillas. Blaed raises an arm to flag down the bartender. While we wait for him to make his way over to us, Blaed turns the questions on me. "No big triathlons for you this weekend?"

I shrug. "Nah, I'll catch the next one," I say with a smile.

I'm about to make a comment about the race Ana and I worked last month when I remember that I told Blaed that I was traveling for work, but not where I had been. Or what my job was.

Blaed leans over the counter and places our order with the bartender. I run through every interaction we've had. I was never wearing anything with the FIRE logo. Neither was Ana. I never mentioned where I worked. What I do. *So how does Blaed know?* I start to sweat through my shirt, and I don't think it is the temperature causing it.

The bar is too crowded, too loud. The latest pop hits are blaring through the speakers. I should feel safe in such a packed room, with all these people to potentially help. Instead, I'm anonymous, easily lost in the throng. If I scream for help, will anyone even notice?

I pull out my phone quickly.

Blaed glances over. "Uh-oh, am I boring you already?" he says into my ear, his hand grazing my shoulder.

Two minutes ago, I would have been thrilled by the idea of this incredibly handsome man who apparently has no dating or romantic bans touching me, flirting with me. Now I can't help but feel boxed in. I give him what I have now named my

Castillo smile, as in "I'm playing nice and flirting back with you but I'm totally not into it" grin.

This is not a date. This is a trap. I can feel it.

I make up a lie. "Just texting Ana; she wanted to make sure you didn't blow me off." Ana is probably asleep by now given the time difference.

"Tell her I say hi," Blaed responds. "But that I'm happy she isn't here," he adds with a wink.

Damn, he is cute and sexy. And apparently, I was totally blinded by it. Honestly, I'm a little happy Ana isn't here too. Because if my suspicions are correct, then I'm glad she is out of the line of danger.

I can't ruminate on all the ways I've been thoughtless lately. I text the one person who I know will come and help me. Even if it means I look foolish to him for not being suspicious sooner.

Charlie Ross

S.O.S.

Danger.

We didn't work out a codeword for this situation, but I'm using the codeword.

Help!

I send along with a pin for my location.

And then I wait for Declan.

33

DECLAN

Boring-ass budget meetings are not my idea of a fun Friday evening. But this is exactly the dull distraction I need.

Since Wednesday I've been ignoring Charlie. Only interacting for necessary business. I shouldn't have gone to check on her. The sooner I sever all friendly attachments, the sooner my heart and my head will accept that she is a distraction. She should be with someone who can date her, give her the relationship she deserves, and not put her in danger.

The word "danger" hangs in my mind. Because I still haven't been able to place the man I saw at the bar in Copenhagen. Something about him irks me. He didn't match any of the images Ian handed me.

Danger because if we don't find those black-market weapons, they will find someone: innocent victims.

My phone pings.

I look down and the word that has been on my mind flashes on my screen.

Charlie Ross

Danger.

I unlock it, not caring if Oliver and Finn think it's rude.

I read Charlie's text messages. Then I read them again.

Without preamble, I stand.

"Is everything OK?" Oliver asks.

Finn is aware of our secret operations, but he's on a need-to-know basis. And he doesn't need to know this until I figure out what is going on. I hand my unlocked phone to Oliver, then head to my office to put my laptop in my messenger bag and leave.

Oliver is moving quickly as well. He walks me out of the office and hands me back my phone. "Bring her back here and we'll sort out her security," he says. I give him a firm nod and do my best to stay calm. Charlie is in control of the situation if she can still message me.

Dammit. I should have pressed her on wearing a tracking dot. Or at least granting location access to me or Ian. I should have taken the time to show her some defensive maneuvers.

I get in my SUV and speed out of the parking lot. My bike is strapped onto the back because I was supposed to go for a training ride after work. A few weeks ago, I would have been annoyed to miss training to help Charlie. Now all I can think of is getting to her.

The GPS on my phone directs me to her quickly. Thankfully, traffic is light and the beach bar it leads me to isn't overfull yet.

I scan the outdoor seating area and don't spot Charlie. No sign of her brown hair and blue-black glasses. What was she wearing earlier? My mind provides an answer. Dark green blouse and white jeans that hugged her ample curves. Even when trying to avoid her, my mind was still cataloging all it could.

I enter the bar discreetly. It's open-air so there isn't a door to walk through, but I want to be cautious. I'm not sure what kind of danger Charlie thinks she is in. My instinct is to find her and throw her over my shoulder to bring her to safety, but I have to think strategically.

I stand near the entrance and do a quick survey of the people around me. The bar is filling, people are talking, the noise level so high I won't be able to hear Charlie.

My eyes find her at the bar; she is sitting there next to . . .

Blaed Johannson.

My mind catches on several things at once.

Blaed used to be in my unit. I haven't seen him since I separated from the navy. There is no way this is a coincidence.

With this assumption, my mind finally places the man we saw in Copenhagen. Without his beard, I might have recognized him sooner. Someone X.C. introduced me to once in passing. An old friend of his from basic training who had been stationed across the world. The man, Shane Ramedia, must have been recruited by the Order as well.

Two guys I used to serve with both now working against FIRE? Was this connection somehow exploited for the trap that was laid in Osaka? How could Blaed betray me and X.C. like that?

I watch Charlie and Blaed. She's smiling as he talks animatedly, then she laughs at whatever joke he just finished. They look like a happy couple on a date. Blaed is flirting with her. It's obvious. My fists clench. Some caveman coding in my DNA wants to get them as far apart as possible.

Charlie is generally a trusting person. I might have trust issues, but I can easily surmise Blaed is working for the Order and therefore a threat. I hate that my mistrust is accurate this one time. I wish this was a case of jealousy or unrequited feelings. But it is more. If Blaed is on a mission, he could be trying to get information from Charlie, or, worse, apprehend her.

The crowd swells and grows louder around me, bringing me out of my inner thoughts. I remind myself that Charlie sent a help signal. She must sense he is dangerous. She must be playing along for the sake of keeping herself safe in this crowded place.

I move toward the side exit and pull out my phone. I send off a text to Charlie.

Declan Davidson

You need to freshen up in the bathroom.

That's all I send. There'll be time for us to go over the details. Right now, my focus is on extraction. I wait for Charlie to approach.

After a minute, Charlie makes her way over to me. We lock eyes and her shoulders relax. A small smile, a genuine one, forms on her lips. She lets out a deep breath.

Charlie opens her mouth to speak and all I want to do is scoop her into my arms and silence her with a kiss once more. It's not the worst way to keep Ms. A Million Questions quiet. Instead, I indicate she should remain silent with a sharp gesture across my throat.

I point to the exit and she follows. I stay behind her, my hand on her shoulder, leading her out of the bar and to my vehicle.

Charlie stays silent, having learned from the incident in Copenhagen. I want to ask her so many questions. *What she was thinking talking to Blaed? Is this the first time she saw him? Have they met before? How did she suspect she was in danger?*

But I save all of it. Because there is no way Blaed Johannson just stumbled on Charlie Ross at a random tiki bar. That I can conclude on my own.

I drive down the road, the Gulf of Mexico to our right. The sun is setting and the water, while beautiful, is blinding. About a mile later, I pull over into a public lot.

I get out of the car and Charlie follows me. I grab a spare towel from the back, one I usually use after a training ride, and march over to the beach. My shoes will be full of sand. I'm not dressed for this location, but it's our best bet right now.

The sound of the waves and the gulls is loud enough to distract me from all I want to say to Charlie. First things first, I need to check for any planted devices.

The thought of Blaed touching her and planting a tracker on her body makes my own skin crawl. I decide to check her bag first.

I lay out the towel and gesture for her purse. Charlie gives me a confused look. I'm too angry to do anything but scowl at her until she hands it to me.

I turn the enormous bag over and the contents spill out. Her wallet. Cell phone. A pack of gum. Receipts. Loose change. A tampon. And then, unmissable: a tracking dot. Small but powerful.

I hold it up to show Charlie. She takes a half-step back. I'm not sure if she is scared of me and the ire I know I must be showing or the device itself.

I turn sharply and fling the device as hard as I can, throwing it into the Gulf of Mexico. Where I wish I could throw Blaed, the still unknown mole, and whoever else is involved in their schemes.

I need to calm down. The anger coursing through me is akin to what I contended with before I completed basic training. It's what I felt immediately after I was burned on that botched mission in Osaka. It's a dangerous feeling and I need to keep my wits about me right now.

I turn back and Charlie is kneeling over the towel and putting everything back into her purse. I should help her. But I still need a moment.

How can she not understand why I am so mad? Blaed is as well trained as I am but has no moral qualms whatsoever about kidnapping, murder, or anything else. *How can she not understand that I care about her and seeing her next to such a dangerous person scares me?* I want to scream at her and hold her in equal measure.

I stride over to her and she looks up. "Do we still have to be quiet now?" Her voice is low, soft.

"No, but I'd appreciate it."

"Declan," Charlie stands, leaving her purse on the towel, "I reached out to you because I was terrified. He knew things about me that I had never told him. I went through my mind for everything I'd said to him over the past month, but I never told him."

Charlie's words hit me like a lead pipe. All the trust I'd invested in her threatens to crumble. They've interacted before, which means he could have planted that device at their first encounter. "When did you two meet?"

"Ana and I met him after my first week and then I ran into him again a week ago." It's a punch to the gut. All this time I'd been falling for Charlie and Blaed was already moving in on her. "Are you mad at me about this? That someone planted a device on me?"

"You should have been smarter about this!" I yell at her.

Charlie takes a step back. I immediately regret my tone, but I am so angry. That Blaed was so close to her. That she looked happy with him. *No, that was a ruse*, I remind myself.

"This guy used to be in the same unit as me, and he was not one of the honorable ones."

Charlie doesn't respond. I can see the implications settling in. She didn't know. How could she have suspected that first week when she was in the dark about our clandestine operations? Still, I look away from her, down at the sand. I put my hands on my hips and shake my head. Because I don't want to know the answer to this next question, but I have to ask it. My stomach turns at the thought of what a "yes" might mean.

"Has he been to your apartment?" I try not to yell at her again, but I know my tone is harsh.

"No!" Charlie answers instantly. Realization dawns across her face. "Wait, do you think he followed me to my house before? Do you think he broke in?"

I did extra training when I began working at FIRE to be able to tell if someone is lying. Charlie is telling the truth. I'm still too mad to try to help quell her rising panic. I exhale and glare at her again.

"Dammit, Ross! I cannot believe you didn't catch this sooner!" I run my hand through my hair. I want to throw something else. To break something. It doesn't matter that I trusted Charlie, because she was unknowingly passing information.

"Sorry I'm not an expert in evasive spy techniques or whatever you'd call it." Charlie crosses her arms, defensive. The sea breeze is whipping her hair about, the dark strands swirl around her face.

"A strange guy pops up multiple times and you don't think it's weird?" I ask.

"It's not exactly a stretch to think a guy is genuinely interested in me." Her mood has shifted; I've hit a nerve. Charlie's face grows red as she speaks. "I thought at worst he was hitting on me, at best maybe I could make a new friend in a new city."

"Did you kiss him?" This has nothing to do with any compromised information and everything to do with what I'm feeling right now, the jealousy bubbling inside me. But I need to know.

Charlie gives me a firm answer. "No."

"Did he touch you?" I picture the worst things my heart could imagine. I need to get all of this out, like poison from a snake bite.

"No," she says calmly.

"So, what, was this a date?"

"Declan, I'm still in my work clothes!" Charlie says but doesn't answer my question.

"Was this a date?" I'm grateful the beach is relatively empty because our voices are loud. To anyone who could hear us, we sound like a couple having a fight.

"Just because YOU have a no-dating rule doesn't mean I have to have one," Charlie spits at me.

I shake my head. How could I have been so dumb to think for a second that I had a chance with Charlie? To have let myself catch feelings for her? To not act sooner? "So it was a date," I say, and it isn't a question; I can't even look at her right now.

"Why do you care? You have your 'no relationship' rule." There is a clip to her voice that catches my attention. I glance at her and her blue eyes brim with tears before she lets out a sigh and blinks them away. "And then you kiss me! And you say nothing about it!"

I wait for her to say more. Will her to say what I am longing to hear. That she wanted to be out with me instead. That she wants *me.*

Charlie glances over at me before focusing her gaze on the water. She lets out a deep exhale and covers her face, hiding her emotions. She shakes her head and crosses her arms. "Whatever. It was for our cover, right?" She snaps her lips shut, forcing herself to stop talking.

I take a step closer to her, then another. I cross the distance between us.

Charlie fidgets, looking every way but mine.

Once I'm next to her, I reach out and touch her arm. She lets out a small gasp and I swear it takes everything in me not to lift her up and pull her close. She glances up at me, and I recognize the look in her eyes before her focus darts to the sand at her feet. She wants me to say it, to say that I wanted to be with her. At least, I hope that's what I'm reading. Because if not, I'm about to embarrass myself.

"That's how it started," I say, and I move my hand from her arm to her chin. I wait until she looks up at me. Once her cobalt eyes are trained on me, I tell her, "That's not how it ended."

I look at her mouth, slightly parted and perfect. I take a deep inhale and take my chance. I close the space between our mouths and take my opportunity to hold the woman I've been fantasizing about all week. As our lips touch, I pull her close. Her body relaxes against mine; she leans into me with her whole being.

The sea breeze is pelting us, spinning around us. I can't get enough of this woman. I let my hands move from her shoulders to her lower back. She presses herself closer to me. One motion of her hips that tells me everything I need to know. She wants this too. In a brief second, when our lips are not touching, she lets out the sweetest moan that sends my mind racing. What other sounds can I bring forth from her? If we stay on this beach until dark, can I lay her down on that towel and get her to release every passionate sound in her? I harden at the thoughts running through my mind. Of me and Charlie and our bodies connecting.

My hips vibrate as my phone rings and for a second I think of our inappropriate conversation the other day. I break our kiss and give her a devilish grin. Her blue eyes are staring up at me, then she bites her lower lip and I'm about to claim her mouth once more.

"Declan," she breathes.

How I long to hear her call my name out loud, uncontrollably.

"Charlie." I smile and press my lips to hers.

To my surprise, she breaks our kiss and says my name again. “Declan,” she utters, and places her hands on my chest, a little pressure to push me a half-inch away from her. My blood is still racing, wanting more.

“Your phone,” she says, and I realize the buzzing in my pocket is still happening. Her lips are slightly swollen and her face red. It is the sexiest look on her. I want to chuck this phone in the water too, but instead I check the caller ID.

It’s Oliver.

My libido is doused in cold water. “Davidson,” I say as an answer, grateful the sea breeze is likely muffling my voice so he can’t hear how husky it is.

Charlie is eyeing me, and her coy smile dissipates when I say, “Yes, she’s with me. We’ll come back to the office now.”

She grabs her bag and shakes out the towel as I finish my brief conversation with Oliver, assuring him we’ll be there as soon as possible.

We walk back to the SUV together and I open the passenger door for her. I’m desperate for answers. I want so badly to find these weapons and put a stop to the Order. But right now all I can think about is getting this information exchange over with in the hopes that Charlie and I might continue the conversation our bodies were just having.

34

CHARLIE

I simply cannot think straight right now. My head is a mess. Confused about who Blaed really is. My mind is warped, realizing my instincts were so incredibly wrong. The past few weeks I've sensed this foreboding. That I was being watched. And it turns out I was. This is way more serious than I thought.

Then there is Declan. Racing to get to me when I signaled for help. His anger and blatant jealousy. And then that kiss. No cover, no hiding our faces, no reason to do it other than we both wanted to. My body is still hot from that embrace. I have that same euphoric runner's high feeling I used to get all the time.

For the car ride back to FIRE headquarters, we are both quiet, letting this be the transition to business mode, giving ourselves time to clear our minds, to focus on this new evidence. I avoid the temptation to hold his hand, to offer mine up to him. I need him to touch me so desperately. But desperation will not find out what the Order is up to. Will not stop this next attack.

We walk silently back into headquarters.

Once we're in the elevator, Declan presses the button for our floor. The tension in the small car is thick. I dare not look over at him, that would tempt another kiss that I know I won't be able to keep brief. Declan is right beside me. I'm safe. For now, that's enough.

He must be reading my mind, though. His fingertips, light, barely there, move from my upper back to my lower and back up again. A gentle soothing touch. A reminder that I'm not alone. I close my eyes and take a deep breath. Then the elevator doors open and we separate.

Uncle Ollie greets us at the entrance. He holds the door open and wraps me in a hug as soon as I'm close enough. "You did the right thing reaching out for help, Charlie," he reassures me. Though I can't help but feel that I've compromised the FIRE missions. Even if it was unknowingly.

We spend the next two hours going over every single detail of my interactions with Blaed. Ian, Declan, and Oliver ask variations of the same questions, trying to see if they can get any more detail out of me. The first time I saw him at happy hour with Ana. The second time I ran into him at the coffee shop before work. The brief interaction tonight where he asked about details I never shared.

I did not mention what happened when Declan came to get me. What happened after he threw the tracking device into the water. Declan doesn't either.

"I'll take the physical description you provided and run it through my database. See if he is working with the Order or is just a run-of-the-mill weirdo," Ian offers. Is Ian trying to dismiss my worry as a girl being too sensitive, reading "the wrong" things into what a man at a bar did or said? Or is he trying to explore all possibilities?

I expect Declan to jump in and explain that Blaed also has a connection to X.C. When he doesn't, I decide to follow his lead and not say anything either.

"Any luck using that software to come up with more matches for our mystery buyer in Copenhagen?" Declan asks Ian.

"Nothing," Ian says with a defeated nod.

Oliver rubs his head, thinking over the situation. "Charlie, you didn't have that purse with you on our mission in Key West, correct?"

I shake my head. I brought a smaller one Ana lent me specifically to match my outfit.

"And you didn't have it with you in Copenhagen?" Declan asks.

"No, I brought a cross-body bag for the flight and a FIRE backpack for my carry-on," I explain.

"So on both of those missions no one would have been able to track you," Oliver explains.

I realize he's right. I think aloud with them. "So perhaps there's another mole? Another tracking device?"

"We can't do daily sweeps of every employee and their personal items for bugs," Declan states.

I think about the incidents Oliver and Declan asked about. Our official missions. I get why the mole would want to sabotage our reconnaissance efforts or subvert our covert missions. But what was the point of locking Declan and me in the storage unit? To scare us? Declan and I were still able to get out unscathed. *The person who closed the door and locked us in knew we were there; why not attack us then? Maybe they were after something inside?* It doesn't make sense. It could have been the security guard at the storage facility just closing it if he thought we were done. Maybe they only wanted us contained for thirty minutes? *But why?* Then a new angle dawns on me.

"Maybe the mole isn't a person," I suggest.

The three of them look at me, waiting for me to elaborate.

"Clearly, whoever planted that device on me was using it for *some* information. But it would have been incomplete. I usually leave my purse in my desk. They would need someone else to fill in any gaps and no one person knows all of those details. But our computer system does."

Declan crosses his arms and leans back against Oliver's desk. "You think it's some kind of computer virus?"

"I mean, all the details of our travel and the executive schedules are on our system," I say. That's something Trey would have access to, so he wouldn't need me out of the picture to get that info. I cross him off my list of suspects. For now. "Why else lock us in the storage unit if not to keep me away from my desk?" I see Declan and Oliver nod, considering this theory.

"You think I'm not constantly sweeping for these kinds of viruses?!" Ian demands. It's the first time I've ever heard him raise his voice.

"Hey." Oliver holds out a hand to calm Ian. I'm glad I'm not the only one who is jarred by his overreaction.

"It's a theory," I explain.

Declan jumps in. "Ian, we know your team is overloaded and working round the clock. It's not unreasonable to think something may have slipped through."

"We *are* working hard," Ian responds, still heated. "Your girlfriend over here doesn't know what she's talking about!"

"Hey!" Declan barks back.

"I didn't mean to imply anything; I just can't see any person on this team willfully putting us in danger," I backpedal.

"You'd be surprised," Declan mutters without looking at any of us. He's referring to Osaka, to the mission that killed X.C. and which nearly took him out too.

"Alright, team," Oliver says, putting an end to the bickering. "It's late. We're all exhausted. Let's get some sleep and regroup in the morning."

I nod. I could fall asleep in one of Uncle Ollie's office chairs right now.

"OK," Ian agrees.

"First, we need to figure out where Charlie is staying tonight."

These words from Uncle Ollie shock me. "Um, I'm staying at my home," I respond.

"If you've been tracked for potentially a month now, Blaed knows where you live. Losing the connection with the tracker, the first place he'll look is your home," Declan explains.

A shiver of fear races through my body. I have been watched, spied on, this whole time. Did I have any private moments to myself?

"You'll stay at the safehouse this weekend; we'll find a more permanent solution on Monday," Uncle Ollie says after taking off his glasses and rubbing his eyes. I've contributed to another mess that the team has to deal with. A mess that will distract us from finding the weapons Castillo bought and preventing them from being used.

"Safehouse?" I say.

"Come on." Declan stands and gestures for me to do the same. "I'll take you there now."

Declan leads me back out of the building and to his car. A lifetime has passed since I left at five to go to the bar.

For the whole drive over to the safehouse, I'm jumpy. My nerves surge at every stoplight. At each set of headlights that pass us. Any of them could be Blaed. Or the mole. Or someone else sent to harm us, to stop us from interfering with the Order.

The crowded streets are too busy, too packed. I can't wait to be in the safehouse, but will I be safe there?

35

DECLAN

On the drive over to the safehouse, I keep my thoughts steady. *One problem at a time. One step at a time.*

"I need to go back and get my car," Charlie says as we wait at a stoplight, her eyes on her lap.

I nod. "Let's plan to pick it up tomorrow." I'll feel better about it in the light of day. Also, I'll want to thoroughly inspect it for tracking devices.

The light changes and I head forwards to the entrance ramp for the highway.

"Wait! I need to grab my clothes, toothbrush, personal items," Charlie protests, pointing back in the direction of her apartment.

I shake my head and keep my focus on the road. "Nope, too risky. We'll have the ops team sweep your place this weekend and clear it for any bugs or traps."

Next to me, Charlie says nothing, but I can hear her breathing louder. Heavier. She is panicking.

"Hey," I say, my right hand reaching for hers. I can't truly comfort her the way I want to. I have to get us to the safehouse in one piece. This is the best I can do right now. She grabs on to my hand and squeezes like her life depends on it. "We'll be there soon," I tell her, and I speed up, aiming to get us off the streets rapidly.

"Why didn't you correct Ian when he offered to find Blaed in the database?" she asks. "We already know his connection to you and X.C. And the buyer in Copenhagen."

"You saw how well Ian handles being corrected or critiqued," I reply.

Ian is a typical tech guy. Has to be the smartest one in the room, a bit of a complex about it. Doesn't like being corrected or questioned. He's a coding wizard, but he lives up to the stereotypes of his profession – the good, the bad, and the neurotic. He definitely overreacted to her questioning the firewall.

"So we're letting him waste time and resources to spare his ego?" I can hear the disdain in Charlie's voice.

"He may turn up new information," I explain. "Blaed should be in the database as a known potential associate. Ian will be able to update his status and potentially give us information on his whereabouts over the past three years since I've seen him. And it's not that much work for Ian. It will take him a few keystrokes to pull up the profiles based on the description you gave. Maybe you'll recognize if anyone else has been tailing you."

"Alright," Charlie concedes. But she says it as if she is still questioning my reasoning. Not fully convinced. What I won't admit is that a small part of my brain is searching for a different explanation. Because if someone else told me this situation, I'd say X.C. was more involved than I realized. But I know that can't be true. No way. Besides, even if he was involved, they killed him. I can't riddle out how X.C. could have been involved with the Order. Did he get too close to stopping them before, so they recruited people he knew? Is that how they eliminated him?

I take the exit for Ybor City and navigate the redbrick streets to our safehouse. A refurbished cigar warehouse rehabbed into an apartment blends in here.

I use the security code to enter the steel-reinforced garage and park.

Charlie hops out and waits for me to open the interior door. The air-conditioning hits me first, which is a welcome reprieve from the humidity that has seeped into the garage. The concrete floors and open-concept design give the safehouse a cavernous echo. The kitchen and living room flow into one another on the first floor, and there is a loft with one bedroom atop a metal spiral staircase.

I close the door behind me and set the security system. Charlie wanders through the space, taking it all in. She gravitates to the kitchen and I realize she probably hasn't eaten anything.

"I think it's mostly stocked with frozen meals," I say, nodding to the refrigerator. There's enough food to last for a full week.

"Good to know," Charlie says quietly. She passes through the kitchen and over to the bookshelf on the far wall. The safehouse is also fully stocked with books. Because you never know how long you have to lay low for. While here, operatives aren't supposed to log into any streaming services or e-reader devices. They ping off the nearest cell tower and any spy worth their salt would triangulate the location easily. It kind of defeats the point of hiding.

Charlie starts to read off the last names of the authors. "King, Patterson, Grisham. Austen, Atwood." She pauses and pulls out a book. "Le Carré? Really?"

"Too on the nose?" I say, trying to lighten the mood.

I let her wander the first floor and I head up to the loft area. There are FIRE-branded clothes in the dresser. They're probably all too big for Charlie, but likely more comfortable than wearing her work clothes.

"Declan?!" Charlie calls out, startled. I tuck the clothes I could find under my arm and thunder down the spiral stairs, careful not to trip.

"What's wrong?" I ask as I set the clothes down and reach for the pistol on my hip.

"Nothing, I just thought you left," she says, staring down at her feet.

"No, not yet. I'll show you how the security system works and then I'll go," I tell her.

Charlie walks over to the couch and takes a seat.

"The security panel is here," I say, pointing to the wall near the garage entrance. "You can seal everything with this button, and close off the windows and doors. It will send an alarm to headquarters, so we'll know to come get you." Charlie isn't so much as looking at what I'm trying to show her.

"Over there –" I point to the massive steel door in the middle of the far redsbrick wall – "is the escape route if the safehouse is breached. The emergency elevator leads into one of the infamous Ybor Tunnels as a last-ditch escape if necessary. It locks once you're inside the tunnel entrance. They can't get in and it puts the house on lockdown. Only a manual override at headquarters can unlock it. It's the ultimate panic button."

"Tunnels? Elevator?" Charlie asks. "Where do they go?"

"If necessary, away from danger," I reply, grateful that at least some of what I'm saying is getting through to her. I can sense her unease, but I continue. "All the entrances and exits are covered by security cameras. You're safe here."

Charlie glances over at the door and then the panel. "Can we assume that whoever the mole is, they know about this place? About these 'secret' tunnels?" she asks, using air quotes.

I want to reassure her. But the truth won't do that, so I don't say anything.

"They would, wouldn't they?" Charlie sits on her hands and starts to rock back and forth on the couch.

"Yes."

Charlie rolls her eyes. "So it's not really that safe?"

Her expression is awash with fear. Given how close Blaed was to her tonight, how easily he could have kidnapped her, I don't blame her. "It is. Ian personally switched out the systems last month, all-new passcodes, all-new wiring. Everything's up to date."

Charlie doesn't answer me, so I continue to point out what she'll need. "I grabbed some clothes for you. All oversized but better than sleeping in jeans." I point to the stack of clothes I've put on the kitchen counter.

She doesn't say anything back.

"Alright, hit this button to set the alarm when I leave," I say, pointing to the control panel. "I'll be back in the morning to check on you."

Charlie jumps off the couch. "You're leaving?!"

I'm shocked by this sudden response after so much silence. "Charlie, you're safe here." I point to one of the cameras to emphasize this.

At this, her chest starts to heave and her breaths grow shallow. Her face is red. "They've been watching me for a month!" she wheezes out. "You think some camera in a corner is going to make me safe? What if they get in here tonight?!"

I close the space between us and wrap her in my arms. "Breathe, Charlie," I remind her. "Breathe." I take a deep slow inhale and then a controlled exhale as I hold her. I do this until her breathing matches mine. The scent of her fruity perfume is faded at the end of a long day but still there. "I'll stay," I tell her. "I'll stay."

Charlie nods once I make this offer. "And no video feed?" This seems to disturb her the most, the surveillance. I understand it, but I don't like it.

"OK, I'll only arm the doors and windows." I know the instant she lets her fear go, as her body relaxes. "Tomorrow, we get your stuff and regroup at headquarters. Sunday, I'll teach you some defensive moves."

Charlie pulls back and glares at me. "I'm a female runner. My dad had me in self-defense classes since I was twelve. It's the guns I can't outrun, Declan."

"OK, then, I'll take you to the shooting range." She opens her mouth, her unease still apparent. "I don't expect you to be a lethal marksman. If nothing else, you'll learn how it works so you can better disarm someone."

Charlie nods and tucks her head back into my chest. I move my hand to cradle her head. "Thank you," she whispers.

"Alright, get cleaned up and I'll get some food made," I say as I let her go. She grabs the clothes on the counter before heading to the bathroom on the far side of the loft.

Since Copenhagen, I've thought of what it would be like to spend the night with Charlie. On opposite ends of the safehouse in inexpensive Ikea furniture did not feature in any of those scenarios. The safehouse has to be functional, not fashionable. It has a minimalist design which could appear to be an aesthetic choice. It is more a result of electing to fund the security features first. This will *not* be a comfortable night of sleep.

Staying here with Charlie may make her feel safer right now, but it is dangerous. I'm distracted by her; I can't keep her safe like this.

And I'm so close to falling for her. I'm at the edge of a cliff. One move and I'll plummet.

36

CHARLIE

The hot water and steam can only wash away so much. Sweat, dirt, makeup.

The fear isn't coming off; it won't fade away.

After I towel off, the bathroom mirror is covered in condensation. I don't make any effort to wipe it away. I don't want to see how I look; I know it will only amplify the dread brewing inside.

I finger-comb my hair and assume I look presentable enough. Declan has already seen me at my worst.

Putting on the baggy borrowed clothes reminds me of all that has happened this evening and all the things before it. In the weeks since I started working for FIRE, I have been bugged, shot at, locked in a storage unit, and tonight – well, who knows what might have happened if Declan hadn't shown up. Blaed didn't say or do anything specifically threatening, but he planted a tracking device on me a month ago. Who's to say what else he might have done? If not tonight, then another time.

My glasses are all steamed up, but when I exit the bathroom they demist. The air-conditioning is on full blast, my skin hot from the shower, so it's a welcome change. I know this evening I'll need an extra blanket or two, though.

As I enter the main living area, the smell of garlic and cheese hits me. My mouth waters and my stomach grumbles. Declan's handgun is on the table in the living-room area. I didn't even know he had one on him. I guess he's always been discreet about it.

"I found some cauliflower-crust frozen pizza," Declan announces. He is in the kitchen and has taken off his button-down shirt, leaving him in a tight white T-shirt that is tucked into his slacks. His lean but firm arm muscles are on display. If I thought he was hot before, he is volcanic now.

And I . . . am a walking pile of laundry. I consider if I should dig for a better-fitting set of clothes when my stomach turns again. "You could have said cardboard-crust frozen pizza and I would have eaten it gladly," I admit.

Declan smiles at me as I sit on one of the barstools by the kitchen counter. The clock on the stove tells me it is about to strike midnight.

Declan offers me a bottle of water and a paper plate with freshly cooked pizza. We eat in silence, Declan leaning on the counter across from me. His mind is busy; he is thinking through all these shreds of information that barely amount to any substantive clues.

"Thank you," I say after I have one piece of pizza in my stomach. Declan looks up at me as he takes a sip of his water. "For saving me earlier," I clarify.

He gives me a nod and says, "We're a team." I guess that's his way of saying "you're welcome."

"Yeah, we are. Aren't we?" I reply, not sure what I want him to respond with.

"This is a lot. I didn't have to deal with all this in my first month on the job and I knew what I was signing up for," Declan says.

I shake my head, because he did have to deal with an explosion killing his mentor and almost finishing him off as well and I don't think there is an appropriate amount of time for that either. "I think this is the part where I question if this job is worth it."

Declan splits the rest of the small pizza between us. "I understand the fear, the danger. But we have to think about those weapons, how many people could be hurt, could die. We have to help."

My mind pictures the crowds that will be at the World Games. I used to envision them chanting my name as I crossed the finish line. Now I can only hear the phantom screams of how they'll react to an impending terror attack. This threat is so heavy. "Do you sometimes think someone else should save the day?"

Declan gives me a devilish smirk. "No."

Of course not. Declan Davidson is a good guy through and through. Even if some of his intentions lead him to be a little overprotective.

I offer to clean up and Declan settles onto the couch to sleep. It doesn't look at all comfortable.

"Are you OK over there?" I ask.

"We're locked in for the night," he tells me before locking his eyes on mine. "I'm not going anywhere."

I nod and turn off the lights in the kitchen before climbing the metal stairs. The entire safehouse is dark, save for the small amount of light coming from the digital clocks in the kitchen and the loft.

I get under the unfamiliar covers of the bed, cocooned in these oversized clothes. Exhaustion demands my full attention. Declares how worn down I am. "OK, goodnight," I call out.

From below, I hear Declan's voice. "Goodnight, Ross."

I take a deep breath and close my eyes.

I'm back at the World Games trials. My legs are sculpted, my body ready. The starting gun fires and the race begins. But I am stuck. I try to move, but nothing happens. The other runners round the oval and I'm standing in the way. They crash into me, as if they can't see me. I'm on the ground, trampled under their racing spikes. I try to roll away, to escape. But I'm frozen. Immovable.

I jolt awake with a scream. I can't see anything in front of me, but I can tell I'm not at home. I hear movement nearby. Feet on concrete, then a rattle on metal.

"Charlie?!" Declan calls out in the darkness. My eyes adjust and I see him reach the top of the stairs.

I'm still gasping for air as I cover my face, embarrassed that my bad dream disturbed Declan, who was already going out of his way to be nice and sleep on a tiny couch because I'm too scared to function right now.

"I'm sorry," I tell him, shaking my head. I try to steady my breath, but I find myself still heaving for air.

Declan crosses over to me, setting his handgun on the bedside table as he passes. He must have grabbed it when he heard me cry out. Declan is now wearing only his undershirt and boxers. *Right. He probably waited to change until I went to sleep.*

Declan sits on the bed next to me and wraps an arm round my shoulder. "It's OK, sweetheart," he says, his lips on the crown of my head. My senses register everything while my eyes still adjust in the dark. Declan's cologne isn't that strong, but his skin is warm against mine. His firm arm muscles hold me as if I am about to crumble.

My body sinks into his. I can't hold this fear and tension when he touches me. It melts away.

"It was just a nightmare," I explain. "I feel so ridiculous."

"Stress is dangerous to our bodies and our brains," Declan offers as an explanation.

"Yeah, but could my stress dreams just be public speaking while naked? Or my teeth falling out? Something embarrassing but not terrifying?" I say, trying to make light of the situation.

"My nightmare is that I'm back in high school and I have to take a final exam I've never studied for," Declan confesses as his thumb rubs my shoulder.

"Nerd," I tease him.

"I mean, I would have aced it, but still stressful," Declan adds. I can hear the smile in his voice.

"Always so confident, always so cocky," I mutter.

Soft lips press into my hair. "You wouldn't want me any other way, sweetheart," Declan says. He's right. And without realizing it, my breathing is normal again, my nightmare forgotten.

I want to apologize for being weak, for being scared. I've told myself a million times that I'm strong. I was an elite athlete. I've tackled endless doctors' appointments to finally get the correct diagnosis. I moved across the country to start a new job and a new life. I know I'm tough and brave. So why is that feeling abandoning me now?

"What's it like to be fearless?" I ask him.

"I'm not fearless," Declan says. "I always run toward danger, to help, to fix things, to make it right. In most cases, that's not fearless or even brave. It's foolish." His words are soft, the gravel in his voice gone. After a deep breath, he admits, "Actually I'm terrified. Because I finally have something to lose." As he says this, he wraps his other arm round me.

I am so safe, caged in his arms. I pull away enough so I can lift my head. My lips find his instinctively, as if we are magnetized. His warm mouth, his strong arms, they are all I need. All I want. I make a silent wish. *Please don't let this be a dream.* His kiss is soft and sweet, caring. He is holding me like I am something to be cherished.

But my mind is confused, even if my body knows exactly what it wants and what to do. I let out a weak laugh. "I thought . . . I thought the other day after you saw me so sick and weak . . ." I wince, thinking about how pathetic I must have appeared. "I thought . . . you had put me in the friend zone."

"I tried to. I needed to. I really should," Declan says, his arms releasing me.

I nod. I shouldn't have said anything.

Then Declan's hands find mine, our fingers interlacing. "You understand the danger of being with me. Of how I have been burned and betrayed. These people will stop at nothing. I could never forgive myself if they hurt you to get to me. If I lost you too."

I nod again, unsure if he can see me. I know this is the most generous way he can let me down easy. Logically.

"If I were a stronger man—" Declan cuts himself off and squeezes my hand.

"I respect your boundaries," I tell him, reminding myself that I need to be strong as well. "Declan, you have a rule. I don't like it. I hate it." I look down at our hands. "But I respect it. I'm not the kind of person to try to make you something you don't want to be."

"Charlie . . ."

The way he tenderly says my name has me fighting back the emotions storming inside me: how much I want him; how much he means to me. Declan disconnects our hands so he can tilt my chin upwards. His eyes lock on mine and I feel too exposed. Like he can read every thought in my mind right now. But I'm unable to look away.

"For years, I had this rule and infatuations came and went. The truth is, no one has ever once tempted me to break this rule like you have. It's more than how much I want you. It's how much I want to be with you at the office, on missions, even after this career is over." As he says it, I can see it all. Work, life, cycling, running, cooking, all the exciting and mundane things. With Declan.

"Charlie, my rule means nothing against the truth I feel when we're together. The truth that says *we* are a rule that can't be broken. That we belong together no matter what." He is saying the most beautiful things. I want to beg him to stop. Because I'll cling to them. I'll recite them to myself as I pine for him. This is worse than him freezing me out. If he is going to say we can't be together, I'd rather be put out of my misery. Tears are coming, but I have to fight them back. I refuse to appear even more fragile.

"I'm weak for you, Charlie," he whispers, and my heart begins to race. He moves his hand from my chin, his fingertips tracing a delicate line along my jaw until he wraps his hand through my hair. He is holding my face so we are eye to eye, making sure I hear him, see him. "I will tear down every wall, break every rule to get to hold you. To be with you."

Spellbound, I don't dare look away from him. Declan releases me and I let out a whimper, disappointed he didn't kiss me.

"After seeing Castillo flirt with you, I was frustrated, offended on your behalf. But I knew we had our roles to play." Declan pauses. His firm hand starts to move in my hair. Massaging my scalp, soothing me. But it is also a possessive action, one that sends heat to my belly. "Tonight, seeing you with Blaed, I almost ran over there and clocked him for daring to be near you." He shifts away from me, his hand leaving my skin. He sits forwards on the edge of the bed.

I should be scared by his confession. But I can't be scared by it when that same feeling fueled him to protect me. I reach out and touch his hand, the same way I did when he told me about the Osaka mission in the storage unit. No one should have to feel alone when they admit their darkest memories or thoughts.

"You deserve something less complicated. Someone who doesn't put you in harm's way," he mumbles.

"Life is complicated, life is dangerous. Every relationship is a risk, a leap. You're the one I want to jump with," I tell him.

Declan squeezes my hand and lifts it to his mouth, giving it a gentle peck. Then he moves his lips to my wrist, my arm. It's so good and so right. I sigh as each kiss lands on my skin. This is absolutely what I want and need right now.

I utter the same word he said back in Copenhagen after our first kiss.

"More."

37

CHARLIE

That one word unleashes something in Declan. In me as well.

His lips move from my arms to my mouth at lightning speed. I reach for him and we are horizontal on the bed seamlessly, as if this is the most natural way for our bodies to be together. His kiss is soft and tender, his hands hungry as they grip me. First my neck and shoulders, then he moves lower to my breasts. I arch into him. His arousal greets me and drives my hunger. I've never known need like this before. It's consuming me, taking over all reason and logic.

The scratch of his stubble prickles my face. I long to feel it all over my skin.

He grinds into me again and I cannot control myself. I let out a moan as Declan squeezes me and teases with each touch.

He gives my lips a playful bite, sucking on my lower lip before releasing it with a *pop*. In a swift motion, he pulls his shirt over his head with one hand. The power and precision of his movements stuns me.

I need him. *Now*.

With a gentle push on his shoulder, Declan rolls onto his back. I straddle him and move my hips. The bundle of nerves between my legs demands another round. Another. I tense at the sensation, the promise of release. Declan's low groan tells me his body agrees with mine.

I lean down and kiss him. His hands grab my forearms, but release as I start to kiss his chin, his neck. I move my body down his so I can kiss his shoulders. His chest. His abs. His chest hair tickles my cheeks as I work my way lower and lower until I reach his navel. "You don't have to," Declan whispers.

I look up at him. "I want to," I say. My voice deep and my breath raspy. Because I want to give this man everything. So he knows how much I need him. To thank his body for protecting mine. For his heart to trust that this is right, that I'm safer with him than without him.

But more than what I want, I *need* to give him this. So that he knows he can lose control with me. He deserves to be able to lose control.

I keep kissing lower and lower until I arrive at the elastic band of his boxers. I give a quick teasing kiss and then reach my hand into the opening. Hot, hard velvet hits my palm.

Oh my. He is thick. And long. I doubt all of him will fit in my mouth. My muscles clench deliciously at the thought of how he'll feel *down there*.

On all fours, I lick my lips as I squeeze his shaft in my hand, making eye contact with him. He gives a nod and I pull him free from his boxers.

I lean my head lower and give him one long lick. Declan's breath catches. I feel powerful. That this man of discipline and rules is unraveling because of me.

I give him a wicked smile and then put him into my mouth, taking as much of him as I can. I start to lick and suck. His hips move in rhythm and I know he likes what I'm doing when he reaches down to twist his fingers in my hair.

"Of all the ways I've ever tried to silence you, this is by far my favorite."

I let out a moan and give his shaft a pull and the tip a flick of my tongue. Declan groans in appreciation.

I get back to work and his hips move to follow the motion of my mouth. We find a rhythm until Declan cries out. "Stop! I won't last if you keep doing that," he tells me.

I slowly release him from my mouth and sit back on my heels. I'm grateful that the bed in this safehouse is soft and sizeable to fit us both.

I take the hem of my shirt and begin to lift it higher and higher. I slide the shirt off and Declan sits up on his elbows, drinking in the sight of me. His eyes travel from my navel up my body. He evaluates me slowly, as if he is memorizing me like a map, studying me for his next mission. Heat courses through my veins, burning for his touch, his mouth.

Once our eyes lock, I can't help but be overwhelmed by his desire. I've never felt this way before. Never been so wanted or seen. Or so eager to be touched and taken.

Dexterously, he scoops me into his arms and his tongue finds my nipple. The way I'm kneeling, my breasts are at the perfect height for his mouth while he sits on the bed. With each touch, my skin awakens. His fingertips are like electricity, bringing life and heat to what was dormant, forgotten.

Every sensation is a gift. After the terrifying time years ago when my body was numb, I vowed to cherish every feeling in my body. Every pinch. Every pain. But this. This touch is everything. It is everything my body needed and more.

With one hand round my waist, his other travels up my legs, past my knee, my thigh, until he reaches my ass. He gives it a firm squeeze before he moves higher. In a tantalizingly slow motion, he dips his fingers beneath the waistband. I didn't want to put my dirty undies back on for sleep, so he has nothing barring his way. His fingers unhurriedly caress my rear before they find their way to my center. I let out a sharp exhale when his fingers meet the slick skin between my legs and he releases my nipple from his mouth.

"All this, for me?" he asks.

"All of me for you," I breathe.

"Trust your body, Charlie," he says as he removes his hand from my pants. He licks the wetness from his fingers.

Declan is efficient at work, and it seems that in bed he is just as methodical and deliberate. My body reacts in sync with my mind, wanting him even more.

His words cause a reaction too, fire pooling in my center. I didn't know I needed to hear them, but I did. Because I've spent years second-guessing everything I feel inside, how my body moves. But this, tonight with Declan, this is exactly what my body was made for.

"It knows what to do; it knows you want me."

"I trust you," I tell him. "I want you."

At this, I lower myself so Declan and I are face to face. He wraps his arms round me and breathes, "Let me taste all of you," before kissing me. I melt into him, relishing the sensation of our skin connecting. Gently, he lowers me onto the bed, his deep kisses claiming me. The tension builds in my body, at the bud of nerves so desperate for his touch. I grind my hips into him and his erection greets me.

Declan is detail-oriented, cataloging each piece of me as evidence. The taste of my nipples, the curves of my skin, the wetness between my legs. All critical data for this thorough man. I wouldn't want it any other way.

Declan raises off of me and gently tugs at the borrowed sweatpants. He drops them to the floor and begins to kiss his way up my body. Starting at my ankles, he places delicate kisses along my legs, my knees. His stubble scratches and tickles the whole way up. He takes his time once he reaches my upper thighs. It's a tantalizing delay, the pressure building within me.

He stops and looks up at me. I bite my lip and give him a nod. With the go-ahead, he pushes my knees apart. The change in his demeanor excites me. His strength and force are a promise of what is to come.

He dips his head down and gives one long deliberate lick, the tip of his tongue hitting my clit sending a shock of sensation through my body. I can't help but writhe and call out.

"Patience, sweetheart," Declan says before he returns his mouth to my center and gets to work. I lift my hips in pleasure and find a rhythm against him. When he moves his body so he can use one of his hands on my thighs, I know I'm about to lose control.

He kneads my inner thigh gently, not losing his focus with his mouth. Centimeter by centimeter, he moves his hand up and up and up. When he finally, gently, places his finger inside me, I clench around him, the cascade of sensation too much.

"Yes, baby," Declan encourages me. One swirl of his fingers, another. And I'm a goner.

My body explodes in pleasure as I cry out for him. Declan doesn't relent, he continues to lick and swirl, as I ride the waves of my orgasm. When my body calms and I lay there panting, I look down at him. He appears both satisfied and hungry.

"I need you," he tells me. "Now."

"Then take me," I breathe.

He lays back on top of me and kisses me with desire. I grind into him, eager to start again.

Abruptly, he hops off of me and over to the nightstand. In the dark, he rummages around and finds what he is searching for. A box of condoms. "Safehouse has to put safety first, right?"

I laugh and bite my lip. "Did you know those were here?"

He shakes his head as he walks back to the bed and sits on the edge. "No, I'm just incredibly –" he pauses and plants a kiss on my lips – "incredibly lucky."

He opens the condom and begins to put it over his tip. I notice his hands are shaking slightly. Perhaps from the adrenaline of the evening or the hormones raging inside us both. I reach over and touch his hand. Then I finish what he started, slowly rolling the condom down his rigid length.

Declan looks over at me with a wicked smile and says, "Good girl" before kissing me and laying me back down.

I wrap my arms round his neck and pull him closer. His tongue slides against mine. His body moves with me. He traces his hand down the side of my body, his fingertips painting a line of electricity that gives me delicious shivers. When he reaches down between my legs again, I gasp.

"Are you sure?" he asks.

"Yes," I tell him. "Take me now."

He waits a moment longer, drawing out my anticipation.

"Please," I breathe.

With those words, he guides himself inside me. He's slow and considerate at first. My muscles expand deliciously to fit him and then contract around him. I flex around him again and again, a wave of pleasure escaping my lips.

We begin to move slowly together. Hips in unison. Lips finding each other before pausing to release a grunt or a moan. Our bodies speak a secret language; we move together without need for further instruction.

Declan starts to move faster, each motion harder. "Mine," Declan growls before shifting our position. He lifts one of my legs and sinks in deeper. I gasp at his size and girth. He begins to pump faster, going as deep as he can. "Charlie, you are all mine." He emphasizes each word with a heavy thrust, bringing me back to the edge of pleasure.

"Yes," I breathe as my body reacts to each movement. Each word.

"Say it," he commands.

"I'm yours," I call out, my body a rush of sensation.

"I'm yours," he echoes as he pumps his hips. With each motion, I think I might explode again.

He moves his hand to touch the spot where our bodies meet, where the bundle of nerves between my legs is in overdrive. He translates what my body needs seamlessly. A sailor, a spy, a cyclist, and a fervent lover. There is no one else I would want.

"That's it, Charlie," he murmurs in my ear as my breathing quickens. "Come for me," he commands. "Come *with* me."

I'm over the edge.

"Declan!" I call out his name and hear him groan. His face tightens and he releases inside of me.

My body is numb with pleasure, my limbs heavy from the hormones released. My orgasm is powerful and renders me powerless.

I've felt this way before. Out of control, unable to move. Then, I was terrified, unsure of how my body was betraying me. This time, in Declan's arms, I am safe, in control. The waves of pleasure are calm and I am able to focus all my energy on him and his pleasure.

"Charlie," he pants before he collapses next to me on the bed. We lay still for a moment before he stands to dispose of the condom. When he lays back down next to me, I place my hand over his chest. His heart beats fast under my touch. Mine is too. He settles in next to me and holds me in the silent darkness.

His lips caress the crown of my head again, a delicate cherishing kiss. I move slowly and look up at him. Our lips connect once more. We are two puzzle pieces who have finally found their match.

A tired, spent, exhausted, grateful kiss goodnight deepens. Becomes passionate once more. Becomes heated and excited.

Declan envelops me again, pinning me to the bed.

This man, who can go all day long on the bike, who has endurance and speed and strength, shows me that he can go all night too.

38

DECLAN

The early-morning light wakes me. I slept well, even if only for a few hours.

Charlie lays next to me, her breath even as she dreams. Her bare shoulder begs to be kissed, but I don't want to wake her.

I get up and put on my boxers before tiptoeing downstairs. I find my undershirt and put that on too.

I set about making breakfast and discover there is oatmeal. And that is it.

Another check of cabinets reveals some peanut butter and a tin can of coffee. It's not decaf so I know Charlie may refuse it, but I certainly need the caffeine.

After yesterday, there is so much for my brain to unpack. The largest topic on my mind is Charlie. She's the one who has been taking up more and more of my headspace the last few weeks. And now it seems – my heart.

I'm happy. I'm smiling and my face hurts from it because I'm not the kind of person who smiles for no reason. My brain is already forming daydreams of future nights with her, of dates and dinners, and all the things I've avoided for years because no one else was worth the risk.

I'm happy and that terrifies me. Giving into each other last night has shifted the world. *What if the Order targets Charlie? What if they get to her? What if in trying to protect the world Charlie is at risk? Or what if I save Charlie but other people are harmed?*

I need to go for a ride on my bike. I do my best thinking there. Charlie isn't a problem to solve. My fears are.

I set the drip coffee to brew when I hear a buzz coming from the living room. I walk over to find my phone rattling on the corkboard and laminate coffee table.

It's Oliver. "Go for Davidson," I say at my usual volume and then wince. I don't want to wake Charlie and the echo in here is kind of ridiculous.

"Declan, we have a new piece of information. One of the stewards on Castillo's yacht let us know they're about to dock in Ostia, Italy."

"That port gets them close to Rome," I confirm.

"Exactly. Apparently, they'll be docked for over a week," Oliver continues, not mentioning or commenting that my voice is now much quieter.

I nod and turn round at the sound of Charlie stirring in the loft. "So Castillo will be at the World Games to either carry out the attack or act as an alibi for the secondary attack."

"Or both," Oliver answers. "Let's all regroup later this morning at headquarters. Let's say two hours from now?"

"Will do," I confirm.

"Can you pick up Charlie from the safehouse on your way in?" he asks, as I watch the woman in question delicately descend the spiral stairs wearing only the oversized T-shirt I watched her take off last night. I can't help but stare at her legs as she takes careful steps. When she reaches the bottom stair, she looks over at me with a smile before blushing and biting her lip. My mouth is dry, my tongue glued in place. My expression must give away my thoughts.

"Uh yeah, I'll pick her up," I lie after clearing my throat.

Oliver disconnects the line and I make my way over to Charlie, who is pouring two glasses of water in the kitchen.

I offer a "good morning," before I plant a kiss on her head.

She smiles as she twists her hair at the nape of her neck. "Morning."

"Sorry I woke you up," I admit.

Charlie brushes this off and starts to assess the breakfast options. I make a bland bowl of oatmeal while Charlie not so elegantly dips a spoon into the jar of peanut butter and begins to nibble at it.

"How are you this morning?" I ask, knowing this open-ended question could refer to any number of things. Physically. Mentally. Does she feel safe? Does she regret last night?

"Well, I do feel protected in this safehouse, but I think that has more to do with the company than the building," she admits. "I'd give your personal security services a five-star rating, but I'd rather keep you all to myself, so maybe I'd lie and post a one-star."

That smart mouth of hers. I give her ass a little tap, making her squeal and jump lightly.

Best possible answer.

"Oliver is already up with fresh intel," I tell her. I relay the updates, and as I do, the twinkle in her eyes dims. The call from Oliver has burst our bubble. Last night, we forgot about everything outside the walls of the safehouse. It was nice to forget that danger was circling. To forget the potential consequences of our missteps in stopping the Order.

Charlie is brooding, the shadows forming again in her mind. I can't protect her from it forever. We have to face what is going on.

For a few more minutes, I can keep her distracted, though. Keep myself distracted.

"Any chance we can get some fresh clothes for me?" Charlie asks.

"I prefer this outfit," I tell her, which elicits an eye roll from Charlie, as she takes another spoonful of peanut butter.

"Somehow I don't think Uncle Ollie will approve." We're both talking round the elephant in the room: the big question of "what are we now?" Because it's too soon and there's so much at stake outside of this safehouse for us to figure out first. *Are we coworkers with benefits? Or something more?*

"There should be more options upstairs," I tell her as I pour out some coffee. "We can get some decaf for you on the way in. After we discuss the fresh intel this morning, I'll go with you to sweep your place."

Charlie takes all of this information in.

She takes a slow and deliberate lick of the peanut butter on her spoon. This captures all of my attention. My exhausted and overworked member twitches in my boxers, somehow ready to go again.

Charlie mindlessly takes another lick; I don't think she is doing this intentionally, but it's driving me mad. All I can think of is how we used our tongues last night, how we tasted one another. How I long to taste her again.

I step closer and put my hands on her arms. "Charlie, today we're going to get a plan together, OK?"

She nods, accepting this.

"And then, after this long but productive day –" I pause and Charlie glances up at me with her clear blue eyes – "I'm going to take you to dinner."

A smile more brilliant than the sunrise breaks across her face. "Yeah?"

"Yeah," I confirm. "If I'm going to break a rule, I'm going to break it the best way I know how." Then I move my mouth right next to her ear and whisper, "But if you lick your spoon like that one more time, I'm going to have to take you right here."

My eyes move in time to catch her face flush, her coy grin fighting back.

She lifts her spoon to her mouth and slowly and deliberately licks it, cocking her eyebrow, daring me to make good on my threat.

I shake my head and mutter, "Insatiable."

I set my mug down delicately and then with both hands grab her hips and place her on the kitchen counter. Her spoon clatters to the floor, but I don't care. My lips are on hers and her legs wrap round my waist.

This incredible woman: headstrong in the streets, playful in the sheets.

Her mouth tastes like peanut butter and I want to devour her. Our tongues glide together. I move my hips so she can feel how hard I am for her. How much I want her again. The sound that releases from her mouth sends me to another level of carnal need.

"Charlie," I say as I kiss her neck and grab her ass. This ass I've been fantasizing about for a month now. This ass that I want to explore and pleasure. "Last night I worshipped the goddess that you are." She sighs at my words and melts in my hands. "I think this morning I have no choice but to *fuck* you."

I let the word ring loud and clear, echoing in the safehouse.

Charlie's breath hitches before she gives my neck a little love bite.

I slap her ass with my whole hand, lightly but enough to make a loud sound. She yelps playfully in my arms. Then, as expertly as I can, I grab her thighs and tell her to "hang on." I lift her from the counter and climb the stairs up to the loft with her balanced against my hips. She nips at my neck the whole way there. Once we're at the foot of the bed, I lean forwards and release her. She flops onto the bed with a bounce, exposing her naked body beneath the borrowed T-shirt. Charlie lets out an excited giggle before I climb on top of her.

"If this is how you punish me for being a bad girl, I don't think I'll have much incentive to be good ever again."

"Noted," I say with a wink before I lean back and kneel between her legs. Could it be that her excitement and eagerness are symptoms of the same thing I have? The same feelings being reciprocated? If it is, then it's a miracle. That in this callous world with weapons and war and waste we ever found each other. Silently, I vow to never let go of this moment, of her.

I savor the view before I touch her hips and use my hands to roll her over. I lower myself and take a playful light bite of her butt cheek.

Charlie wiggles and moans.

I kiss my way up her back slowly, taking my time. When I reach her neck, Charlie is smiling. She is enjoying this. Which is good. I like knowing that she wants to play a little with me, that we can put the outside world out of our minds and focus on this. I move my body to grind against hers, my dick rock hard and ready to go again.

"Ross, I've had this exact fantasy about you," I whisper in her ear. She exhales a sweet moan as my hand slides between her legs. "I'm going to take my time and enjoy this," I tell her.

Her hips move into mine; we already know each other so well and connect so perfectly.

"Are you ready?" I ask.

"Yes," Charlie says with a tilt of her hips, inviting me to take her from behind.

With that one word, I plunge into her and show her that I am a man of my word.

39

CHARLIE

I pull on a new set of spare clothes that fit me much better.

This outfit is all black. The sweatpants are from some sports drink company with their logo running up the leg and the shirt is from one of our shorter-distance females-only run series. They are both slightly bigger than what I would usually wear, but they'll do just fine for today.

Was Declan nervous last night and picked the first thing he could find, or did he want to give me extra-baggy clothes for modesty? *Or ease of access*, I think.

I didn't expect this rush of feelings. Not just for Declan and how my heart is wanting him, but the joy at the muscle ache. The wonderous happiness that I have missed. My body worked *for* me, and each ache is a blissful reminder – not only of a long night in bed with Declan but of what my body can do. I want all the muscle aches. From running. From working. From loving.

Declan is in the safehouse garage getting his bike gear set for a morning ride. He offered to leave me with his handgun, but I told him I'd be more afraid of accidentally shooting myself if I needed to use it. "Shooting range. Tomorrow," he'd said with finality before walking through the door.

After a few minutes, Declan comes back in wearing his cycling kit. The one he planned to wear on a training ride yesterday evening. Dark blue with white stripes looks good on him. He's striking with the front unzipped and his lean muscles and dark chest hair showing.

"Are you sure you want to get a training ride in now?" I ask.

"Athens is only a month away and I do my best thinking on the bike," he explains.

I get it. I'm proud of him for sticking to his plan.

"I guess there is a lot to riddle out right now," I say. He looks over at me with a curious expression. "About Blaed, and the Order, and the World Games," I remind him, shocked that I need to.

"Yes," he agrees. Then I realize that he may want to think about me, *about us*. If there is an us. My shoulders slump involuntarily. I didn't have to think about it. I'm all his if he wants me.

Declan walks over and grabs my hands in his, interlocking our fingers. When I meet his eyes, he tells me, "I can't think clearly when I'm around you, Ross. And after last night –" he pauses and smiles – "and this morning –" he kisses my cheek – "I'm especially distracted. I need to think about this case."

I beam up at him. How is he able to read my mind and ease my fears?

"The one thing I don't have to think about, the one thing that makes sense right now," he continues, "is this." He gives me a long slow kiss and my body reacts the way it did last night. Curling into him. Wanting more. But also desperately needing rest.

He pulls away and walks back to the door leading to the garage. "We'll leave for headquarters as soon as I get back," he reassures me.

"OK, will you be safe?"

"Of course. And remember, you're locking yourself in. Don't let anyone else in but me."

We agreed to turn on the video-monitoring system since I would be alone, and then I could see him come and go. I nod and show him I'm ready to press the button the second the door closes.

"Just ten miles, OK?" he assures me.

I know it will take him around thirty-five minutes, so I let him get going.

I watch him walk out and then, on the screen from the closed-circuit security feed, I see the garage door open. Declan strolls out with his bike and clasps his helmet on before he mounts the bike and speeds away. I push the button to close the garage and set the security system.

I know the time will fly by, so I do my best to tidy. I pull the sheets from the bed and drop them in a hamper along with the clothes from last night. I'm not sure who does the cleaning here, but I want to make it easy for them. As I put things back the way I found them, I wonder what I'll say the next time I talk to my parents and they ask me about work. Or what I will say to Ana when she gets back to the office on Monday. She's certainly picked up on the vibes between me and Declan and now I have updates! *Or do I?* I so want to chat with her about this. How can I disclose this development without spilling the beans on the secret operations?

I move to the living-room area and gather some of Declan's things. I grab my cavernous purse, the traitor that it is for hiding that tiny tracking device, and pack away my work clothes and Declan's as well. I'm guessing he'll go to the office in his cycling kit.

About twenty minutes after Declan leaves, the front door buzzes. I know Declan is an excellent athlete, but there is no way he finished that quickly, even if he sprinted the whole time.

I see Ian through the security feed. "Charlie, I've got breakfast and updates," he announces through the intercom. He has a pink box in his arm that is likely filled with glutenous pastries I shouldn't have.

"Is this man trying to kill me?" I mutter to myself and press the buzzer to let him in.

I pad barefoot over to the front door and wait for him to enter.

"Hi, Ian," I say brightly as he enters. "There's coffee in the pot if you want some." Then I continue to gather up my items.

"Thank you, Charlie," Ian replies and he heads to the kitchen in my peripheral view. He sets the pink box on the counter and opens it.

"Sure thing," I respond. "What's the update?" I ask, half listening, half tidying. I relock the safehouse just as Declan showed me.

"There's been a security breach," Ian tells me as he stands across the counter from me. *No shit*, I think, given the tracking device we discovered last night. But maybe Ian is referring to a new one. The smell of fresh pastries wafts over to me.

The kitchen is the last room for me to clean up. I need to wash the dishes we used and sweep away some crumbs. I reach for my cell phone in the pockets of the borrowed pants. "Let me tell Declan so we can get on this right away," I say.

"Oh, don't worry," Ian says.

His words catch me by surprise. I stop what I am doing and look up at him. That's when Ian pulls a gun out of the pink box and a silencer as well. He methodically twists the silencer onto the front of the gun as he walks toward me.

"Declan won't be back in time to help," Ian adds matter-of-factly before he takes aim at me.

40

CHARLIE

I don't have seconds to think, or even milliseconds. I have to act.

The dirty oatmeal bowl in front of me is my only weapon. I chuck the bowl at Ian's head and it connects, knocking him back and then shattering on the ground. He stumbles and goes down as well.

I don't have time to check what damage it did to him; I have to run.

If I head for the front door, which I first have to unlock via the security panel, I will cross Ian. If he has any degree of consciousness, he could easily shoot me before I leave.

The tunnels! I race for the back wall and don't dare look behind me. I make it to the massive door and heave it open. I think I can hear Ian moving, but I have to ignore it. Once I'm in the tunnel, I pull the door as hard as I can.

OK, that noise is definitely Ian moving. I have seconds before he can stop me from shutting the door.

The metal door is hefty, but I lean back with all my weight to get it to close. I'm not sure if it latched. I move the wheel lock to try to seal it, but it won't budge.

Shit!

I lean and pull again. *Thud.* Something has landed against the other side of the door. Ian.

He pounds on it. That is what snaps the final centimeter closed. The door *thunks* into place and I push on the wheel.

The lock engages and I take a deep exhale. I'm safe.

An alarm starts to sound on the other side of the door, dampened by the thick metal barrier.

Ian is contained.

But so am I.

The tunnel is dark. I pull my phone out of the pockets of the sweatpants. My battery is low since I didn't get to charge it last night and I have no bars for service. But the flashlight still works. I only need it to last until I get out of this tunnel.

If I get out of this tunnel.

What Declan called an elevator is actually a rudimentary dumbwaiter that has barely enough space for me to fit. I worry it's the original machine used when the tunnel was constructed a century and a half ago, but the rope holds my weight and lands softly on the earthen floor of the tunnel. The acrid air is still. It's like I'm disturbing the tomb of long-buried secrets below the city.

My bare feet are tentative on the cold muddy ground. The passageway is unfinished. I'm not sure when the last person was here.

I have no sense of direction, so I go the only way I can: forwards.

My breath steadies. Ian is locked in. Declan will see the alarm.

My heart stutters as his image floods my mind. He'll blame himself for leaving me. He'll be angry at me a little for letting Ian in. I'm such an idiot. My blind trust has put me in a dangerous situation twice now.

And Ian. *Ian!* Of all people. I will have to figure out how he bypassed us this whole time. How he fooled not just me, but Declan and Oliver as well.

I have to get out of these tunnels. I try not to focus on the sounds around me. It's likely vermin that would dwell below ground. My bare feet and arms are hypersensitive; I'm ready to jump at the first trace of any bugs, snakes, or worse.

Fifty feet later, I come to a wider passage where the air is less stale. I look up and see a ladder. *A way out!*

I pocket my phone and climb. The temperature rises with each rung. I can taste the fresh air, even if I can't see daylight yet.

When I hit the top of the ladder, I balance and reach for the wheel lock. It's stiff.

I try it again, terrified it may only unlock from the outside.

There's no give. I try again and again.

I may have escaped Ian for now, but a new terror starts to sink in – that I may never be able to escape this tunnel. That once my phone dies and there is no light, I'll be plunged into darkness. And then what? How long can I survive down here?

Panic sets in and I pull with everything I have. But it isn't enough.

41

DECLAN

My body is resisting me today. I won't hit my mile goal, so I'll need to turn round at the fifteen-minute mark regardless of my distance. Lack of sleep is the cause. But I can't be mad about it.

Getting out of the safehouse has helped me clear my mind and think. Charlie is a beautiful distraction. She has been since she showed up at FIRE. With what happened last night, I'm hoping she will be less of a distraction. That if we continue down this path, we'll be able to focus at work on work, and focus outside of work on . . . other things.

This past week has changed everything. I used to think I wanted to be alone. Easier to tackle missions. Easier to train. Easier to have no connections. You can't lose what you don't have. But since that kiss in Copenhagen, it's like everything I was pushing down, every thought and feeling I'd ignored, has forced itself to the surface. And it feels good to want someone, to have them – to have more than just a job or a calling. To have someone to share it with.

But first we need to stop the Order from carrying out the attack at the World Games – or elsewhere.

I run through the facts in my mind as I approach the end of Bayshore Boulevard and have to turn back toward Ybor. The sky is a brilliant cloudless blue, the kind they capture in postcards of Florida. This sun will only add to my biker's tan.

As I hit the turn, my phone begins to buzz and beep.

The alarm at the safehouse was triggered.

I stop the bike and grab my phone from the mount. *Did Charlie hit the button because she needed to or was it a mistake?*

I read the notification. It's the tunnel alarm. Someone went into the tunnel and locked the door, sealing the safehouse. *That could not be a mistake.*

I try to think like the Order.

If someone broke into the safehouse to hurt Charlie, they would want to get her out of there if they weren't familiar with the security system. Chances are that Charlie won't be at the safehouse much longer. Unless she's in the tunnels, in which case she's on the move.

I dial her number. The line rings and rings before cutting off. *Maybe there's no reception in the tunnels. Or the phone is still in the safehouse.*

Charlie doesn't have a tracking device on her. *If* she has her phone with her, I could have been able to locate her *if* we had shared locations. *Damn.*

There are too many variables to make any educated guesses. I mount the phone again and get pedaling. I fly down the mixed-use sidewalk, swerving to avoid early-morning runners. Then I think of a way into her phone to track her: hack it. I skid to a stop and find Ian in my contacts. I'll ask him if he can help crack into Charlie's phone to find where it is. It's illegal, and hacking her phone would usually fall under the behavior of someone with trust issues, but it might save her.

Ian's contact card is easy to find and I am about to hit send when something tickles in my mind. Ian has shared his location with me, but I hardly ever need to use it myself. I enabled it so he could track me while on missions. My brain is telling me to look this time.

I click over to his location and see that he is at the safehouse.

There is no way he arrived there to help Charlie already. He must have been there *before* the alarm went off. Charlie would have let him in and then . . .

I play back the past months in my mind.

Ian – who called me to make sure I was in place for the Mexico City rendezvous.

Ian – not able to get us a clear license plate on the motorcyclist who shot at me and Charlie.

Ian – who lost the footage from the Castillo mission.

Ian – who rescued me and Charlie from the storage unit.

Ian – who provided me with images when I needed to identify the buyer from Copenhagen instead of giving me access to the database.

Ian – defensive when Charlie hypothesized a hole in our firewall.

I try to tell myself this can't be true. He has had plenty of opportunity to eliminate me or Charlie or Oliver. Why make a move to capture Charlie now? We've trusted Ian with so much of our operations; he is in the perfect position to do the most damage.

My gut is telling me that Ian has been our mole this whole time. My head is telling me that he can't have been so easily swayed by the Order. But so many already have.

I can only hope that Charlie is in the tunnels and isn't trapped in there with Ian.

I need to think. I need a plan.

I need to save Charlie.

42

CHARLIE

It feels as if I'll never escape when I feel a small torque. It's not much, but it is something. I'm sweating through my clothes. The hot air is working its usual evil magic on me. My hands are slick, a line of sweat meandering its way down my forehead, threatening to sting my eyes. The hair let loose from my bun is sticking to my face.

Another twist and the wheel gives a bit more. I grunt and will the lock to move with everything I have.

The lock releases and I push open the hatch.

Air.

Open air.

Sunlight.

I pop my head out of the hatch and come eye to eye with a perplexed rooster. He pecks at the ground and then struts away. I pull myself out and close the hatch behind me. I want to lay down on the ground and soak in the beautiful daylight, taking gulps of the fresh morning air, but there's no time. I need to figure out where I am so I can get to safety. I can't stay here. Because Ian certainly wasn't acting alone. The sooner I can get to Declan, the better.

I spin and see a monument in the center of a park square. Centennial Park.

Ybor City is known for several things. Nightlife, but the bars and restaurants in my eyeline are closed. It's also known for cigars, hence the safehouse in the rehabbed warehouse. It is a couple miles from Downtown Tampa. If I keep moving, maybe I can catch Declan on his way back to the safehouse.

I take off down one street that looks fine enough. It's too early for any of these businesses to be open yet. My bare feet are sensitive on the brick sidewalks. Most of the hexagon bricks are intact, but the broken ones jut out and hit the tender skin on my soles. I used to run barefoot all the time at my dad's insistence. It helped me with excellent run form, but my callouses have long since healed.

I will myself to pick a direction. I stop again and survey the area. *Think, Charlie, think!* And then I remember my phone!

I pull it out and I have maybe five percent battery left. I do one quick search to help orient myself. Once I know where I am, I head left toward Downtown Tampa. If I can get to Kennedy Boulevard, I can figure out how to get to headquarters. Which will give out first, my feet or my phone battery?

I navigate to my contacts as I keep going down the sidewalk and turn left.

My thumb presses the button to dial Declan and give him an update before this phone dies on me. When I round the corner, I run smack into someone and drop my phone. It's a man a few inches taller than me. He smells like the cologne my dad wears. He steadies himself by holding my arms. This works and neither of us falls down.

"Oh my gosh! I am so, so sorry," I apologize reflexively. I must look like a total mess, with mud and sweat all over my too big borrowed clothes.

"Gotta watch where you're going," the man says. He has kind hazel eyes set into sunworn skin; the kind of tan you get from years spent outside.

"I'm so sorry. I'm glad you're not hurt," I say, repeating my apology, before a plea begins to form on my lips, to ask this man for help, to explain that someone is after me.

Then everything begins to move slowly.

It's a phenomenon I spent time looking up on one of my many hospital visits. I would sense it just before my limbs would go numb. When I told my doctors, they said it only seemed that time was moving slowly because my brain was busy capturing every facet of a stressful moment. It happens to people during car accidents or other physical traumas. They say they can recall every minute detail of the seconds leading up to it, the brain working in overdrive. So when I could recount the exact patches of light peeking through the canopy, the leaves falling into puddles on the course, it wasn't part of my condition. It was a stress response to a traumatic event: losing all control of my limbs.

The first time my legs went completely numb on a training run, I was on a steep trail. I hit the deck and rolled over tree roots and twigs. I knew something was badly wrong. After crawling on my elbows to find the team, my dad hurried over with the first-aid kit. The antiseptic wipes didn't sting. Didn't cool. Didn't do anything. I remember every terrifying millisecond of that ordeal and the moments just before. The crunch of the leaves under me, the sound of my body thumping against the ground, the look on my teammates' faces.

Right now, with this man's hands on my arms, I experience the same sense of time drawing to a stop. A bird flits from one magnolia tree to the next. In the distance, a rooster is crowing. A white van rolls down the street. But I can feel his hands on my arms. I can feel the scratchy gravel beneath my feet, warm but not hot enough to burn yet. This isn't an episode, so why does time feel like molasses?

"Oh, not a problem, Charlie. You're just who I was looking for."

The same heaviness I experienced last night at the bar with Blaed sets over me. The street spins while I stand still. In my periphery, the van slows to a stop and the door rolls open. The grip on my arms tightens like an arm-pressure cuff.

"It's about time we were properly introduced. I'm Xander, but everyone calls me X.C."

All my self-defense practice did nothing to prepare me for this encounter. My mind is telling me to wind my arms round and break his hold. But I'm frozen. All that practice and now I'm too terrified to use it.

He pulls something out of his jacket pocket and covers my face.

Oh, this is what chloroform smells like, I think before everything goes dark.

43

DECLAN

My thumb hovers over the phone screen. I want to break it with my hands. But doing so won't crush Ian. It will only slow me down.

I dial Oliver instead.

He answers after one ring. "It appears as if it's only Ian in the safehouse. I have a view of every angle and I don't see her," is how he greets me. He must be watching the security feed from headquarters.

"I'm on a training ride. I wanted to clear my mind before diving in today," I offer as an explanation and an apology for why I'm not there already.

"It's good you didn't leave to get Charlie right after I called. Could have been both of you there when Ian arrived."

Oliver's relief only fuels my guilt. I should still have been there with her. I shouldn't have left her. But then would Ian have tried to take me out? Shot me first?

"I'll pick you up," Oliver says, not acknowledging my silence.

"Ian is the mole." I say this hard-to-swallow truth aloud.

"Yeah. I did a rewind on the video log from just before the alarm sounded. He took aim at Charlie and she fought back. After she fled to the tunnels, Ian tried to pull out the security panel and mess with the wiring, but it appears he electrocuted himself. Then he threw around most of the small furniture pieces trying to break the windows. They're not going to budge. Now I can see him pacing," Oliver says, growling through the phone.

The alarm went off four minutes ago, maybe five. I can picture Ian covering his ears as the piercing sound repeats over and over. It's a small justice to know the noise may drive him mad.

"Did you suspect?" I ask, recalling that Oliver did not tell Ian about his decoy attack theory earlier this week.

"I've suspected everyone at one time or another. You're not the only one who was betrayed in Osaka. I ignored my gut. I thought it was just—" Oliver cuts himself off.

He doesn't have to fill in the rest. I know exactly what he's trying to say. After Osaka, I've questioned everyone over and over again. I've been testing and retesting everyone around me. I could have told Ian yesterday evening, told him I knew exactly who Blaed was. Was I testing Ian? My gut – my instincts – suspected before I was aware.

We hang up and I wait for Oliver. I remove my helmet and try my best not to pace, not to panic.

Charlie isn't in the safehouse. Confirmed.

Would she stay in the tunnels? Or would she find a way out?

Some cafés should be opening up soon. If she's outside, she'll know to seek a crowded space. I worry about her running blind through the streets. Her body would already be primed for exhaustion and now aimless, countless miles running to safety. This is not going to be good for her.

Come on, Charlie. Where are you?

Oliver pulls up in his silver luxury SUV and pops the back hatch. I place my bike in the back and get in. I don't care if my sweaty cycling kit damages his leather seats. It's been ten minutes since the alarm sounded now. We still haven't located Charlie, but we have time. I keep telling myself that over and over. *We have time.*

My phone buzzes. It's Charlie!

I answer and put her on speakerphone immediately. "Charlie," I call out. But it sounds like she is far away. Is her phone in her pocket?

Someone is with her. I can't hear anything, so I turn up the volume as loud as it can go. And that's when a familiar voice fills the car.

"I'm Xander, but everyone calls me X.C."

"What the . . ." Oliver mutters next to me.

I hear the sounds of footsteps and a car door slamming and then the line disconnects. But I can't move. I can't think.

Because that was X.C. I'd know that voice anywhere.

But X.C. died in Osaka.

I try to think back to that evening. The fog obscuring our view of the bay. The rendezvous that was beyond delayed. We should have gotten out of there way earlier. X.C. said he heard something and walked further down the dock. And then the blast and I was in the water.

But if he's still alive, then what happened? He didn't come back to headquarters. Didn't come to pull me from the water, but he knows I'm a strong swimmer. I try to make the puzzle pieces fit with who I know X.C. to be. Old loyalties die hard. But the mental picture of what happened that night and, in the months since, is ash in my hands.

Oliver's voice breaks through to me. "Declan, you know what this means?" he asks, but it's a rhetorical question. He has riddled it out before I can.

"He betrayed us," I manage to say, although I still can't believe it.

It was X.C. who sabotaged the mission. X.C. who set the dock to explode and let me stand there, knowing full well I could have died. X.C. who walked away without seeing me exit the water, who assumed I'd drowned. X.C. who recruited Ian to spy for him. X.C. who built his own cartel of mercenaries who would do his bidding, no matter who was footing the bill.

"Betrayal" is such a small word for the depth of the pain he has caused.

"Yes, and now he has Charlie." Oliver's words are clear and urgent.

Her name snaps me out of my spiral. *Charlie.*

X.C. is alive and that lying motherfucker has Charlie!

44

CHARLIE

I open my eyes to more darkness. Not complete total pitch black but a hazy gray. There are thin lines of light in the distance, sliding under whatever doorways or windows it can. It is enough to tease me with the promise of outside – of freedom. The air here is stale, like it has been trapped and left to rot for years. I know it isn't the tunnels because it smells metallic with a hint of diesel.

I move my sore muscles slowly, but I can't budge more than a half-inch. The unmistakable scratch of rope digs into my wrists and ankles. I suspect whatever is keeping me in place is another rope against my chest. Thankfully, these clothes from the safehouse are thick and protect my skin. Cold hard metal against my bare arms tells me I am, in fact, tied to a chair. How fucking clichéd is Xander Caruso?

I fidget more, hoping to find a weak spot in the knots. I don't find any give. Then I remember both X.C. and Blaed are ex-navy. Sailors are good at knots. I grunt in frustration. My head hurts and my stomach is queasy. *Does chloroform make you feel sick too?*

My motion must have caught someone's attention. Footsteps echo off whatever space we are in. Intuitively, I know that whoever is coming will not help me. There is no point calling out and asking who is there. It's X.C. or Ian or Blaed or someone else I want nothing to do with.

With a resounding *thunk*, harsh light pours over me. My eyes, accustomed to the dark, beg for relief behind my eyelids. I hear the distinct shutter click of a smartphone. Cool. Whatever else this creep is into, they now have a photo of me bound.

I hazard to open my eyes. More lights have been engaged. They look like those construction-site lights: bare bulbs in a metal cage.

"Charlie Ross," says the man I ran into in Ybor, taunting me. The man who I thought, stupidly, might be able to help. Xander Caruso. The jerk who betrayed Declan, Oliver, FIRE, and his own morals.

I grunt, not willing to give him any satisfaction. He is outlined in light, his figure a shadow.

A second set of footsteps approaches. I'm outnumbered.

A familiar figure steps into the light. Blaed. He mutters something to Xander, their voices so low I can't make anything out. They conclude their brief exchange and Blaed turns and gives me a wink before walking off. If looks could kill, he would be vapor right now. X.C. would be next.

"Is this where you tell me your evil plan before you kill me?" I say, putting on my bravest voice as I test the ropes again. The rope keeping me to the chair isn't as tight as the others. If I stand, I could probably get up. But my ankles being tied would ensure a faceplant. Honestly, I wouldn't mind an explanation. X.C. is alive, so clearly his "death" in Osaka was faked. But why? And was it necessary to almost kill Declan as well? Or was that his goal all along? I highly doubt he's about to tell me that he's so deep undercover that he has to "play" the bad guy. I'm bound and restrained after being kidnapped. He's the bad guy, alright.

X.C. laughs. "You're clever. I can see why Oliver hired you. But you're much more valuable alive. For now, at least."

I'm not relieved by these words. "What do you want?" Why would he tell me? And would I actually trust anything he said? Still, I want to know.

"To complete the job I've been tasked with by some very *powerful* friends," X.C. says as if this should be obvious. *The Order, he's been working for them all along.*

I correct him. "To let a massive cache of black-market arms loose and watch as innocent people die?"

X.C. laughs again. "Oliver wants to play James Bond. Let him. But developing the underdeveloped world takes money and resources. It's done by businesses, not charities."

"So why the weapons?" I ask, since I'm pretty sure weapons destroy; they don't build anything.

X.C. stalks closer to me, a smirk on his face. "Underdeveloped countries are easily overthrown by the warlord with the biggest hoard. He who provides the arms to the one in power gets the contract. Are you keeping up with me, Ms. Ross?"

His patronizing tone makes me want to spit in his face. But he has a gun in his hip holster, so I decide to not antagonize him.

"All of the weapons are being used to buy off politicians?" I clarify.

"Warlords, not politicians," X.C. says. "But, really, a suit and tie are the only difference between the two. And no, not everything is for exchanges. We have one special set ready to make a big impact." He sounds almost giddy about this. I want to ask him about the oaths he swore, about his duty to America, to the world. Did he forget all of that when he retired from the navy? But I don't think I'm in any place to psychoanalyze him.

"At the World Games?" I try to confirm. At least I'll have intel if I ever get out of here.

My stomach clenches. I have no idea how late it is, or if this is a side effect of the chloroform.

X.C. examines the dirt under his fingernails, as if speaking to me is lower than this on his priority list. "Oh, we've got something planned for the Games, but not what you think. Our little surprise is . . ." He leans closer to me, his fetid breath finding my nostrils. "Well, let's call it a fireworks show. Emphasis on *FIRE*."

I narrow my eyes at him, parsing out the meaning. FIRE is the target. Will it be our headquarters? An upcoming event?

Exponential Endurance Championships? My mind races with the possibilities.

"FIRE may mean well, but the operations Declan is running for Oliver are starting to spoil the Order's plans." X.C. purses his lips. "I respect Declan. I started to test the waters with him, to see if he might be persuaded to join me. But he loves playing superhero too much. I knew he'd only be a hindrance. Poor timing on my part that the bomb didn't finish him off." He tilts his head to the side before shaking it with disapproval. There are so many layers of messed-up in the dynamic between Declan and X.C. Commanding officer and soldier. Mentor and follower. A pseudo-father figure and a young man eager to prove his worth. Hearing X.C. speak of killing Declan as if it was another task on his list makes my heart hurt.

"Still, FIRE must be stopped," X.C. continues as he begins to pace, proud to spell out his plans. "And could you imagine if a charitable donation of leftover shirts going to innocent children was rigged with explosives?" He feigns shock and his features reveal a wicked smile. "The outrage! The cry for accountability and answers. The company who caters to the wealthy, who has a perpetual problem of mostly serving rich white males, implicated in the deaths of innocent children, all clamoring for their free King Cool goodies."

X.C. takes one of the hanging bulbs and shines it to my right. The locks on the shipping container next to us belong to FIRE.

The shirts! That's what someone – likely Ian – was messing with in the storage unit. Locking me and Declan in there wasn't about trapping us or even bugging our computers; it was about *implicating* us.

I realize where we are. I'm tied to a chair in a hallway created by stacks of shipping containers. That dank smell is the damp of the ship. The uneasy feeling in my stomach is from the imperceptible rocking of the vessel we're on.

"What does Raj have to do with this?"

"Ah, I hear I have you to thank for that, Charlie," X.C. says, sneering like the Grinch with a wicked plan. "Ian told me you were so happy to coordinate the leftover FIRE shirts to go to Raj's charity. Here I was wracking my brain for a way to eliminate him and you give me this gift. Two problems, one explosion. Not only is his do-gooder nature making my clients, like Frank Castillo and the rest of the Order, look bad, but he's building infrastructure with other local charities, helping 'the people' help themselves. Which means the companies run by members of the Order aren't getting the business. They don't get any exclusive contracts for power, internet, the works.

"With Raj and his charity in shreds, people will seek out established brands, like the ones my clients run. And then we'll do a little reputation management by eliminating Raj. If not in the actual explosion, then by the same PR nightmare FIRE will be facing. When your shipment of donations kills the deserving children, there'll be enquiries. Raj will be ruined, if not actually killed. Pity. FIRE will be under a microscope.

Declan and Oliver and their little spy plans will have to be put on hold."

I glare at him, speechless at the depravity of his plan. How does someone go from leading soldiers and being an exemplary officer to this? What could possibly justify this? Then I remember Raj being delayed en route to Kalispell. His medicine was stolen; his bags routed incorrectly. Was X.C. unsuccessfully sabotaging him before?

"We can't have FIRE ruining our plans," X.C. continues. "We'll finalize payment for the arms deal in Rome when every world leader is present. While the world is cheering for their favorite sports, the explosion in Côte d'Ivoire will draw international outrage. We can't have Raj helping to develop these nations without the Order's resources and materials."

I am without words. The scale of this plan, the seamless nature of it. It's truly that evil form of genius.

X.C. keeps elaborating. "And once Oliver and Declan know that the only way to prevent your untimely demise is to sit tight and not say a word to the authorities in Italy or Côte d'Ivoire, we expect full cooperation."

X.C. and the Order are discrediting FIRE and eliminating Raj. It's cruel but well thought-out.

X.C. stops his pacing when I say the only words I can form. "Damn, that's a good plan."

45

DECLAN

We drive a few blocks before pulling over. Oliver parks and we hash out our theories. It's been twelve minutes since Charlie called. "Let's determine where we think he might take her before we head back to headquarters. I may send you back out on your bike to go find her," he tells me.

We need to find her first, then we can address Ian's deception and figure out just how long X.C. was working against us before he staged his death.

"We could message one of Ian's team to ask if they could hack his computer for us . . ." I begin.

Ian may have secret messages from X.C. that could give us some clue, but I'm not sure I trust any of his team until we can re-evaluate anyone our head of IT hired in the last year. The look Oliver gives me confirms he has the same qualms.

My phone chimes, as does Oliver's.

I check my device and it is a message from Charlie. I tap open the message at the same time Oliver murmurs "Jesus!" under his breath.

The message loads on my phone. It's an image.

Charlie is tied to a chair. Her face is tight. She is wincing in pain, or perhaps at the harsh light on her.

Charlie Ross

Tampa shipyards. Now.

That's all the text below the image reads.

"It's X.C.," I say aloud.

I want to scream. I want to rage and pound my fists against Oliver's luxurious dashboard. I want to end X.C. for all he has done to hurt and betray me, and now he has Charlie! I wanted to punch Blaed and Castillo for being flirty with her. But this?! Kidnapping her? Tying her up? I will murder this man if I ever see him again. It is a fact.

Oliver starts the car and navigates to the other side of town. Each stoplight is a personal affront. Every slow driver is culpable, an accomplice to Charlie's kidnapping.

This is a nightmare. This is the epitome of terror.

My greatest fear has been realized, and not even twelve hours have passed since I decided to break my steadfast rule. Since I let Charlie in and let myself love her, and now she has already been taken. My subconscious is playing out in real time. My anger subsides to let in a crushing wave of sadness and loss. Can we get there in time? Can we save her? What if we can't?

Lock it up, Davidson, I chide myself. There will be time for emotions later. Not now. I need to focus and think. To use my specialized skills to save her.

My mind races with options. Can I trade myself for Charlie? Whatever fate X.C. has planned for her, I'll step in and take it. The man wanted me dead before anyways.

Stress radiates from Oliver as well. "I'll never forgive myself," he mumbles as we sit at the longest red light known to man.

I feel the same exact way. I shouldn't have left. To go on a training ride? Yes, it was to clear my head so I could think straight. But I shouldn't have left her.

Our conversation from last night replays in my mind. "Do you sometimes think someone else could save the day?" she'd asked me. I'd reflexively answered no because all I've ever wanted to do was help, to save people. It's who I am. And when it comes to Charlie, I'll be damned if I don't try to save her now. I get what she was after, though. Can someone else take all the risk? Can I let my life be dedicated to something else? For once in my life, the answer to letting someone else be the hero is both no and yes. I want to be the one to save the day, but I also don't want the day to have to be saved at all.

We near the port and I ask Oliver, "What's our plan? Come in hot? Split up?"

Oliver gestures for me to pop open the glove compartment. One handgun is in there. I check and it's loaded. "I have another in the back."

I nod, grateful that I don't have to tell him my handgun is in the glove compartment of my SUV, which is at the safehouse because I spent the night there.

"We have a shipment of leftover shirts heading out today from the Tampa shipyards," Oliver explains. "I don't believe in coincidences. I bet whatever ship it's on, that's where they're keeping Charlie."

I remember this now; Charlie was managing something about it when we were in the storage unit.

"Have you neutralized Ian?" I ask Oliver.

He pulls up his phone and the video feed for the safehouse. Ian is rocking on the floor next to the metal door to the tunnels, his face scrunched in pain.

"He isn't the only one who knows his way around a keyboard," Oliver says with a wink. "Jammed the wireless signal. Even with his unlimited data, he's not getting a message in or out of there. And I'm not about to let up on the alarm either. Let him burst an eardrum for his trouble." Oliver pockets his phone.

I give him a nod, because it's not my place to tell my boss "good work!" but with Ian contained, we now know there shouldn't be any extra surprises waiting for us inside.

The shipyard is locked on a Saturday morning so Oliver parks outside. I get out and tuck the handgun into the pouch at the back of my cycling jersey. Oliver heads to the back of his SUV and opens his toolbox. Roadside tools, a set of shears, and a spare gun are what he needs.

First, we use the jack to prop the car and Oliver turns on the hazard lights, giving us a plausible explanation for the car being on this stretch of road. The shears cut a perfect line in the fence so we can sneak in. Now all we have to do is find the right ship.

I give a nod to Oliver and we get moving. There's no time to waste.

I'm coming for you, Charlie.

46

CHARLIE

X.C. recoils from my comment about his plan being good. I don't mean good as in altruistic or beneficial; I mean good as in elegant, air-tight, and deviously well planned.

He narrows his eyes, assessing me.

"What made you this way? To think this is OK? You want to create chaos to pave the way for billionaires to make more money?" I can't hide the disgust in my voice.

"I want to see the world developed, and this is the way it gets done. Business. The way it always has. People bitch about colonialism, but, hey, it worked." X.C. gestures around him, as if the interior of this ship were somehow evidence of peak civilization.

I am rendered speechless by his disregard for lives lost and history forever altered by greed.

"Didn't you used to have ideals? Wasn't there a reason you joined the navy?"

I think of Declan. How he does the right thing because it is the right thing to do – even when no one is watching. How his idea of rebelling as a teen was to join the Naval Academy instead of West Point. How did X.C. ever disguise his true self from Declan, and for so long?

X.C. huffs in frustration. "Yes, for service and duty. And after nineteen years, I was honorably discharged."

This man has no honor, is all I can think.

My silence invites him to elaborate further. "Nineteen years. Not twenty. No pension. No lifetime healthcare benefit. A parting 'fuck you' for my years of service. So now I'm working for a team that pays. Up front and in full."

Money. Money has corrupted him, like so many men before him. Like waking to find myself tied to a chair, it's a pathetic cliché.

X.C. resumes his pacing, done with our conversation.

His shoes make this annoying squeak every time he turns. The sound refuses to fade into white noise, demanding my attention.

My legs and arms vacillate between the tingles of my limbs falling asleep and the deep pain of being stuck in this position. I wiggle my torso and roll my shoulders. I move my stiff neck from side to side. The satisfying crack is nothing compared to the slight jump X.C. gives at the sound. *Good*.

My options are slim. Do I bargain for my life? Do I offer to join the Order and become a double agent just to escape and deal with the consequences later?

Uncle Ollie and Declan will never agree to sit quietly and ignore the impending attacks. They would never let innocent people die if they could stop it. I know, deep down, when X.C. asks them to trade my one life for the lives of many that they will agree, but keep working to find the arms, thwart the threat, and save as many people as possible. They'll fight to save everyone – including me, because they aren't going to take this man at his word.

I don't either. Which is why I know that even if I live through the summer, I don't trust X.C. to release me once the attacks are carried out. No way.

At best, Oliver and Declan acquiescing buys me a few extra weeks as the ship makes its way from Tampa to Africa to find a way to escape. Once these terror attacks and arms exchange are complete, I'll be collateral damage.

I tell myself this is good. I can surely think of a way to escape in all that time. Declan and Oliver will make it happen.

X.C. arrives back in front of me again. His sidearm is on display. The survival instinct in my mind tells me I need to get my hands on that weapon.

The realist in me recognizes that another scenario could play out. Uncle Ollie and Declan could refuse X.C.'s scheme and vow to stop the Order. At which point, X.C. (or Blaed, wherever he has disappeared to) could pull a gun out and kill me. It is a true no-win situation. *Yeah, this sucks.*

I do another visual survey. The lights give me a better outline of the shape of the interior holding space. There's a cargo bay door ahead, maybe thirty feet away. Forty? If I can get up and somehow untie my feet, I can get to freedom. Of all the times I've lamented that I couldn't run, this is the one time I truly, physically, can't.

The irony would kill me, if X.C. weren't likely to do so in the near future.

47

DECLAN

The Port of Tampa is not big by any means, but the ships waiting to be launched are. The docks can only accommodate a handful of shipping vessels given their size, though I used to be stationed at massive naval bases that dwarf this port on much smaller ships.

The shipyard, however, is surprisingly empty, but the ship isn't due to set sail until this evening. Perhaps the crew hasn't arrived yet.

The morning cool has baked off and the sun is beginning its work in earnest. No longer calm and humid, the heat is here. The ships only provide a sliver of shade when we are next to them. The concrete and rusting shipping containers are sun-bleached. I'm sure the same process is happening to my skin, my eyes.

Oliver leads the way to the imposing vessel discreetly. I keep an eye out as we approach, ready to engage with anyone X.C. might have with him.

Once we're topside, Oliver and I assess our options. Our primary goal is to find where X.C. is holding Charlie. From the photo, it appears she's inside the hull. It is clear that to have any hope of finding her we need to split up.

We duck behind a container. The high stacks of metal blocks are daunting. As if they could topple at any moment.

"You ready for this?" Oliver asks as he eyes the narrow walkway between the containers.

I nod. "Now that I know that asshole left me for dead, oh, I'm ready."

Oliver lets out a sharp exhale. "That's what I was worried about. Use your head, Davidson. Our goal is to get Charlie. If we can locate any of the explosives and neutralize them, that would be great too, but the first goal is Charlie. Revenge is further down the list." Oliver's words are exactly what I need to hear. Because my anger, my rage toward Xander, was blinding me. The image he sent us, of Charlie tied up and wincing, flashes in my mind. I may never forget it as long as I live.

"Understood. Let's get our girl," I say.

Oliver stares at me blankly before giving me a stern nod. I don't have time to wonder if I may have given away my feelings for Charlie in just a few words.

He heads down the path between the containers, searching for some way into the hull. I move to the edge of the ship to check the perimeter for an entrance.

X.C. demanded we meet but gave us no further instruction. It has the hallmarks of a double cross. I guess that's his specialty now.

As I continue to the stern, I pass the massive structure that leads to the bridge. It towers above the already dizzying heights of the containers.

Where would X.C. have the best strategic advantage? Inside that elevated bridge, he would have an unobstructed view, but it would be difficult to escape – for Charlie, for me, or for himself.

I keep an ear out for any sounds. Aside from my own breath and footsteps, I hear nothing. As if this is a ghost ship, as if Charlie may already be gone. I press on, hoping this mission doesn't end like it did in Osaka, with me in the water and X.C. getting away.

48

CHARLIE

No one ever tells you that being a hostage is infuriatingly boring. The silence. The lack of information.

Despite all the insipid waiting, I have still not riddled a way out of this. The situation or my ropes.

I have no way to track time. The thin slivers of daylight coming in from the outside are getting shorter. The sun is higher. With this, the temperature rises. While there is no light coming in to add any heat, there is also no air-conditioning. This ship was meant to haul stuff, not humans. Sweat trickles onto my lips. It's the only thing I've had to drink since my meager breakfast of peanut butter and water.

I think I might be delirious when the first muffled *thud* calls my attention. It sounds both close and far.

Blaed walks up to X.C., his brisk footsteps drowning out whatever I thought I heard. They converse quickly. I can't make out any of the words, which is annoying.

Blaed exits once more, this time down a narrow opening to my left.

I hear the noise again.

A few things occur to me at once.

1. X.C. specifically named Oliver and Declan in his plan. He must intend to tell them he has me captive, or he already has. He expects them to come for me.

2. While my hands, ankles, and torso are bound, my mouth is not covered. Is X.C. counting on me to call out for help? To draw them in? For what? A verbal spat? Or perhaps a more lethal showdown, given that both Blaed and X.C. are armed.

3. The noise I am hearing must be either Oliver or Declan. They are so close, my heart is singing. But this is a bad situation. One or all of us could be shot or killed. The consequences of what I say and when I say it matter.

I think on it before the noise sounds again. *Thud*. Should I stare ahead coolly, as if this is exactly what I expected? As if help is right on time. It might unnerve X.C. or he could call my bluff.

My immediate default would be to call out "I'm in here!" Which *duh, captain obvious*. Not helpful. It's not going to give Oliver or Declan any useful information that the sound of my voice wouldn't already provide.

The noise rings out again, this time much louder. Closer. I hear the grating scrape of metal on metal.

X.C. turns to face me, a sinister glow in his eye. He palms his handgun and unlatches the safety.

"There's only two—" is all I manage to scream out before Blaed returns and covers my mouth from behind me.

X.C. shakes his head. Blaed's strong hand covers both my mouth and nose. X.C. helps him to untie my ankles. Once my legs are free, I begin to kick wildly.

X.C. backs away before I can make contact. His gun is raised, ready to take aim once he locates his target.

Blaed uses his free arm to lift me from the chair. The rope round my torso drops to the ground once I'm standing and a new sensation touches my back. Even through my clothes, I can make out the shape. Round and hard. The muzzle of his gun.

We wait for whoever is here to enter.

"Charlie!" The only voice that would make me happier is Declan's, but hearing Oliver is great too.

I don't want to be shot. I really, really don't want to be shot. But I need to let Uncle Ollie know I'm here. I do the first thing that comes to mind and stick out my tongue. Blaed jolts his hand a few millimeters. It's enough, and then I open wider and bite down on his hand as hard as I can.

"Bitch!" he cries out.

"Don't shoot!" X.C. hisses at Blaed. "We have no leverage without her!"

Blaed curses under his breath and wraps his arms round my neck, his gun again at my back. I'm a human shield now. I can't believe I ever thought this guy was cute or nice. His touch makes my skin crawl.

"I'm coming, Charlie!" Uncle Ollie calls out once more. I can't see where he is, but knowing he's near gives me hope.

X.C. is on edge, turning this way and that to see where Oliver will come from. He's terrified right now. That's an advantage.

A *bang* rings out to my right. X.C. and Blaed both turn to face it. Then another *clang* to the left.

They shift again, me with them.

The recognizable *thump thump thump* of running feet approaches. Uncle Ollie grunts and then slams into X.C. Xander hits one of the metal bins hard and his weapon drops and so does he. The sound of the impact reverberates.

Then Uncle Ollie turns toward Blaed.

This is all wrong. Blaed has a clear open shot on Uncle Ollie; he needs to move. Another set of distant thuds begins to sound. *Declan!* My heart sings, hoping it is him. Blaed tightens his arm round my neck. I want to pull his arm down, but my hands are still tied behind my back.

I need to act quickly because this standoff between Uncle Ollie and Blaed has to end somehow. And both guns are pointed directly at or very close to me. I give my uncle as subtle a nod as I can and hope he catches it.

With all the force I have, I pick up my right leg, my power leg, my starting leg for every race, and smash my bare foot down onto Blaed's foot. Sure, if I had a steel-reinforced boot or my running spikes it might have more impact. But I'm working with what I have.

Blaed lists to one side for a second and I kick backwards, hoping to hit his most sensitive bits. Instead, Blaed releases my neck and grabs my ankle, stalling my momentum and causing me to faceplant. I expect the bruise to be gnarly.

Before I hit the ground, Uncle Ollie lunges.

Blaed fires off a shot but misses. The bullet hits the metal. The ricochet echoes around us. Another metal-on-metal whine.

"Declan . . ." My parched lips scratch out his name.

X.C., who was down on the ground, stands and runs down the dark passageway. *Coward.*

I don't hear any more signs of Declan's approach; I can no longer hear anything over the grunting between Blaed and Uncle Ollie.

Even with my arms tied, I find my way up to standing. The metal chair I was bound to is in front of me. I make a knee-jerk decision to kick it over. As Oliver and Blaed dance around each other, knowing someone has to shoot first. The sound of metal against concrete is loud and both Oliver and Blaed flinch, but Oliver clocks what I'm doing. The next motions happen too fast for Blaed to move out of the way.

Oliver takes a half-step forwards and Blaed steps back and topples over the chair. A bullet flies up to the ceiling. I duck and try to cover, hoping that if it ricochets back to the ground, it won't hit me. Then, with Blaed on his back, I do the ugliest thing I've ever done as a human. I kick. My bare feet are taking a beating themselves because Blaed's body is rock hard. But I know I land a few solid blows when he calls out in pain. Oliver grabs Blaed's gun and pockets it. Quickly, before Blaed can stand, my uncle uses his pocketknife to cut my wrists free.

My shoulders are unforgiving as I bring my arms forwards. Oliver places a spare gun in my shaking hands as he stands over Blaed.

"Uncle Ollie," I whisper, my head light. From the lack of food, heat, sudden and powerful movements, the fact that there is a gun in my hand. One of these factors, all of these factors. I've never felt this way before. Drained after a race, sure? I've gone numb and tingly with my episodes. But this is new, and whatever it is, it's not good. But I need to help. Right now, we have Blaed outgunned. That could still change. In the distance, I hear the telltale whine of sirens.

Uncle Ollie gently guides my hand so I am pointing the gun at Blaed. *Oh God, I hope I don't have to use it.*

While I stand over Blaed, my uncle uses the ropes that once tied me to bind him.

I keep telling myself I have to focus for just one more minute. Just one more.

"This is not the kind of dynamic work environment I was looking for, Uncle Ollie," I pant with less conviction than I intend. My voice is whisper thin, but it still merits a smirk from my boss.

The sirens are getting louder. Closer.

Quick footsteps behind me are a reminder that they aren't here yet.

I turn toward the sound. Declan is running along the narrow pathway that X.C. escaped down. Bright white spots dot my vision, and I am so light but also so heavy at the same time.

I hit the floor before I can even touch Declan. Before he can reach me.

49

DECLAN

My eyes beg for sleep. My head announces a headache will arrive soon if I don't rest. Still, I get back to work. A few more emails and then I can stop. I tap out the necessary messages and shut down the screen I've been staring at for two hours.

Today has been relentless. Even though the authorities arrived to take Blaed into custody earlier today, Oliver and I stayed on site to respond to every question they had for us. We gave answers. Some more forthcoming than others.

They were also dispatched to apprehend a trespasser in a company-owned property. The cavalry went to the safehouse to take Ian in. Neither Oliver nor I wanted to see him. I've spent the past hour ensuring his access to any FIRE systems was thoroughly revoked.

Oliver was able to back up everything he said with security footage. Ian went to the property and pointed a gun at Charlie. She escaped, only to be taken by Xander Caruso and Blaed Johannson. They're now involving the federal authorities to track down X.C., who fled like a little bitch. No mention of their motive, though.

And Charlie. My breath catches and I tell myself to push it aside. The fear, the self-loathing. I don't have the luxury of letting that crash over me. Not yet. It feels like a week has passed since I woke up next to Charlie in the safehouse this morning. How blissful the day began is a cruel reminder of how quickly it devolved.

I close my laptop and set it on the coffee table before standing.

Being in Charlie's apartment is like we're in stasis; we're in a cocoon of safety. Within this home, I can forget everything outside. We can stay here and nothing can get to us. But that's not reality.

I make my way down the hallway to her room. Charlie is asleep on her bed, where I tucked her into her pink frilly duvet.

She lost consciousness on the container ship. The paramedics checked her. Her blood sugar was dangerously low. Thankfully, she was able to eat and relay her story to the police before they drove her to the hospital for further examination. Blood tests, a walking cast for her foot, and a follow-up appointment with a podiatrist scheduled, and she was released.

Oliver and I didn't get to the hospital until she was nearly ready to be discharged. When it was time to leave, Oliver offered Charlie a ride home. We all piled into his car and I asked him to drop me off at the safehouse to get my SUV. Oliver didn't ask about how my vehicle got there before it went on lockdown. He didn't show his suspicions, which would have been confirmed when Charlie changed vehicles and asked me to drive her home.

I lean against the doorframe and watch her rest. *She's safe*, I remind myself. For now, she is safe.

As if Charlie can sense my presence, she stirs, gently opening her eyes. "Hey," she coos, reaching for her glasses out of habit.

I walk over so I can hand them to her. The bruises on her wrists from the ropes catch my attention. The welt on her face is already purple, though the ice pack I left her with has kept the swelling down. I raised her foot up on one of her throw pillows, her new boot waiting for her at the edge of her bed. Seeing her injuries, my anger builds again. "I got it," I tell her as I sit next to her on the bed.

She puts on her glasses and props her head up on her elbow, still lying down. "Thank you," she says, as her free hand stretches for mine.

I have so much to say and I don't want to say any of it, so I swallow my words.

"Any updates?" she asks. Her memory of this morning must be fuzzy.

I nod. "Yeah, Oliver and Celine are handling the local papers to make sure FIRE isn't mentioned in any coverage. She drove up from our Miami event to sort it out. We removed the container heading to Côte d'Ivoire, and the bomb squad is going through it meticulously to remove the explosives." A deep breath escapes me and I rub my eyes.

"I should contact Raj and his team. Better to forget the damn shirts at this point," she mutters and reaches for her phone.

"Already on it," I assure her.

Charlie glances at the clock on her bedside table. It's late afternoon. "You've been working this whole time?"

"You know me," I respond.

"Declan," she says before taking a deep breath. I know what's coming. She will apologize and explain. But she isn't to blame for any of this. I already start to shake my head, rejecting her apology.

"I'll never forgive myself," I whisper, hoping this strong woman doesn't see me for the weak coward that I am.

"It's not your fault." She squeezes my hand. "I'm a big girl. At any point, I could have quit. After you locked me out. After we were shot at. After being stuck in a storage unit. After any of it. I could have quit my job, broken my lease, and run back home."

I watch her as she says this. The color has returned to her cheeks, the light in her eyes is bright.

"I stayed because I want to help. I want my life to mean something."

"But the risk, the danger . . ." I begin.

"Life is risk. Life is danger. I could have risked an autoimmune flare by going for a run or eating something my body doesn't like. I could have been hit by a bus any day this week. If I'm living this life, I want to live it."

I silently consider her words.

"And you should too."

I shake my head. "I had a rule for a reason. My worst fears played out today. Charlie, I've only had a brief moment to care for you, and you were taken from me. They could have killed you."

"Declan," she says.

"I can't," I admit. "I can't let this happen again. I care for you too much." I stop speaking because I know I'm about to cry. "I think I might –" I stop myself before I say "love" because the word is too powerful. Once I say it, I know my heart will accept it. And that will make this all the more difficult. I glance down at her hand, the one that's intertwined in mine. The one that is bruised and bandaged.

"Declan, they were coming after me anyways," she murmurs.

I look at her, willing this to be true, but shake my head. "No."

"Yes. That Blaed guy planted a device on me in my first week. When I was Oliver's assistant. Before anything with us started."

"But they knew what you mean to me," I explain. "They sent a picture to my phone of you tied up because they knew how much it would hurt me."

"Now they know what we mean to *each other*," she corrects, "they'd still come after me to get to you or go after you to get to me. Should we both be miserable staying apart from each other *and* have to contend with that?"

I had everything I wanted last night and today it's frightening to hope again.

"Declan, I can't do this without you. It will be torture to not be with you. To see you fall out of love with me." Her mention of the word has my attention jumping from her hands to her eyes. "To see you one day decide that someone else is worth breaking your rule for." Her blue eyes are swimming with tears. I want to kiss them all away. "I won't beg you to be with me, Declan." She shakes her head. "If you set this boundary, I'll respect it. Even if I hate it." She looks away, as her tears spill over. "I know you want what's good for me," she says as though she's explaining it to herself. This woman in front of me is so strong. She'll do what's "right" for her, even if it feels wrong. She quit her passion for running because it was best for her health. And she'll quit me too if I demand it.

But I don't want what is good for her. I want her to live a great life. And I want one too. Sometimes good is the enemy of great. A steady string of tears silently spills down her cheek.

My heart snaps. *I made her cry*. It's the worst thing I've ever done. And I promise myself it will never happen again.

All this time I've wanted to be the hero, to save the day. It's always stressful and it makes me stronger; my walls go up higher. But this time I literally just rushed in to try to save the girl. And sitting here next to Charlie, seeing how tough she is underneath her sweet demeanor, I think maybe she's throwing me a lifeline. I can choose for her to rescue me. From my isolation. From my self-imposed, self-important rules.

This is it. This is the moment I'll regret for the rest of my life if I leave her now. I will know this is where I made my biggest mistake. Not many people can pinpoint that moment in real time.

I can change this, I tell myself.

"No," I say. "I want this. I want *us*. I'm willing to take the risk if you are," I say as I gently rub her hand. There are tears on my cheeks, but there's no taking them back now. Not when we are balanced on this razor-thin precipice. I'm not ashamed to cry; I'm just not used to it. "Because the pain is worth it."

At these words, echoing hers earlier this week, her eyes snap back to mine.

"It is," she replies, and with a weak smile I know we are going to be OK.

I lean down and kiss her. I want to be gentle, not sure how much of her is hurting. Our lips touch and I swear we are melting together. It's a sweet and slow kiss. The kind you savor, which works as a balm, healing everything within me. I break our kiss to wipe the tears off her face. She reaches up and does the same for me.

Charlie wraps her arms round my neck and guides me on top of her. We kiss. We touch. And then we sleep. I spend the afternoon holding Charlie tight, afraid this dream will end again.

When I wake, she is there, and it feels like the beginning of a new era. The clock reads 8:30 p.m.

Charlie stirs next to me; I didn't mean to wake her.

"So, about that date," she mumbles, her voice thick with sleep.

"How about a night in tonight and I make reservations for when you're all healed?"

I hate to disappoint her, but I don't think either of us are up for a night on the town.

"Sold!" Charlie says before turning her face to kiss me.

Me too, Ross.

50

CHARLIE

"Welcome back, Charlie!" Shauna greets me as she breezes into Oliver's office. In my absence, he hasn't had anyone to enforce his daily schedule. I let the head of HR go in and know I'll have to return to my usual gatekeeping after this impromptu meeting.

Oliver told those who asked that I was recovering from a training injury. I'm a runner and my foot was in a walking cast. Believable enough. It's a version of the truth, if you consider kidnapping on-the-job training for being a spy. No one outside of strategic operations knew that I was working from home while my bruises healed. Remote work was nice, but I missed the team.

"There you are." Ana walks up to my desk, her arms full with an oversized cardboard box. Neon-colored T-shirts are on the brim of spilling out.

"You need help with that?" I ask, as I stand and walk round my desk to grab the box from her.

"Yes, let's get these to the break room," she tells me, and I lead the way. "We're switching our T-shirt sponsor for next year, so all these blank ones from the old sponsor aren't needed."

The reminder of our previous batch of leftover shirts sends shivers up my spine.

I set the box on the table in the break room and Ana tapes a note on the table. FREE.

"Whatever's left at the end of the day, I'll drop at my church; they do a lot of outreach to the homeless," Ana assures me.

I fix my face, snapping out of my impending spiral. "That's a great idea!"

While I did share *a lot* of updates with Ana after she returned from Europe, I didn't tell her everything.

That I was injured and working from home, yes. How I was injured and the circumstances leading to my kidnapping, no.

I also requested that she bring over burritos one night so we could talk about Declan.

Because what's the point in falling for the hot guy at work, and he's also into you, if you can't tell your best friend about it? Ana has sworn her secrecy, but I'm not sure how much longer it will keep anyways.

As if summoned by my thoughts, the one person I desperately want to keep this secret from waltzes into the break room.

“Hello, Celine,” I say as she passes us to make herself a cup of coffee.

“Good day, Charlie,” Celine says with a cheerful voice. “Ana.” She gives our coworker a friendly nod before coming over to examine the box of shirts.

Celine hands me a folded newspaper and pulls out a highlighter-yellow tank top. The newspaper is today’s *Miami Herald*. The headline above the fold reads: KILBRIDE IN CUSTODY. The subheading is a quote from the police chief of Miami-Dade County: THE CHARGES WILL STICK THIS TIME!

It’s been all over the news, so I was already aware. Ex-senator and current inmate awaiting arraignment Titus Kilbride has been taken into custody based on new evidence.

“Ana, what do you think? Is this my color?” Celine asks, holding up a shirt to her chin. Ana gives her decisive opinion while I scan the article.

It’s a clever way for Celine to give me an update with Ana in the room. While Oliver, Declan, and I were fighting X.C. and Blaed, Celine was in Miami for our triathlon event. She met with local newspapers, ensured our pro athletes had good coverage, and she executed the mission that I suggested in my first week here: to get Kilbride to confess to his crimes.

Learning that Celine was operating on the secret missions was surprising. But nothing shocked me quite as much as the news that ex-senator and now confirmed sexual predator Titus Kilbride admitted his crimes to Celine over drinks at a hotel bar. She recorded the whole thing and even got him to admit which police officer he bribed to destroy the critical evidence that resulted in his case being thrown out. It was a good day for justice.

I look up at Celine and Ana chatting about the various colors. "I bet you could pull any of these off, Celine," I tell her.

I'm not only speaking about the bright fabrics. I've learned that Celine is not only one of the good guys but that she is ridiculously good at her job. She was skeptical of a new team member for the same reasons Declan was. I'll trust her for now, but I'm not completely willing to let her off the hook for being a grade-A bitch to me.

Celine makes a small motion with her shoulders. "Thank you, Charlie," she coos. "I love your hair today." I'm equal parts stunned and validated.

"Thanks," Ana and I respond at the same time. I finally decided to give into the humidity and stop fighting it. Ana showed me how she does her beachy waves, so she deserves some credit for it. It's a good look and it's earned me the approval of more than just our office's resident fashionista.

Celine decides on bright orange and exits the break room.

Ana and I exchange a look that reads "hey, that's an improvement." We're giving Celine another chance, but we won't be surprised if she proves us wrong again.

I guess it goes to show you can never really judge someone by a terrible first impression. They reveal their character one action at a time. Turns out Celine is one of the good ones, even if she is slightly territorial. But, then again, I'm in love with someone who's very territorial too.

I make Oliver his morning cup of mushroom coffee and bring it over. He waves me in. "Catch the door and sit down," he says, pointing in the direction of a chair while wrapping up an email. I close the office door and take a seat.

The past two weeks have been a whirlwind. I thought being kidnapped and held for ransom would be the biggest news, but life has continued to throw more my way. Mostly good things, though. Still, I haven't had much time to think. Being forced to sit quietly, even for a minute, is a gift.

For starters, my new doctor was happy to hear that I was testing my limits with more physical activity and dietary changes. I wasn't forthcoming about the kidnapping; I just said I'd been getting in some sprints as well as longer runs. The bloodwork he ordered showed my eosinophil levels were normal and that I continued to be in remission. He reminded me that it may not last forever, though, and his realism was sobering. I thought living carefully had kept my flares at bay. Maybe I can control them, but maybe I can't. And since this new doctor is working with the University of South Florida to launch a long-term study on my condition, I gladly signed up. Because I can't control a lot of things about my body, but I can do this. I can help. And, in a way, I'm winning back some control.

"Alright," Oliver says as he locks his computer screen, "Charlie, we need to discuss your position with FIRE."

His words send a shock of fear through me. *Oh goodness, am I being fired? I've only been here for two months.*

His next words soothe me. "You've done an amazing job in your current role." I can sense a "but" coming. "You've shown an interest in our extra operations."

"Interest" is an amusing word choice. Did I show an interest or was it thrust upon me?

"We both know this job was supposed to be a launching point. Ideally, you would work over the next six months to a year to seamlessly transition into any other role within the organization. So how about strategic operations liaison?"

I won't make a snap decision. There are factors to consider. There are complications to officially working on the strategic operations team. Namely who my boss will be.

I look through the all-glass office door, at my desk waiting for me. Surely if I transitioned roles, I'd have a new seating arrangement. Then my eyes catch the quote above my desk: *Quitters never earn a line in the history books.* I grin. The whole time I've been here, I've regarded this quote with shame, as if it were browbeating me into self-loathing. Today it's just words on a wall.

I can stay. But this time my name won't be in history books for a good reason. A secretive one.

I turn my attention back to my uncle, who's waiting for my response. I give a nod. "Sounds like a plan."

We shake hands, making our plan official. There's only one person I can think to share the news with.

I close Oliver's door behind me and saunter to the office across from my desk.

"Hey," I say to catch his attention.

Declan peers up at me and his smile says it all. Bright, brilliant, the kind of smile that cannot be contained. The dimples that distract me, the eyes that communicate safety. Of all the things I thought I would reclaim with this job, this adventure on the other side of the country, it was my confidence, my independence, my trust in my body and my instincts. I wanted to own an identity outside of running and my need to walk away from it. I never expected this. These emotions. This man. Once, he infuriated and exasperated me; now he has me connecting with my inner goddess.

"Hey," Declan responds.

I saw him last this morning when he left my bed early for a training ride. It's only been a few hours, but it feels too long. I lock my thoughts of last night away so I can focus. "I have some news," I share, unsure if he already knows.

"You said yes?" Declan asks, and I'm guessing he and Oliver already discussed the potential new role.

I nod. I want to walk over and sit on his lap and hug him. I want to kiss him, I'm so happy. But I do neither of these things, because I am a professional, dammit.

Declan's computer chimes. He glances over at the notification and grimaces. "Oliver already sent an email to Shauna with us on copy saying we need to meet with her first thing."

“About the job? Oliver said I’d be transitioning for half a year or more.”

Declan raises his eyebrows as if to say, *Not about that*.

I let out a soft laugh. Clearly, Oliver wants us to disclose our relationship to HR, the relationship we thought we were keeping under wraps. No secrets among spies, I suppose. Turns out we don’t actually have a non-fraternization policy here; Celine was just trying to keep me away from her crush. “Is this his way of asking your intentions?” I joke with Declan.

He stands and grabs his travel mug. “Yeah, I guess,” he says as he passes closer to me.

I’m still in the doorway, blocking his way. “And what are your intentions? Are they honorable?” I bite my lips because I know I’m playfully skirting the line we’ve drawn.

“Mostly,” Declan says with a wink as he pinches my hip.

51

DECLAN

"Alright, let's get to it," I mutter after I take a sip of fresh hot coffee. The caffeine is necessary for this morning's task.

Charlie groans and we head over to Ian's office. It's remained locked for two weeks now. Shauna sent the discreet "Ian Turner is no longer with the company" email. Void of details.

The rumor mill did its thing. Everyone thinks Ian was sabotaging our athlete-tracking app to force Oliver to sign with a new platform partner, that Ian would get a kickback. Some theories said he needed the money for gambling debts and that is somehow related to his arrest. A few people are theorizing that Ian tried to kill Oliver to get the CEO job. Or something like that. Gossip is always oddly specific and yet very vague. People make up their own stories and it never gets close to the messy truth.

Everyone on Ian's team has been fully screened. Several have been put on standard duties for the time being so we can assess if they're potentially leaking any information.

Ian is already out on bail. He's been charged with trespassing and attempted murder with a deadly weapon. Since these are his "first offenses" and he has friends in high places connected to the Order, he will likely get a slap on the wrist and probation. Charlie has a restraining order, but paper doesn't do much to stop bullets. We expect he'll flee to join X.C. whenever his trial concludes. Oliver said Ian's lawyer will likely have him sign a plea deal for lesser charges to get the whole thing over with.

In the meantime, FIRE is stuck with unraveling what he left behind. We did a full technology reset – again – and I'm confident we left no backdoor code for him to infiltrate.

His office is another story.

Charlie approaches Ian's workbench. "What a mess," she mumbles.

I agree. It's chaotic. Though I once thought it was a sign of his ordered brain, his ability to track everything without filing it.

Charlie picks up one of the papers. I should get busy packing up his hard drives, organizing the files into normal FIRE business and potentially sensitive documents about our missions. Instead, I walk up behind Charlie. I place my hands on the workbench, pressing our bodies together, and delight in the pleasant "hmm" she releases.

After checking that no one is walking by, I bury my nose in her hair. The smell of her fruity perfume fills my nose. It is a distinctly Charlie aroma, a smell that has now found its way into the fibers of my pillows. Even on the nights she hasn't stayed over, her scent lingers. My world smells like Charlie now and I love it. *I love her.*

I move my head so I can plant a kiss on her neck.

We made a new set of rules, promises to keep our relationship out of the office. But we're alone in this completely closed-off space. I figure we can steal one or two moments. I plant another kiss on her shoulder. I stiffen against her, memories of last night filling my brain.

"Not here," Charlie whispers before biting into her delicious lips. The blush on her cheeks tells me she's thinking what I am, but she has better restraint.

She's right. I plant a chaste kiss on her shoulder and walk to the other end of the table. Charlie busies herself with the documents before she looks over at me, the pink of her cheeks still not fully receded. I wink and watch her neck and face go into a full flush.

Charlie clears her throat. "How about you take that side and I focus over here?" She turns away from the table and starts to go through documents. I know she's keeping us on task. Her work ethic is unparalleled, and it's one of many things I appreciate about this strong woman.

Without any windows, it's hard to keep track of time while we sort through Ian's materials.

"Who else is going to Rome next week?" I ask to break the silence. I swear if I have to look at one more technology contract, I'll need to borrow Charlie's glasses to see straight.

Charlie begins to rattle off the names. "You, me, Oliver, Celine, Ana . . ."

Obviously, our pro-athlete liaison is going, trying to covert some of the shorter distance athletes to move to our events. Because while the World Games are elite and the average person wouldn't dream of trying out, many runners, triathletes, and cyclists live for the endurance events.

"We'll need to keep an eye out for some potential recruits for our team too," I add.

Charlie looks up from her stack of documents. "Anyone you have in mind? Are we sitting in the stands for all the sharp shooting and archery events?"

She's trying to be sarcastic. While those athletes would have skills we need in our line of work – the spy side of things – we want those who have more access to the upper echelons, the parts of society where the Order operates.

"I'm thinking dressage, gymnastics, and fencing," I reply.

Charlie nods, accepting this explanation. I'm sure she'll have a new itinerary for us by the end of the day. She moves to another stack on the far side of Ian's workbench. Some loose papers and a few spare parts. "Declan, come look at this," she says, her eyes examining the paper.

I walk over and peer at what's in her hands. Schematics. It appears to be some kind of device Ian was tinkering with. A new mechanism he was creating. Beneath it is a Metro map of Rome and an overlay of the city with World Games events and their locations.

"Are we sure we got all the explosives Castillo purchased in Argentina?" Charlie asks as she flips one of the maps over to reveal a yellow sticky note with two words written on it: "opening ceremony."

"Yes," I respond. Castillo's yacht is still impounded by the Italian Coast Guard as well, in case any munitions were hidden within any secret compartments. I check the schematic. "This doesn't look like a weapon, though. It's some kind of recording device." I'm confused even as the words leave my mouth.

My mind turns over this new information. X.C. told Charlie that only some of the munitions would be used to eliminate Raj and cause a nightmare for FIRE, so we assumed that the anticipated fallout would be a cover for whatever arms deal Castillo intended to make at the World Games. But what if both of those were supposed to be the distraction? Something to keep us busy, from seeing what they really have planned. Charlie said X.C. had something different planned for the World Games. Could this device be the big plan?

It never ends. That's the frustrating part. Evil never sleeps. The layers of subterfuge peel back to reveal more.

Then again, I'm an athlete. I live for a finish line that feels impossible. Espionage is an endurance sport. Marathons and ultras, triathlon, road biking, the miles are endless when you're out there. Sure, there are aid stations every so often, but it doesn't change the fact that the longer you're in it, the further away the finish line appears. That's why crossing it feels so good.

The world is always teetering on the edge of disaster. The bad guys are well funded. But something has changed. And it's Charlie. Because now I have a reason to want to keep the world safe. For her. For us. Not just my hero complex.

Our work isn't done yet. There's still a threat to neutralize. I get that itch to get out there and stop it.

I glance up at Charlie and see a shine in her eyes. She has it too.

"Looks like we have our next mission," I say.

Charlie reaches for my hand. "We sure do," she says with a wink.

THE FINISH LINE

Acknowledgements

The acknowledgements are pretty important. It's the very last thing a reader will see in a book. No pressure, or whatever.

First and foremost, I want to thank: You! You took time out of your day to read this book. Do you know how amazing that is? And you're the kind of reader who reads the acknowledgements too. You're awesome! Thank you!

What follows are the names of those I'd like to thank that have been released from the spy-vault:

I'd like to start by thanking Ruth Bennett, Aimee White, and the amazing team at Ink Road and Bonnier Books UK. Thank you for believing in my silly sporty spies and bringing out the best in them. Your notes and your dedication to this story and characters have been invaluable.

Thank you to Isabel Lineberry for your patience and thoughtful insights to help take this from wild idea to finished book. Thank you to Kristina Perez for taking a chance on me. A big thank you to the entire team at Perez Literary and Entertainment and to Dana Spector at CAA for handling film and TV rights.

This book wouldn't exist without the help of several important people. When I needed the time to write, Miss Ashley and Miss Lisa at Romp n' Roll St. Pete kept my little one entertained while I typed at a new word-per-minute record in the lobby.

Thank you to the readers who have followed me since day one of my indie science fiction novels and those who read everything I write, regardless of the genre. And thank you to the book clubs who have selected my books for your monthly read. You have excellent taste and your charcuterie boards are epic!

I'd also like to thank my dedicated followers and readers who stepped up when I asked for name suggestions for some of the B-level villains in this book. Thank you to Stephanie Michella, Barbara and Casey Sloan, Michelle Pearl, and Audrie. Seriously, guys, the names are the hardest part.

Writing is an individual sport, but much like running, triathlon, and cycling – you need a support crew. A big thank you to the Shakespeare's Sisters, especially Lauren Beltz. I love the sisterhood and support from the ladies who go the distance: Harriet, Casey, and Sara. Also, a big thank you to the best hype squad any author could have – online friends I've never met IRL: Allie and Kristen – you guys rock! Thank you to the 2026 Debut Discord server for answering my questions and a source for so many new author friends!

Next, I want to thank the real ones who have been putting up with my crazy story ideas – and reading them! – since high school: Tori, Chelsea, Sophia, Linzy, and Nora.

I'd also like to thank my friends and coworkers at the real-life largest endurance sports company in the world. You made it fun to work there and the best parts of that job made their way into these pages: Stephanie, Christine, Garge, Michael, Tara, Natalie, Mylia, Jasmine, Ali, Dorsey, Trent, and [REDACTED SPY STUFF]. The endurance sports community is incredibly welcoming and loving, even if the miles on course are intimidating. Thank you to the athletes, announcers, and site crew for embracing me and this book!

Next, I want to thank my family, who have always encouraged me: Mom, who instilled a love of reading. Debbie and Jeff, who have supported me through the many long years of writing, editing, and revising. My Aunt Kathy – yes, critical acclaim for this book would be a dream come true. But in my over-large boisterous family, Aunt Kathy is the artist. She has encouraged all of us to follow our creative passions. And as long as she likes this book, it feels like a win.

Don't you dare play the wrap-up music yet! The most important ones are next:

To my star child. You make this life so much more fun, messy, exhausting, and silly. I love you so much. You make me proud every day, I only hope I can keep doing right by you and making you proud too. If you're reading this, it means you're all grown up or you've snuck into Mommy's office to read things you shouldn't yet.

And the person who deserves the most thanks and appreciation is Jason. My rock, my first-reader, and my consigliere – I couldn't do any of it without you. Writing, living, training for half marathons. You inspire the best of what I create. You've been my biggest cheerleader in writing and in fighting for my health. Thank you doesn't even begin to cover it!

About the Author

Kate Williams worked for four years at the largest endurance race company in the world and is *95%* sure none of her previous coworkers is a spy. Er . . . *90%* sure. Originally from Philadelphia, she now lives in sunny and stormy St. Petersburg, FL. Williams is an avid runner and has published speculative and science fiction under her other pen names. This is her first romance.